Sex
Becomes
Her

Books by Regina Cole

Sex Becomes Her

Sexy Living
(coming soon)

Sex Becomes Her

REGINA COLE

KENSINGTON BOOKS
www.kensingtonbooks.com

KENSINGTON BOOKS are published by

Kensington Publishing Corp.
119 West 40th Street
New York, NY 10018

All Kensington titles, imprints, and distributed lines are available at special quantity discounts for bulk purchases for sales promotion, premiums, fund-raising, educational, or institutional use.

Special book excerpts or customized printings can also be created to fit specific needs. For details, write or phone the office of the Kensington Sales Manager: Attn. Sales Department. Kensington Publishing Corp., 119 West 40th Street, New York, NY 10018. Phone: 1-800-221-2647.

eISBN-13: 978-1-61773-781-7
eISBN-10: 1-61773-781-X
First Kensington Electronic Edition: July 2015

ISBN-13: 978-1-61773-780-0
ISBN-10: 1-61773-780-1
First Kensington Trade Paperback Printing: July 2015

10 9 8 7 6 5 4 3 2 1

Printed in the United States of America

For the man who is my everything. I love you, bean!

My thanks goes to:

Jodi and Gabe, my resident chemists, for their valuable help in this book.

My fabulous agent, Nicole, for helping me develop this idea.

My lovely editor, Peter, for helping me bring Eliza and Chandler to life.

And to my family, for putting up with my deadline-brain.

And most of all, to everyone who reads this book. Thank you for letting my stories entertain you.

1

The cart had a flat spot on one wheel, and the *thump* was driving Eliza insane. But there was no way she was going to take the time to go back to the front of the small grocery store and swap it out. She'd already seen three people she knew, and two of them had looked away almost instantly. After this much time it shouldn't hurt, but it still did. Being a pariah in her hometown wasn't exactly how she'd pictured living her life, but it was her reality now.

Setting her jaw, Eliza moved through the produce section and checked her list. Spinach, cucumbers, tomatoes . . . If she shopped smart, she wouldn't have to do this again for a month. Getting fresh veggies only once a month wasn't ideal, but neither was living in a town that was convinced she was some kind of sexual deviant.

Her ratty sneakers didn't make a sound on the polished floor of the grocery store. The cart was half-full, and as she rounded the final corner toward the registers, her name smacked her in the back of the head like a mallet.

"Eliza Jackson! Oh my God, it *is* you."

She winced, then turned. "Oh, hey, Marshall." Eliza crossed

her arms to cover the worst of the holes in her Green Day T-shirt. Part of the fun of being a chemist was ruined clothes when coworkers weren't as careful with chemicals as they should be. "How are you?"

Marshall looked her up and down, a somewhat leering smile on his face as he adjusted his grocery basket. "I'm doing great. You still at Quality Testing?"

"Yeah. I'm lead chemist in the pharmaceutical division." Eliza smiled politely, even though her insides were shaking. She wasn't stupid. This wasn't an old high school friend interested in catching up. This was something else entirely. "What about you?"

"Eh, I'm at Eubank Financial. Anyway, I heard you dated Tyler Hagans for a while. He's a buddy of mine."

Eliza's hands tightened into fists, and her smile froze.

Marshall continued, oblivious to her discomfort. "I have to say, I didn't know you were gay."

Her teeth hurt as she clamped them together hard. Her words were muffled as she spoke without releasing the clench of her jaw. "I'm not gay."

Marshall's laugh was mocking. "From what I heard, liking girls is the least weird thing about you. Anyway, you go do what you do. Have fun, but watch out. I've heard some of that kinky stuff you're into is illegal."

With a wink, Marshall turned and walked away, leaving Eliza to stare after him in shock and hurt.

When she could breathe without her chest feeling like it was cracking in half, Eliza turned and pushed her thumping grocery cart to the checkout line. But before she could start loading her items onto the conveyer belt, the cashier flipped off the lighted number 1 sign.

"Sorry," she said, giving Eliza a distrustful look. "This lane is closed."

Closing her eyes for a second, Eliza took a deep breath, then pulled her cart to the express lane, which was the only one left open. The red-shirted manager gave her a look, but started scanning her items anyway.

"Thanks," Eliza muttered as she accepted her change and receipt. The guy didn't say anything, just gave her a tight-lipped smile before cheerfully greeting the customer behind her.

Blasting her favorite band's latest album all the way home didn't help improve Eliza's mood. It hurt, damn it, and she was tired of pretending it didn't. By the time she made the left onto her street, her jaw ached and her eyes stung.

She hadn't done anything wrong. She'd just been honest about her fantasies, and when she and Tyler had broken up over it, he'd trumpeted her most secret desire to the world, complete with embellishments. It was the worst kind of betrayal, and even now, six months later, she wasn't sure how to deal with the hurt. Other than to hide in her house and vow to spend the rest of her life as a celibate hermit, that is.

Throwing the gearshift into Park, Eliza released her seat belt in the same motion. Silence fell over her like a blanket as she cut the engine. Her skull thumped back against the headrest and she blew out a breath. This was nothing new.

"It doesn't matter," Eliza grunted as she shoved open the car door. The cool breeze hit her skin, raising goose bumps in its wake. Trudging across her lawn with her grocery bags dangling from her forearms, Eliza fumbled through her keys to find the one for her front door. She was so distracted that she almost tripped over the box on her front steps.

"What the hell?"

Bending low, she examined the label. It had come from North Carolina. Maybe it was Bree? A shot of excitement tore through her, and she trotted up the stairs and pushed through the front door in a matter of seconds.

Dumping her bags and keys at the table by the door, Eliza turned and headed back to the stoop. Her blood pumped with anticipation as she carried the package through her messy house and straight to the kitchen table. Grabbing one of the knives from the butcher block on the counter, she grinned.

"What have you sent me, Sabrina?"

The sharp knife made quick, neat slices through the packing tape, then clattered to the table as Eliza abandoned it to pull open the cardboard flaps.

"What in the world is this?"

It was pink. Not just pink—pink was much too tame a name for this color. As Eliza withdrew the scraps of fabric from the box, dangling from their tiny strings, she decided that the only real name she could give that color was fuchsia. Or maybe magenta. Or maybe a color off the spectrum that hadn't been named yet. She had to blink three times to ease the pain from the brightness. And it wasn't just pink, it was a pink bikini.

Digging through the rest of the box, which contained the other half of the magenta monstrosity, a bottle of sunscreen, and a tank top with some sparkly letters on it, Eliza finally came up with an envelope from the bottom of the box. Her name was written in Bree's extra-swirly cursive.

The paper crinkled as Eliza ripped open the envelope and unfolded the letter. A plane ticket fell out. Eliza barely glanced at it; she was already reading.

> *Liza,*
> *I hope you like the little care package I sent you! If you've already read the tank top, you know that I'm asking you to be my bridesmaid. I know it's kind of presumptuous to buy your plane ticket without asking you first, but you're always complaining that you never get to go anywhere, so here it is! I'm flying you out to Hawaii for our wedding, which is November 9th. You can stay the whole week, our treat! You're such a good*

friend, Liza, please say you'll come and be my bridesmaid.

Love you bunches! Call me after you're done reading so we can celebrate together!

Bree

When she realized that her tongue was actually drying out, Eliza closed her mouth and let the paper flutter to the tabletop.

She'd known Bree was dating a guy, but she hadn't known it was serious. And a wedding in Hawaii, only a month away? Eliza shook her head. Damn. Bree didn't waste any time.

After yanking open the refrigerator and taking a regenerating swig of apple juice, Eliza went down the hall to retrieve her cell phone. A mound of bags in front of the door jogged her memory. Oh yeah, the groceries. She should probably start putting those away.

Tucking the phone in the crook of her shoulder, she hauled the bags to the kitchen.

"Oh my God, Liza! Hey!"

"Hey Bree, I got your little box of goodies." Eliza winced at Bree's delighted squeal, which went straight through her eardrum.

"Ohmygod, isn't it the best news ever? You can come, though, right?"

"Well," Eliza drew out the word as she pulled open the door to her pantry. "I'm not sure."

"Why not?"

Eliza sighed, her arms full of canned goods. "It's a long way away, and I'm not sure if I can get off work—"

"Horseshit." Bree's tone was firm. "You haven't taken a vacation in three years, and I know it. They can do without you for a week."

"I'm just not sure if I feel comfortable. I don't really know any of your family other than your crazy mom, so I'll be kind of lonely, and—"

"If you can honestly tell me you're not lonely there at home, then I'll lay off you."

Bree had been the one friend Eliza had confided in after the shit with Tyler blew up. She knew how miserable Eliza had been, had even begged her to move down to North Carolina and work for her father's company. The offer had been tempting, but Eliza couldn't stand the thought of leaving her hometown. Even if that same hometown hated her.

"Fine," Eliza groaned. "I'll go. But I'm going to regret it. I've got to go shopping, find stuff to wear so I won't embarrass you."

"You won't. It's going to be awesome."

"And no fixing me up. Promise me, Bree."

The silence on the other end of the line was suspect, and Eliza raised her brow. "Bree . . ."

"Fine." Bree's exasperated tone made Eliza grin. "Deal. But promise me you'll keep an open mind, all right? There are a few guys there that I think would be perfect for you. You know that Tyler was a small-minded asshole, and there are tons of guys who'd kill for someone more adventurous in bed."

Eliza pretended not to hear that last part. "Okay, let me get going. I've got a lot to do if I'm going to be ready to go in, oh, twenty-four days."

Once the call was disconnected, Eliza took a deep breath. Okay. She could do this. And the more she thought about it, the better it felt. Get away from all the small-minded small-town people? Maybe she could even pretend to be someone else, someone confident, who owned their slightly unorthodox sexuality.

She allowed herself a small, genuine smile. Maybe Eliza the hermit could become Eliza the bombshell for a few days.

24 Days Later . . .

Eliza's heels clicked against the tiled floor of the airport. Shifting the strap of her carry-on on her shoulder, she wobbled just a little, but pulled it back before it turned into a stumble.

Why the hell had she thought it'd be a good idea to wear high-heeled boots to fly? Waiting until she'd actually reached Hawaii to begin her bombshell routine seemed like a much better idea now. She'd held up the TSA security line for a good three minutes while she fumbled with the zipper on the left one. They were still new and kind of stiff, which didn't exactly make for easy removal. And then her gate had been all the way at the ass end of the airport. Of course. After that, though, the first leg of her trip had been fine. Now she just had to make it to her connecting flight without falling on her face. Hopefully she'd get used to walking in these monsters before she showed up at the resort. There, the last thing she wanted to look like was herself.

"Sneakers," she said beneath her breath as she glanced at the flight monitors mounted to the wall. "Sneakers for the return flight. That or flip-flops. I don't care if it's November."

A speaker crackled overhead, barely audible over the noise and chatter of the busy airport. Eliza pulled at her dove-gray pencil skirt, which was trying to ride up as she walked. She needed to hustle; the flight would be boarding sometime in the next ten minutes, and she was still five or six gates away. It was gate C-4, wasn't it? She should probably check.

Shoving her long brown hair back out of the way for about the twentieth time that day, she unzipped her bag and started to dig through it. Of course she'd had to pull everything out at the security desk because of the whole boot fiasco, and her other boarding pass had been shoved in there somewhere. But walking and digging through her bag at the same time wasn't the easiest thing to do in three-inch heels.

Glancing back to make sure nobody was close behind her, Eliza ducked to the side of the busy corridor and started digging in earnest. Was it maybe in her medicine bag? Nope, just her vitamins, Tylenol, various just-in-case cold and flu meds. Oh, maybe she'd stuck it in the little lingerie bag. No, not there, either. After another minute, her bag was in shambles and she still hadn't laid a finger on her boarding pass.

"Wait a minute," Eliza said, yanking open the side zipper. "Aha!"

The boarding pass wasn't the only thing in that pocket, though, and before she could snag the pass and pull it free, the weight of her tablet pulled the zippered flap out of her hand. A clatter rang through the corridor as her tablet landed face-first on the polished floor.

"Ohmygod," she moaned as she bent over to pick it up, praying that the protective case had taken the brunt of the fall.

"Here, let me get that for you." An incredibly deep voice from right behind her made her jump. The bag slipped from her shoulder and bounced free, pill bottles and panties scattering in a four-foot radius.

"Did I startle you? I'm so sorry."

She looked up then. The sexy voice belonged to an extremely well-muscled guy in dark-washed jeans and a sage-green sweater that almost matched his eyes. His light brown hair was tousled in that careless but gorgeous way, and as he knelt down beside her she had the strangest urge to run her fingers through it.

"I saw your tablet fall, thought I could lend a hand since you've got yours full. Looks like I just made it worse, though. Here, let me help you." He reached for the nearest object that had fallen out of her bag, which just happened to be one of her brand-new black lace thongs.

"No!" she squawked in alarm. "No, don't touch that."

"Hey, I didn't mean—"

"Please, just let me get it." Not trusting her ankles to support her with the damn heels, Eliza began the humiliating task of crawling on the airport floor to retrieve her belongings.

"I'd be happy to help you; after all, it's my fault." The guy reached for her bag.

She jerked it back, her nerves jangling. "No, no, please, really. It's fine." She shoved stuff into her bag as fast as she could, well aware that the burning in her cheeks meant they were a nuclear shade of pink. Hell, she might even be as pink as that bikini. That might be a good name for it—*mortification magenta.*

"All right, if you're sure." The guy looked a little disappointed, but Eliza couldn't form the words of an apology. It was like a giant wad of idiocy had wedged itself in her throat. She'd made an ass of herself in this huge airport, and now she was going to be late to catch her connection if she didn't hurry. What the hell would she do if she missed her flight? He watched her for a while, but then with an apologetic smile, turned and walked away. She couldn't help but mentally kick herself as she watched him leave.

Once everything was shoved back into her bag—including her thankfully undamaged tablet—she couldn't zip it anymore, but she struggled to her feet and hustled to the gate anyway. When she finally arrived at C-4, boarding had already begun, so she joined the last of the line.

"Have a nice flight," the gate attendant said as he scanned her pass.

"Thanks." Eliza caught a glimpse of her reflection in the window. At least that fall hadn't messed up her new outfit. And her hair, which she'd taken a helluva long time to flat-iron that morning before leaving, still looked shiny and bouncy. That little dose of relief lasted all the way down the Jetway and even as she stepped onto the plane.

But as she moved down the aisle, looking for seat 22B, her relief burned up and the smoke turned into a mixture of embarrassment and despair.

The hot guy who had caused her to spill her whole bag in the middle of the terminal was sitting in none other than seat 22A.

This was a five-hour flight. She was going to have to sit next to this guy for five freaking hours, all the while remembering how she'd acted like a total klutz.

Sometimes life really sucked.

2

A sudden noise made Chandler Morse glance upward. There, in the aisle, stood the woman he'd tried to help earlier. Her cheeks were red, the corners of her full lips pulled down as she sank into the seat beside him.

Well, this is a nice surprise. The sight of her pert ass as she bent over to pick up her tablet had fired him like nothing had in a very long time. His divorce had strung out over a year, and while he couldn't deny that it was the best thing for him, he couldn't bring himself to break the vows he'd sworn to until the ink was dry. But for some reason this woman had drawn his eye. Maybe it was the blush. Or the way her full hips flared, framed so well by that form-fitting skirt. He couldn't deny things hadn't gone well earlier, but he'd done his best to apologize. Maybe being stuck beside him on a plane for a few hours would help her forget about that unfortunate accident.

"Hey, nice to see you again," Chandler said, but she didn't look over at him. Her cheeks reddened further as she shoved her open bag beneath the seat in front of her.

His lips curled into a smile as she fumbled in her bag, trying to rearrange the contents so it would zip again. Her black sweater was V-necked, the loose knit large enough that he could occasionally see flashes of skin. Her dark hair swung with her movements, catching the late morning light that shone through the small window beside him. And her ass, well, that was curved and tight and his palms fairly itched to touch it.

She sat up then, and he pretended to be very interested in the flight attendant giving the safety talk at the front of the plane.

"Mind shutting the window shade?"

He glanced over at her. She was squinting in the brightness that glared off the airplane wing.

"Sure," Chandler said with an easy smile. He slid the shade down.

"Thanks." She unfolded her boarding pass and smoothed it across her lap. It was easy to read her name.

Eliza Jackson. He tried it out silently. It suited her. *Eliza. Liza.* Nice name for a beautiful woman.

"So, where are you from?"

Chandler's question was met with silence as the plane rounded onto the runway.

Finally, Eliza glanced over at him, her dark lashes shuttering her eyes. "Um, the Midwest."

Undaunted by her non-answer, Chandler smiled. "Nice. I'm from North Carolina. Thus the slight drawl." He gave his trademark grin, the one that never failed to get a woman to smile back at him even if she didn't want to.

Nothing from Eliza. She seemed determined to focus on the floor, or the seat back in front of her. Basically anything to keep from looking at him. Of course, he couldn't really blame her, but he was disappointed anyway. Had his failed marriage screwed up his game that bad? The aircraft picked up speed as it moved down the runway.

He tried again. "I live near the coast, the Outer Banks. You ever been? They're some of the most beautiful beaches in the world."

"No. I haven't." She closed her eyes as the plane lifted off, her knuckles white as they gripped the armrests.

Chandler watched her as the plane trembled with the effort of its ascent. A little line appeared between her brows, as if she wasn't entirely comfortable with the process of flying. He wanted to reach over and grab her hand, reassure her, maybe even see if her lips were as soft as they looked.

Instead, he opted for conversation.

"Ever been to Hawaii before?"

She shook her head, not bothering to open her eyes.

Undaunted, he continued. "Me, either. It's kind of a forced vacation for me." He snorted a little. Working vacation, more like. His cousin was getting married, and Chandler had been roped into playing the role of best man. Fortunately, his job as private investigator could be flexible, when he needed it to be. "Are you vacationing?"

"Not really," she bit out as the plane hit a decent-sized bump. She tucked her chin into her chest. Like she was trying to make herself as small as possible until this was over.

A longing built in his chest, and he almost reached over to pull her tight against his side, protect her from the fear. He crossed his arms to keep from doing something stupid. So what if they had chemistry? Right now she obviously needed to get through the takeoff. He'd wait until the plane had leveled off, and then he'd attempt conversation again. Draw her out. Get her phone number, if the fates were kind.

But when she finally opened her eyes, Eliza reached into the seat pocket and grabbed the first magazine she came to. Crossing her legs away from him, she turned on one hip, clearly marking their conversation as over.

Chandler blew out a breath. Oh well. He'd fucked that one

royally when he scared her into dropping her panties all over LAX. The mental image caused him to smile again. She'd squawked like a chicken when he almost grabbed that thong. It was worth it to see her beautiful cheeks go pink.

Closing his eyes, he let his head fall back against the seat. Might as well get some rest. There was a dinner tonight at the resort so the wedding party could get to know one another. And if he knew Gregory, it would be wild, full of booze, and run really late. A nap was definitely in his best interest.

Too bad Eliza wouldn't be joining him. A little bedtime fun with her would definitely make his dreams sweeter.

The sudden jolt of the flight's touchdown woke him. Chandler blinked blearily, then stretched as much as the small area allowed him to. His arm brushed by Eliza's, and as he started to mumble an apology, he was struck by the sight of her face.

She was looking straight into his eyes. Her irises were such a deep, dark brown, like expensive chocolates. Caught in her gaze for a moment, he waited.

"Nice nap?"

"It was," Chandler said, stretching as the plane slowed its headlong roll up the landing strip. "Did you enjoy the flight?"

"Not really," she said, fumbling with her seat belt. "Flying's not really my thing."

"You should fly next to me more." He grinned. "I'll keep you safe."

The smarmy line was meant to prick her, and it did the job.

"By the way, you snore," she snapped and bent down to retrieve her bag.

"You're lying," he said calmly as he unfastened his belt. "I've never snored in my life."

She had the good grace to blush, and Chandler grinned at the sight. But the instant the plane stopped, she launched herself out of her seat to move into the aisle. Unfortunately for her, the rest of the passengers had the same idea, and she was forced to stand there, halfway in the aisle, with nowhere to go until the line started moving.

Well, it was unlucky for her, but it was damn incredible for Chandler. Her ass was now at eye level, and he definitely enjoyed the view.

Her toe tapped impatiently, and when the crowd of people finally began to thin, Chandler stood and moved behind her into the aisle.

"I'm Chandler, by the way."

"Nice to meet you, Chandler, but I've got to grab my bag and catch the shuttle. So, see ya. Have a good trip."

She turned left inside the terminal, taking short, choppy steps that echoed inside the crowded Hawaiian airport. Sensing that now wasn't the time to push her, Chandler waited a minute or two before following.

Hell, it wasn't his fault his shuttle was in the same direction. And besides, now he could continue to enjoy the view.

Eliza wanted to punch something. God, could that have gone any worse? While her sexy neighbor slept, she'd centered herself, intending to practice her bombshell routine on him when he woke. It had started out promising enough, but then he'd had to pick at her. She'd promised herself on this trip she'd be confident, happy, completely the opposite of Eliza from Appledale, Ohio. But that plan had imploded as soon as Chandler started teasing her.

A groan escaped her and she stopped right in front of a Coke machine. It was probably just self-defense. For the last few months, any time a guy had come up to her, she'd tried her best to keep them at arm's length. After her relationship with Tyler had gone down the crapper, she couldn't stand the thought of letting another man that close. But Chandler . . . He was nice. He seemed normal. He was hotter than hell, and sweet, and funny. Everything inside her had screamed he looked way too good for her, and she should stay far, far away.

Biting her lip, Eliza glanced over her shoulder. Maybe she should go find Chandler and apologize for snapping at him. It wasn't his fault she'd completely lost all interpersonal skills over the past six months.

The crowd shifted and moved, and she had to duck sideways to avoid being run over by one of those golf-cart security cars. No sign of Chandler. Oh well. Maybe it was for the best, so she didn't embarrass herself in front of him again. There was still time for her to salvage this trip, so she'd do it. New Eliza mask firmly in place, she turned down the corridor toward the baggage claim.

Bree had said that the resort shuttle would be there to pick up her and another wedding party member, and she didn't want to keep anyone waiting.

The baggage claim area was crowded, and Eliza scanned the moving carousel for her bag. It tumbled to the bottom of the wheel all the way on the other side. Eliza muttered, "Excuse me," about seventeen times before she was able to get to the edge of the conveyor belt.

Her bag was on top of another, and as she reached for it a kid climbed onto the edge, overbalancing and knocking into her. Her outstretched hand grabbed for the handle and missed as she righted herself.

"Are you okay?" Her question to the kid went unanswered as the child's mother grabbed his arm and dragged him back from the carousel, yelling the whole time. Poor boy. Eliza turned back to the conveyer belt and sighed. Now she'd have to wait for it to come around again.

"This is yours, right?"

"Chandler?"

It was him—big, incredible smile; broad shoulders; and all. He'd grabbed her bag and was now holding it out to her.

"I saw that kid bump into you. It's not your day, is it?"

"Um, it's not that bad." Eliza smiled as she took the bag from him. "Thanks a lot, I really appreciate it."

"No problem. It was the least I could do."

Together they moved through the crowd at the baggage claim toward the airport exit. Tucking her hair behind her ear, Eliza glanced up at Chandler. This was her chance. His eyes were bright as they looked forward, strong, defined jaw dusted with just a hint of five o'clock shadow. God, he was hot. He was way out of her league. But maybe . . .

"Listen, I should really . . ."

She was about to say "apologize" when she caught sight of the van at the curb. The driver was holding a sign that said "Jackson" and "Morse." The clear escape route definitely appealed to her inner coward. A few more minutes of prep would go a long way to helping her conquer her doubts. Not with Chandler, but maybe the next guy would be easier for her to communicate with.

"Sorry, that's me. But it was really nice to meet you. Thanks for everything," she said, and hustled over to the van. Yeah, so she'd meant to explain, but this was a neat way to get out of it. There'd been enough humiliation in her life over the past half a year without adding this particular slice of humble pie to it. She'd make it to the resort in plenty of time to change for the evening's dinner party, and never have to see the handsome Chandler again.

She wasn't sure if that was a good thing or a bad thing.

"Hi," she said to the driver as he took her bag. "I'm Eliza Jackson, for the Hough-Trailwick wedding?"

"Of course." He smiled. "Welcome to Hawaii. Please, take a seat inside."

With the aid of the handle by the door, she climbed into the van, choosing to take the bench nearer the back of the vehicle. Her hands trembled a little as she unzipped her bag and started digging for her cell phone. It was kind of a relief to know that the awkwardness with Chandler was over. He'd been way too nice, too attractive. It was damn intimidating. A shaky sigh escaped her as she pulled her phone free. She needed to start small, and Chandler had been anything but.

Hopefully Bree was right, and there would be single guys at the wedding she could try again with. This week was supposed to be about letting go of the past and being a completely new Eliza. And she could do that now, if she focused and tried really hard to forget about her awkward—

"Hey there." Chandler grinned at her as he climbed into the van. "I guess we're going to the same resort. My cousin Gregory is getting married there this weekend, to Sabrina Hough."

"Oh shit," Eliza said, then clapped a hand over her mouth.

Chandler barked a laugh as he settled into the bench in front of her. "That good, huh?"

The van door slammed as the driver moved around the vehicle, finally climbing into the front seat. "Next stop, Hau'oli Resort!"

Eliza tried to focus on regulating her breathing, but it was hard to do. Chandler started up a friendly conversation with the driver, and she couldn't be happier to be left out of the chat. God, this was a nightmare.

How was she supposed to be this different, confident person when he would be there all week long? He'd seen her clumsy, awkward, blushing like a fool. She wanted to melt into the seat cushions and disappear.

When the van finally pulled into the lot of the resort, she almost screamed with relief. All she wanted was to run to her room and hide for the rest of the day, possibly the rest of her life.

Chandler climbed out of the van first, and stood there waiting.

"Please move. Just walk to the back of the van, grab your

bag, and go," Eliza begged in a tiny whisper as she yanked her bag onto her shoulder.

But he didn't respond to her pleas for mercy, just stood there and waited for her to emerge from the van door. And when he extended his hand to help her down, damn it, she couldn't help but be grateful for his assistance.

"Thanks," she said, not daring to look him in the eye.

"My pleasure." His accent was soft, not twangy at all, giving a pleasing, lengthy mellowness to his words. And as she passed by to retrieve her suitcase, the cologne that had been teasing her the entire flight tantalized her nostrils. It was light but musky, a delicious masculine scent that made her want to burrow her head against his chest and breathe him in.

"See you later," she said, then grabbed her suitcase, threw the driver a tip, and booked it into the resort.

She was a chickenshit, but that wasn't news. But now she had some extra work to do to get ready for tonight. Chandler would be at that party, and somehow she was going to have to come up with a way to make up for her complete lack of grace and manners during their first meeting.

Too bad he'd already seen her thongs.

3

Chandler's lips curled into a smile as he watched Eliza scurry away like a scalded cat. Her ass twitched as she hauled her suitcase through the doors held open by a uniformed resort employee, and he died to know how that perky ass would feel in his hands.

The sound of his suitcase's wheels against the sidewalk turned his attention back to the shuttle driver, who'd just set Chandler's luggage on the curb.

"Thanks a lot," Chandler said, slipping the man a tip.

"My pleasure, sir. Enjoy your stay." Nodding his head, his face disappearing into the wrinkles of his smile, the driver rounded the van and climbed in.

Chandler took his time wandering into the hotel. As much as he'd like to stand in line behind Eliza, he knew that would probably be a bad idea. She was still raw from the awkwardness of their meeting, and allowing her time to gather herself was more than likely the best idea. It was damn cute, the way the woman blushed and fussed and acted coy and shy in turns around him. It made him feel good—and it had been far too long since he felt good about anything. Oh sure, other women had offered to "console" him in the wake of his divorce, but he hadn't been interested. But something about this sweet little wedding guest stirred parts of him that hadn't moved in a long time.

So he ducked down a side hallway off the lobby, his suitcase's wheels *clack*ing against the joints in the marble-tiled floor.

It was a beautiful resort, with a large central building with restaurant, bar, meeting facilities, as well as a nice pool. Three buildings surrounded it, each ten stories plus. His room was in one of them, he supposed. Chandler stopped by a wide window and took in the sight of waving palms and a clear blue sea. Villas were sprinkled along the edges of the beach, perched high among the dunes, their white exteriors looking calm and serene.

A deep breath filled Chandler's lungs, and he let his lids slide closed. Why had he been unsure about coming here? This was just what he needed. Home and its problems seemed very far away.

Making up his mind, Chandler turned and headed back toward the registration desk. Eliza had to be gone by now. He'd go up to his room, change clothes, and then head down to the beach for some much-needed solitude. And then, tonight, he'd put his investigational skills to work. He wanted to know more about Eliza Jackson.

The check-in process was smooth, the smiling girl behind the counter more than accommodating, and as Chandler headed toward his assigned room in the large building behind the lobby, a sudden call made him pause.

"Chandler!"

A grin spread across his face, and he turned. "Greg, you son of a bitch."

Gregory trotted across the small drive and gripped Chandler's hand in a firm shake. "So glad you could make it, best man."

They pulled in for a hug, back slapping and good-natured arm punching. Gregory grinned as he rubbed his sore bicep.

"You been working out hard lately, I can tell."

Chandler nodded. "Keeps me busy."

Gregory's face sobered a bit. "Sorry. I know things are still rough on you after the shit with Andrea. Hopefully this time away will be good for you."

The memory of Eliza's ass wiggling as she walked away wrenched an unexpected grin from Chandler. "Actually, I think I might be ready to move on."

"Good to hear." Gregory nodded toward Chandler's suitcase. "Don't mean to keep you from settling in."

"No problem. Walk with me if you want."

Gregory fell into step beside Chandler, and they walked down the sidewalk to the building's entrance. Flowers grew all along the walk in beds covered with lava rock at their bases, fragrant scents tickling Chandler's nose as the sea breeze carried them along. They were quiet for a few minutes as they entered the building, a rush of cooled air blasting against them when they pushed through the double doors.

Once the elevator doors had closed behind them, and Chandler punched the button for the seventh floor, he looked over at his cousin.

"I met this woman on the flight over here, and she's here for the wedding."

"Really?" Gregory crossed his arms over his chest, straining his light blue tee over his biceps. Apparently he'd been hitting the gym as hard as Chandler over the last few months.

"Yeah. Her name's Eliza Jackson. Didn't get much of a chance to get to know her, though." The elevator halted, and the doors slid open.

"Eliza?" A funny look crossed Gregory's face as he preceded Chandler out of the elevator.

"Yeah, that was her name." Chandler lifted an eyebrow over at his cousin as he walked down the plush-carpeted hall. "Why do you look weird all of a sudden?"

"I don't. Eliza's great." Gregory's smile looked a little fake, and Chandler's instincts instantly started prickling.

"What's the rest of the story there? What do you know?"

Gregory held up his hands as Chandler pulled his room key from his pocket. "I don't know anything specific, I promise. Just didn't think she was your type."

"What's not to like? She's hot as hell, bro. We didn't really get off on the right foot, but I intend to make up for that at dinner tonight."

Chandler entered the room, Gregory following. The curtains hung open, and sunlight glittered off the clear blue waves outside. Damn, this was nice.

"This is great. Thanks for dragging me out here."

Gregory waved away Chandler's thanks. "Don't worry about it. You need a vacation, I need a best man, it works out."

He set his suitcase on the table against the wall and a sudden idea struck him. "Hey, Greg, do you think you can do me a favor?"

Gregory leaned against the wall and blew out a heavy breath. "Why do I get the feeling whatever you're going to ask me is going to get me in trouble?"

"It shouldn't. I'll be a perfect gentleman, I promise. Two things." Chandler held up two fingers. "One, I want to sit next to Eliza at dinner tonight."

With an eye roll and a shake of his head, Gregory sighed. "No problem. I'll talk to Bree."

"Great. Second, I want you to talk to your fiancée. Get me

some information on Eliza. What she does, where's she from, what's she into."

At that, Gregory made a strangled sound that turned into a fake-sounding cough.

Scowling, Chandler thumped his cousin in the back. "Are you done?"

A red-faced Gregory nodded. "Sure, fine. Sorry. Yeah, I'll do that, too."

The tension that had been lining Chandler's shoulders relaxed, and he smiled. "Thanks man, I owe you one. Well, another one."

Gregory pinched his temples for a second, then smiled resignedly at Chandler. "Don't worry about it. You'd do the same for me."

"In a heartbeat."

With a quick fist-bump, Gregory left the room, leaving Chandler to look out over the beauty of the white-sand beach only fifty yards away.

Sliding open the balcony door, Chandler dragged a deep breath of sea air into his lungs. It was cleansing, refreshing, renewing. Tonight was full of possibilities, and he intended to pursue them.

Especially that intriguing possibility named Eliza Jackson.

Eliza bit her lip as she studied her reflection in the hotel room's full-length mirror. She'd opted to pin her hair up, letting a few messy tendrils fall by her ears. The slinky black dress that the saleslady had assured her wasn't too low or form-fitting had a neckline that fell to her damn navel, and showed off every curve she'd ever thought about having.

Jerking the neckline up a little, Eliza pursed her lips and blew. Damn it, she was supposed to be owning this. *Bombshell, remember?* With a roll of her eyes and a "fuck it," she yanked the dress back where it was supposed to go. With her breasts pushed up by the strapless bra, the sweetheart neckline only served to frame her boobs like they were ready for their close-up. It would have been pretty convincing except for the wariness in her eyes.

Confidence. That was the look she was going for, and she was already blowing it. What about all the single guys whom Bree had promised her would be attending? But as she tucked her lipstick into the tiny silver evening bag, a shiver went straight up her exposed back, one that had nothing to do with the room's powerful air conditioner.

Chandler's mischievous grin had popped into her head, and damn it, she wanted to see him smile again. Only this time without her blushing and feeling like a complete idiot.

One last glance in the mirror, a determined squaring of her shoulders, and she was out the door. Head held high, mile-high pumps not showing a trace of a wobble.

As the elevator descended, she practiced some deep-breathing exercises, reciting her personal mantra in her brain.

Nobody knows me here. Nobody knows those rumors Tyler started. Clean slate. I'm confident, beautiful, and I can talk to anyone I want. Flirt with everybody. I'm a fucking bombshell.

She laughed to herself as the doors whooshed open.

"Care to share the joke?"

The deep voice glued her shoes to the floor, and Chandler had to slap his palm against the door to keep it from closing in her face. Clearing her throat, she thanked him, then exited the elevator.

"Sorry, just remembering something funny." Painting a bright smile on her face, she took him in. A plain white tee stretched over his biceps, dampness nearly turning it transparent. He wore blue swim trunks that slung low on his hips. Sand clung to the bronzed skin of his legs, and he leaned against the door to keep it from closing.

"You look amazing," he said, a light in his eyes as his gaze raked her up and down. Eliza fought a shiver.

"Thanks. Are you coming to dinner?" She hoped her voice was suitably calm, without the trace of nervous excitement that was currently rampaging through her innards.

"Yeah, I'll be there in a bit. Lost track of time on the beach. It's really beautiful out there."

She imagined Chandler shirtless, swimming through the waves; it truly was a sight to behold. And it would definitely be even better if he lost the trunks. The thought nearly made her swallow her tongue, and she coughed.

"Sorry," she gasped, doing her best to clear her throat. "I need to grab some water. See you later?"

"Of course, but are you sure you're okay?"

She smiled, even though her eyes were kind of streaming. *Charming, damn it, be charming, you idiot!*

"I'm fine. Seriously. See you soon."

With oxygen finally flowing clearly to her lungs, Eliza gave a jaunty wave and walked away, making sure to swing her hips like the foyer was a catwalk. It took several seconds for the doors to whir their way shut. She allowed herself a small smile of triumph.

Smooth? Nope. But she'd gotten his attention. And it had been less painful than the airport, so things were definitely looking up.

Her heels clicked and echoed down the long corridor, and she gripped her bag a little tighter as she neared the end. A flower-festooned sign beside a set of double doors read "Hough-Trailwick Wedding Welcome Dinner."

She closed her eyes for a second, and dragged in a deep breath.

The first hurdle, seeing Chandler again, had been cleared. Now she just had to enter this room full of strangers and pretend that she was a normal, confident human being. No small task, really.

"I can do this," Eliza whispered, then gripped the door handle. Music and laughter greeted her as the heavy door swung open, and she walked in like she owned the joint.

"Liza!"

Oh, thank God, it's Bree. Eliza's smile turned much more genuine as she wove her way through tables and chairs over to her friend's side. The redhead had a half-full glass of champagne, and a large purple flower was tucked behind one ear. She grinned as she enveloped Eliza in a huge hug.

"I'm so glad to see you," Eliza said, wrapping her arms around Bree.

"You came! Oh my God, Liza, I'm so glad you're here. You're going to have the best time, I promise." Bree pulled back just enough to grip Eliza's shoulder. "Holy crap, you look amazing. Where'd you get this dress? I've never seen you in something so cute."

Her cheeks heated a little, but Eliza nodded. "I know. It came from a little boutique a couple towns over, in Hannington. I wasn't sure about it, but the saleslady said it looked great."

"She was right. You look like a model." Drawing Eliza in close to her side, Bree grinned. "And tonight's the night to look as good as you do. Dinner will be a little bigger than anticipated. A few of Dad's friends are here, and he invited them to join us tonight. Apparently some of his partners have a time share." Bree rolled her eyes. "But anyway, there are six single guys here, and they're all hot. And one of them might already be into you." Bree winked just as Eliza's heart leapt straight into her esophagus.

"Really?"

Chandler. It had to be him. She hadn't met anyone else.

"C'mere. Let me show you where you're going to sit."

Bree grabbed Eliza's hand, and together they made their way through the room. Large floral centerpieces graced three circular tables that edged a central dance floor. The lights were soft pink and purple, and each time they passed below one, Eliza's sparkly purse threw a glittery pattern on the polished wood dance floor. Bree waved at a couple of people clustered in one corner of the room, then stopped to introduce Eliza to her father. It was a nice conversation, but it seemed to last forever. Once they finally escaped, Eliza glanced at her watch.

Damn, I must have been really early.

She said as much to Bree, who shook her head.

"Nope, it's good. We planned a cocktail hour before the meal anyway. A few people had delayed flights." Bree shrugged as she stopped at a table to the left of the center one. "Here you are!"

Eliza glanced at the center table, then back. A little lick of nervousness danced along her spine. "I'd hoped to sit with you."

With a knowing smile, Bree propped a hand on her hip. "I'm just at the next table. Besides, I think you're going to be just fine." She pointed at the name cards circling the table.

The one right in front of them said *Eliza Jackson*. Following Bree's finger over to the right, Eliza read the next one.

Chandler Morse.

Her mouth fell open. Holy shit. Could she really be that lucky? Or cursed? Or maybe Chandler had asked to sit next to her. Now, that would be an interesting development. It would have to have happened before he'd seen her in the elevator. She hadn't even apologized for acting like an idiot, and he still wanted to sit beside her and get to know her.

A warm feeling bloomed in the pit of her stomach, and she had to fight the urge to put her hand against her throat and grin like a teenager with a crush.

"Wow," she said, because she couldn't think of anything else to say. "That's . . . wow."

A happy sigh escaped Bree. "Come on, girl. I think you need a glass of champagne." She turned toward the door, then stopped short. Eliza almost bumped into her.

"And there's just the guy to bring you one."

If she'd been taken aback at how he looked damp and covered in sand, she was stunned at Chandler all cleaned up. His hair was a bit wet, but his khaki pants were pressed and immaculate. A sky-blue shirt was open at the throat, revealing just a hint of his tanned chest. It made his eyes look even greener, somehow. Shiny brown loafers completed the outfit.

Damn. Eliza's tongue darted out to wet her lips. She'd intended to flirt with several guys tonight, but right now, she doubted she'd be able to look away from Chandler for the rest of the evening.

"Um, I think I'm going to go chat with my cousin for a few. I was going to introduce you, but that can wait for later. I think you'll be in good hands." Bree laughed.

"Wait," Eliza said weakly, but it was too late. Bree was already halfway across the dance floor, and Chandler was approaching her, an appreciative look in his eyes.

"Eliza," he said warmly.

"Hi, Chandler," she returned, hoping he couldn't hear that little nervous squeak in her voice. "Want to get me a drink?" She winked boldly, then inwardly blanched. Oh God, she was so rusty at flirting.

But fortunately, he laughed. "I'd be delighted." He offered his arm, and Eliza slipped her hand through, resting her palm on his forearm. Damn, the man had muscles on muscles.

This was going to be a really interesting evening, especially if that tingling in the pit of her belly was any indication. Just being this close to Chandler was firing her blood, and she resisted the urge to run her nails up and down his arm.

Easy, girl.

But that sane inner voice wasn't anywhere near as much fun as the horny devil on her shoulder. And she had a pretty good feeling that tonight the devil would win hands-down.

4

As they walked together across the room toward the small bar set up along the side wall, Chandler tried to decide if Eliza's mercurial attitude was more surprising or exciting. They damn well tied in his mind. He'd expected to have some resistance to his advances. After all, she'd been embarrassed and prickly the whole time he'd known her.

But when he saw her in the elevator earlier, dressed to kill and flirting with him? Hope had flared. As he showered quickly and threw on some clothes, he'd almost convinced himself that he'd imagined the difference in her reaction to him. But clearly something was changed with her.

"Champagne?" He looked down at her and caught her eye almost instantly. Her cheeks colored and she looked away. Was she embarrassed that he'd caught her looking at him?

"Yes, thanks." Her soft answer was almost lost against a burst of laughter from the center of the room.

He didn't suppress the smile that curled his lips. "Two champagnes, please." The bartender made quick work of pouring, and Chandler tucked a tip into the jar atop the bar before handing one of the slender flutes to Eliza.

She took a sip almost instantly, the glass pressing against her full lower lip. Chandler watched as her throat worked, a small crease appearing between her brows as the bubbles beaded on her upper lip.

"Thanks. I needed that." The pleasure was plain in her voice. "Rough day?"

He quirked a brow at her, smiling to make sure she knew he was kidding. The champagne was chilled perfectly, and Chandler tried to focus on that instead of the way Eliza shifted from foot to foot. The room was filling quickly around them, and though what he really wanted to do was grab her hand and lead her outside to the beautiful patio where the view of the sunset glowed fiery red on the horizon, he instead suggested that they go find their seats.

"Sure," Eliza said, handing him the empty glass he gestured for. "We're on the other side of the room. You're next to me, right beside the patio doors there."

Chandler gave a little laugh as he held their glasses while the waiter refilled them. He passed Eliza's back to her and they started across the floor. "So you've already scoped out my spot, huh. Should I be flattered?"

Her eyes glittered as she tossed a teasing glance over her shoulder at him. "Maybe."

Anticipation tightened Chandler's stomach as he followed her. Damn. He'd hoped she'd be interested, but she seemed more than interested. Was she really that eager?

So far this trip was definitely turning out to be worth his while.

"Hey, man," a voice behind Chandler stopped him. Greg's hand fell on his shoulder.

"Greg," Chandler said warmly. His cousin had obviously come through for him with the seating plan. Eliza stopped, hanging back slightly. "This is Eliza. We met on the plane over here. Eliza, my cousin the groom, Gregory Trailwick."

"Nice to finally meet you," Greg said, his smile slightly strained as he shook Eliza's hand. "I've heard a lot about you."

"Really?" Eliza's expression became shuttered, the light dimming in her eyes.

"All good," Greg said with a nervous laugh. "Mind if I have a word with my best man? I'll return him quickly, I promise."

"He's not mine, so do what you want." Eliza turned and walked toward the table she'd pointed at earlier, her shoulders hunched forward slightly as if she was hiding from something.

Chandler frowned and rounded on Greg. "What was that about?"

"I don't know. You'll have to ask her. But listen, Chandler, I don't mean to be prying into your personal choices, just be careful."

"You warning me away from her?"

"No, I'm not. I'm just telling you to keep your eyes and ears open."

"I'd be a shit PI if I didn't."

Greg laughed, and the sound dissipated a bit of the tension between them. "True enough, man. True enough."

Chandler glanced toward the head table, where people were beginning to take their seats. "I think your fiancée is trying to get your attention."

Greg looked in the direction of Chandler's nod. "Yeah. I'd better get back to work."

"Work?" Chandler snorted. "I doubt that marrying a woman like that is a chore."

A half smile curled Greg's lips. "You might be right. Time will tell."

With a last slap on Chandler's back, Greg moved toward the beautiful redhead who was laughing as she accepted a glass of champagne from a short, round woman.

For a moment, Chandler didn't move. There was something there, some weird undercurrent in the proceedings that needled his senses. That same nagging drive that sent him searching for lies, for half truths and cover-ups. Greg wasn't himself. Not when he talked about Eliza, not when he looked at his beautiful bride-to-be.

"Excuse me," a woman mumbled as she bumped into Chandler's arm.

"My fault," Chandler said, smiling easily as he steadied her. "I'm just standing in the way."

Firmly tucking his doubts in the back of his mind, Chandler started toward the table nearest the patio doors. Eliza was seated there, the corners of her full lips drawn down just a touch. She toyed with a hibiscus that had either fallen or been plucked from the table arrangement.

She was beautiful, and she was into him.

Fuck his doubts. And Greg's half-baked warnings. He was going to spend the next couple of hours getting to know this beautiful woman and apologizing for the misunderstandings they'd had earlier. And then?

Well, then they'd see where the night went. He wasn't arrogant enough to think this was a sure thing. But he'd do his best to make sure the evening ended where they both wanted it to.

"Sorry about that," Chandler said smoothly as he sat in the seat next to Eliza. "Wedding jitters."

Without looking up from the delicate flower in her hands, Eliza answered, "Gregory doesn't seem like the kind of guy who'd be nervous at a wedding."

"Normally you'd be right. But this is his first wedding. That can shake a guy." That nagging feeling came back, a tickling at the base of Chandler's brain that begged him to look further into his cousin's odd behavior. Something else was there, something more than cold feet. He ignored it.

After greeting the elderly couple who sank down beside

them, Chandler turned his attention back to Eliza. "So, do you have someone special back home?"

Her alarmed gaze flew up at him and the flower dropped to the table. "Why would you ask that?"

He kept his voice smooth and even to calm her. "Because I'm interested in you. And I don't make a habit of chasing women who are attached."

His reply evidently stunned her, because she stayed silent for several moments. Eventually, she stammered out an, "Oh."

A waiter appeared by their table and began placing salads down in front of them. Chandler busied himself spreading his napkin over his knee. She needed time. He'd certainly given her some food for thought, and with the way she'd been so skittish earlier, he needed to be patient with her.

Patience he could handle. When the reward promised to be as sweet as the one flicking blue cheese out of the salad next to him, he could afford to play it slow.

Eliza picked at her salad, wondering what in the hell she was going to do now. It was easy enough to imagine catching Chandler and having a crazy vacation hookup in the fantasy realm, but now that he was clearly and obviously interested? Somehow his putting it into words made it much too real. And the real was intimidating her.

The buzz of laughter and conversation around her made her even more self-conscious. She looked like a fool dressed in this way-too-revealing gown. Why did they have to put moldy cheese on her salad? Was she even using the right fork?

"You must not have heard me. I said, why can't they just put normal cheese on the salad?"

Eliza blinked and looked to her left, where the friendly voice was coming from. A round-faced, smiling woman was there. She looked young, probably younger than she really was thanks to her rosy, apple-shaped cheeks. Her dress didn't fit quite right, stretching over the shape of her arms like it was a size too small in the sleeves. A small mound of blue cheese was growing on her bread plate, just like Eliza's.

"I'm Stacey, Bree's cousin."

Eliza smiled, thankful to have someone to talk to other than Chandler. He was making her insides turn too many flips to be comfortable. "I'm Eliza, Bree's friend. Bridesmaid."

Stacey rolled her eyes as she flicked a large crumble of blue cheese off her mound of spinach and tomatoes. "Me too. Well, maid of honor. Even though I begged to get out of it. Bree is merciless."

"She can be," Eliza agreed with a smile.

"It wouldn't be so bad if there was some leeway in the dresses. But spaghetti straps? With these arms?" Stacey poked the flesh of her upper arm with a disgusted wrinkle of her nose. "A girl can't even get a pity shawl?"

"I'm sorry," Eliza said lamely. "For what it's worth, I think the color will look better on you than it does me. That pale blue will look really good with your strawberry-blond coloring."

"I think anything would look gorgeous on you." Stacey smiled. "I don't think I was your size even when I was in junior high. Bree definitely got the more genetically gifted side of the family tree."

Stacey nodded toward the table in the center of the room, and a twinge of sympathy struck Eliza. Bree's family was seated there, her father looking like a silver-haired Hollywood leading man, her brother just as handsome, and her mother a slightly older, but still ridiculously attractive, version of Sabrina. Gregory's family members looked sallow and, well, bland next to the striking blondeness of their counterparts.

A burst of laughter from behind Eliza turned her attention back to Chandler. He wiped his mouth with his napkin while the older woman beside him still chortled.

"My goodness, we've strangled him, Leonard."

"No, no, it's okay," Chandler said, red-faced as he took a sip of water. "Just surprised me, that's all."

"So you aren't seeing the young lady beside you then? Leonard might be interested." The old woman winked Eliza's way.

"Erm—" Eliza wanted to swallow her tongue. "Well, see, I—"

"We're in negotiations." Chandler's statement drew an "ooh" from the woman beside him, and the erstwhile Leonard, who had the grace to look a little embarrassed at his companion.

Eliza didn't know what else to say after that, so she stuffed a bite of salad into her mouth, wincing when a crumb of blue cheese hit her tongue. She chewed stalwartly anyway. This was awkward, but it wasn't as awkward as being cornered in the pharmacy and called ugly names. This she could handle, weird as it was.

The older woman, obviously one of Sabrina's dad's friends, eventually fell into conversation with Leonard and the man seated on the other side of him, and Stacey started talking to the guy on her left, so Eliza and Chandler were finally sort of alone again.

What should she say? Where did they go from there? Maybe she should make it clear that she was just looking for some fun on her trip, nothing long-term. Or maybe if she did, he'd presume that she was trying to save face because she really wanted more? Her stomach did flip-flops, more from the thought of Chandler's reaction than the bitterness of the salad greens.

God, maybe she was trying too hard. Maybe she should just pretend that nothing was happening between them and be polite and say good night as soon as the dessert plates landed on the table. Okay, she was definitely overthinking things. But how could she stop? It'd been so long since things were effortless, were easy, that she really didn't know how to handle them at all.

But thankfully, Chandler stayed quiet. The waiter removed their salad plates and replaced them with their entrées, chicken for her and fish for him. The clink of cutlery seemed extra loud, even though voices and music buzzed through the room. But there, between her and this man, there was nothing but silence.

Why did she have to be so damn weird? Other women didn't have this problem, did they? Flirting was something she'd done when she was younger, more confident. Now when she tried she felt like a phony.

Oh well, fake it till you make it, right?

"I guess I should thank you for running interference. I don't know that Leonard is really my type."

Chandler laughed a little as he cast a glance in Leonard's direction. Eliza followed his gaze. The man was seventy-five if he was a day, and it looked like he and his lady friend had downed at least a bottle of wine each.

"I think Leonard's salving his wounds by checking out the other available women. Of course, I can't fault his taste. He did pick the most beautiful woman in the room to set his sights on first."

"Now you're just being outrageous."

"Nope." The look on his face was completely serious as he laid his fork down by his plate. "I mean it. You look incredible tonight."

Eliza's cheeks went hot, and she put her fork down to keep her hand from trembling. "You're coming on kind of strong."

"Does that bother you?"

"Honestly?" She asked just to buy her some time.

He nodded.

"I don't know what to do with you."

"I know what I'd like you to do with me."

The hunger in his voice sent a pang straight to her lower belly, and she clenched her thighs together to keep the throbbing from shivering through her body. Her mind descended into dark, passionate images of Chandler undressing her, laying her down, pressing her body against his long, hard heat.

Her mouth went dry and she reached for her wineglass. It was empty.

"Allow me," Chandler said, and rose.

"Bring a bottle," Eliza said, her voice shaking slightly. She hoped he couldn't hear it. Casting a glance over her shoulder, she was glad to see that the sun had finally sunk below the horizon. "Let's walk on the beach together."

His eyes lit with excited promise. "If that's what you want."

Her nod was definite. "Yeah. I'll meet you on the patio."

Chandler made his way toward the bar. Eliza watched him go. Her heart thumped hard against her ribs, and she closed her eyes for a second to calm it.

"Are you okay?" Stacey's voice floated to her.

"Yeah, I'm fine. I'm going to take a walk." Scraping her chair back, Eliza smiled at the woman's concerned face. "Seriously, don't worry about me."

She grabbed both her and Chandler's empty glasses and stood.

"Ah," Stacey said, a wistful note in her voice. "Okay, I get it."

"See you later?"

Stacey nodded, biting her lip. "Yeah. Have fun!"

"Don't worry, I will." Eliza winked, then darted out the patio doors behind them. Sliding the glass door closed, she placed the glasses on a nearby low wall and took a heavy breath.

Okay. She could do this. Spontaneous sex kitten. That was who she was on this trip. Her past didn't matter, and neither did anything else.

Chandler was smoking hot and into her. So why not let go and have some fun?

"Shut up," she hissed at her stomach, which was grumbling

nervously. She'd eaten at least half of her entrée, so the noise had to be due to nerves, not hunger. But it needed to stop now.

The music, which had been muffled due to the closed doors, suddenly became loud again as Chandler slid the door open.

Eliza pinned a seductive smile to her face. This was going to be incredible. There wasn't another option. Failing again was completely nonnegotiable.

No matter what, she was going to have fun tonight.

5

The bottle was cold in Chandler's hands, and he tried to pretend that it was the condensation trickling down his palm that caused the shiver in his gut. It wasn't. It was that smile on Eliza's face as she stepped forward, wineglasses in hand.

Thank God Greg had encouraged him to come to this wedding.

"I grabbed a bottle of champagne. It was the closest thing to the edge of the bar."

"Sounds good to me," Eliza said, the glow of the outside light shining softly against her hair.

"There's a little veranda down the steps over there. I saw it when I was going down to the beach this afternoon. Looked private. Would you like to take a drink there?"

Eliza nodded, so Chandler led the way.

Their steps echoed against the stone wall edging the walkway, ferns spilling over their boundaries and trailing down the concrete stairs. Small flowers filled a huge planter, their colored faces looking washed out in the muted gray of the evening.

Laughter and music faded behind them, almost imperceptible by the time they reached the partially hidden veranda.

"Wow," Eliza said, looking around as Chandler set the champagne bottle on a glass-topped table. "This is gorgeous. Are you sure it's okay that we're here?"

"There's a schedule on the wall over there." Chandler gestured with the neck of the champagne bottle before trapping it in a tight grip and popping the cork. "There was an event here this morning, and not another one until Saturday."

"Then I guess we've got it all to ourselves."

He hoped he wasn't mistaking the sultry note of seduction in her voice. She pressed a palm against the table, leaning back and jutting her hip out slightly toward him. His throat went dry as he poured each of them a glass of champagne.

"Appears that way."

She accepted the glass from him and took a long, slow sip.

"You know, you never answered me."

"What?"

"Before. When I asked you if you were seeing anyone."

"Oh." Her glance darted away, and a small shred of nervous energy trembled down his neck. Had he misunderstood somehow? The signs had all pointed to go since she'd appeared in front of him at the elevators, but he still couldn't shake the worry that he'd misread the signals.

He tightened his fist. He'd done a lot of that with women in the past. His ex's face popped briefly into his mind's eye. It was hard to pinpoint exactly what had gone wrong there—was he doomed to repeat the same mistakes? Spreading his fingers deliberately, he relaxed. Damn it, things were different now. He was different now. And he wouldn't let the mistakes of his marriage continue to haunt him here, half a world away from home.

"If this is too much for you, I get it. If there's someone back home that you care about, I'm the last man who's going to interfere. If you want me to leave, just say the word," he said, reaching for Eliza's hand. "But if not, then come with me."

He waited, hardly daring to breathe for a minute or two. Her eyes were dark, glittering softly as she stared at him. The oxygen seemed to freeze inside his lungs, not moving in or out. It was fine. He'd breathe later. For now, all he wanted was to hear her answer.

"I'm not seeing anyone."

Her words seemed to push air back into his lungs. She threaded her fingers through his, and a small *clink* rent the air as she set her wineglass down next to his.

"Good."

She smiled wryly, looking at the ground as they began walking down the steps to the beach. "You don't have to sound so smug about it."

"Why shouldn't I be? I'm on the most beautiful beach on the planet beneath a bright moon, and a gorgeous woman who just happens to be single is choosing to walk with me. If anybody's got a right to be happy at the moment, it's me."

She snorted, but let it pass.

They walked slowly, picking their way down the lighted path to the beach. After a minute or two, Eliza pulled her hand free from his grip. Chandler turned.

"Everything okay?"

"These damn heels are awful in the sand." She put a palm on his shoulder to steady herself while she removed the offending shoes. "I keep sinking up to my ankles."

"Here." Chandler took the shoes from her, tucking his fingers into the heel straps. "Hold on to me while you walk. I'll steady you."

Even in the shallow yellow glow of the path light, her large eyes were beautiful. "I can manage just fine."

"I know you can. But it was a clever ploy to keep holding your hand."

"Giving away trade secrets?"

"Every one I can." He grinned as he took her hand again. A slight tremble shook her fingers in his, and he tightened his grip. They'd reached the shoreline now, and the scent of the ocean breeze was full in his nostrils. Waves crashed one after another, spreading their foamy fingers onto the sand. Eliza was on his right, closer to the water. One particular wave rushed toward them. Chandler pulled her back, but she just laughed and squealed as the water hit her toes.

"Ooh, it's warmer than I expected. Mmm, feels like bathwater."

The mental image of Eliza, naked, her beautiful body sunk neck-deep in bubbly water, her dark hair piled high on her head, her pinkened nipples barely visible beneath the soapy foam . . .

"Ooh, too close, too close! I'm going to get soaked!"

His reflexes kicked in, which was a good thing because his brain was still locked in that bath-time fantasy. Running backward, he pulled Eliza after him out of the way of the waves, but not before they'd both been soaked to the thighs. She bent over and dusted sand from her hem.

"I can't believe I got this dress wet! Ugh, that's what I get for spending so much on a piece of fabric that I'll never wear again."

"What do you mean? You look great in that dress."

Eliza looked up at him from her bent-over position, squeezing seawater from the hem of her dress. "This is a special occasion. I got this dress just for Bree's wedding."

"What do you normally wear, then?"

"Lab coats, usually." She stopped there, as if there was more to say, but she didn't continue.

"Lab coat? Are you in the medical field?"

She shot him a pained look, and he almost wished he'd swallowed the question. But damn it, he wanted to know more about her. Maybe giving her some information about him would make her feel better about sharing.

He shrugged. "I'm a private investigator. Never done anything that needed a lab coat."

Eliza stood then, and crossed her arms over her middle as if she was uncomfortable. The change in her was definite, and he wasn't sure he liked it. "It's not medical. I'm a chemist. I do testing on pharmaceuticals, consumer products, lots of different things."

As she spoke, she didn't look at him. Damn it. He was smarter than this. Maybe Eliza was using this trip the same way he was—to get away from home, from the problems and worries that plagued her there. He wouldn't like it if someone prodded him for the ugly details of his divorce while he was on vacation and trying to have a good time. There might be something in her past just as painful. Even though he really wanted to know more about her, he shoved his curiosity into the back of his mind and stepped toward her.

She looked up at him without dropping her arms. Her hands gripped her sides lightly.

"That's fascinating, but right now there's something else that fascinates me more."

One corner of her lips curled up, and he almost cheered aloud at the sight. "Oh yeah? What's that?"

Pressing a palm against her cheek, he took a step toward her, halving the distance between them. She trembled slightly, dropping her arms to her sides. His pulse pounded loud in his ears, roaring like the waves that crashed only a few yards away.

He bent his head, hovering only centimeters from her mouth.

"The idea of kissing you."

His words blew over her lips, and her lashes fluttered closed.

"Can I kiss you, Liza?"

Her tongue darted out to wet her lips, a shaky breath emanating from her open mouth.

"Yes."

It was the answer he'd craved.

Eliza could barely believe she'd agreed. Not that she didn't desperately want Chandler's kiss—she did. But somewhere between believing she could be a sex kitten during this trip and the actuality of making out with what was, essentially, a complete stranger, she'd been convinced she'd lose her nerve.

But now, with Chandler's head bending down to hers, and her own chin tilting upward to meet his imminent kiss, her bravery seemed to surge. This was what she'd wanted. The past wasn't here on this beautiful beach. Only the two of them stood on the cool sand, arms winding around one another as their lips met for the very first time.

She closed her eyes and gave herself over to sensation. His lips were a bit cool from the evening breeze, the sharp tang of salt greeting her tongue. He moved slowly at first, the strong softness of his mouth on Eliza's calming and coaxing. It was a sweet first kiss, but Eliza didn't want sweet. She opened her mouth to him, beckoning him closer. She wanted his tongue, his taste, his arms bringing her closer to his body. The man had muscles, and she wanted to explore every last inch of him.

And thank God, he was a mind reader. His tongue delved into her mouth, tasting and exploring her smoothly. His arms wound around her back, one hand splayed over her lower spine. Eliza's hips tilted forward as her lower stomach began throbbing with want. Heat filled her limbs and she moaned into his mouth.

Their tongues met, their bodies aligned, and Eliza delighted in the feel of Chandler's growing erection against her stomach. He wanted her like she wanted him. For once in her life, she'd done things right. And if this was her reward, she was more than satisfied.

At least, she would be when he took her to bed.

"Mmm," she moaned in regret as he tore his mouth away from hers. But she didn't get the time to ask why he'd stopped kissing her. His mouth dropped to her jaw, and he pressed a searing line of kisses across the tender skin there, not stopping until he'd trailed down the column of her throat, over to the sensitive skin of her neck.

Eliza clenched her thighs together, which only fed the want burning between her legs. Moisture seeped into her panties, her body screaming for his entry. The roar of the ocean behind her seemed to twine with the thunder of her heartbeat in her ears. Sensation was carrying her away as Chandler's hand slipped lower to cup her ass. His large hand squeezed and lifted her against his hardness.

"Eliza," he muttered against her collarbone, "can I drop your shoes?"

She blinked, then laughed. "Of course."

"Good," he growled, then tossed her pumps up on top of a nearby dune. With both hands unencumbered, Chandler changed. Before, he'd been careful, moving slowly, like he was approaching a wild creature. Now? His hands were everywhere, caressing her ass, moving up the sides of her waist, thumbs brushing the undersides of her breasts.

Wherever he touched, tingles pricked her skin. Goose bumps rose on her arms, and her nipples tightened painfully as he nipped at her ear. Gripping his shoulders was more an act of self-preservation than desire, but as her fingers gripped the taut muscles there her focus redirected.

"God," she said, staring up at the sky as her greedy fingers roamed his shoulders. His flesh was firm, hot, his muscles flexing as his hands moved to her hips. Curling her nails into his biceps, Eliza gasped as he grasped behind her knee and hitched her leg up on his hip.

"I want you."

His words sailed straight into her throbbing core, and she pressed her body tighter against his. The length that had prodded her stomach before was now lined up with her most sensitive flesh, and she almost purred as she rubbed against him.

"I want you, too."

He kissed her again, a wild, unmeasured kiss this time, his tongue delving deep as he thrust against her. She moaned as the head of his dick brushed her clit. God, she was going to go off like a bottle rocket if he kept that up.

"Should we go to my room?"

His question was logical, but Eliza's brain couldn't really handle the thought of delaying this. She was wet, she was ready, and he really thought stopping now to go to the hotel room was the best option?

She looked around wildly. Surely there was somewhere they could be unobserved around here. There wasn't anyone else on the beach, but even in her lust-soaked brain she knew it was a bad idea to just lie on the beach and have sex.

Fortunately, her gaze lit on a row of cabanas nearby.

"There." She pointed, staggering back from him. God, she couldn't wait much longer. It had been forever since she'd had sex, it seemed. She'd made do with her trusty vibrator, but right now with the proximity of Chandler's body and touch, she knew exactly what she was missing. She didn't intend to miss it tonight. "Come on."

Hand in hand they ran across the sand to the small blue-and-white-striped tent on the end of the row. Chandler yanked open the flap, and Eliza almost swooned when she saw what was inside.

A large hammock took up the center of the cabana, canvas

pillows strewn across the white cotton netting. Clear panels in the ceiling let moonlight inside, and a string of solar-powered lights hung from the ceiling beams. It was almost as if it was designed for a romantic tryst.

Eliza laughed aloud as Chandler pulled her inside.

"It looks like someone knew we were coming." Chandler grinned as he unbuttoned his shirt.

"I don't mind this kind of welcome." Eliza sank onto the edge of the hammock. The wooden slat at the end of the netting gave a small groan of protest at her weight.

Chandler tossed his shirt aside, and Eliza bit her lip as she took in the sight of his bare torso. Broad shoulders tapered to slim hips, the classic V of his body proclaiming strength and fitness. His pecs were defined, a slight dusting of hair decorating them, thickening as it ran down his flat abdomen. The happy trail disappeared beneath the waistband of his slacks. She couldn't wait to see the treasure at the end of that particular rainbow.

"You've got an incredible body."

Her honest admission seemed to surprise him. He angled an eyebrow at her and quirked a small smile.

"I'd like to return the compliment, and I think I can, but I'll need to conduct some research to make sure."

"Does that mean you want me to take off my dress?" She tucked her feet onto the edge of the hammock with her, not bothering to adjust her dress. Chandler's nostrils flared as he took in the sight of her thighs, and probably her panties as her hem fell high against her.

"I don't mind helping." He took a step forward.

"It's okay. Stand there and watch." She reached down and grabbed the bottom of her skirt, pulling upward. She smiled inside the sheath of her dress as she heard his sharp intake of breath. That was definitely gratifying. It seemed like he was just as affected by the sight of her as she was of him.

When the dress was free of her head, she tossed it aside. There in her strapless bra and panties, she scooted to the middle of the hammock and patted the space beside her.

"There's enough room for two here. Care to join me?"

His fingers flew to the buckle of his belt, and his pants joined the rest of the discarded clothing on the sandy floor of the cabana. It was hard to see exactly what color his boxer-briefs were, but that wasn't what drew her gaze.

It was the sizable bulge that jutted straight toward her that kept her attention.

Chandler climbed onto the hammock beside her, and their bodies stretched out along the length of it. The cottony bed swayed back and forth as Chandler kissed her, deeply, thoroughly, as if the two of them were the only ones in the world, as if time had stopped and he had forever to explore her mouth.

As much as she loved that, she couldn't stop her hand from wandering down his stomach, tracing the line of hair, until her palm rested on the thick, hard length of his cock.

She wanted him. She wanted this. And she was ready now.

6

————————

Chandler had been trying so hard to keep things slow, to ensure that she really wanted this. But when her hand closed around his erection it was all he could do to keep from embarrassing himself.

Damn. He hadn't wanted a woman this badly since—well, ever.

"I'm not going to last long if you keep that up." His voice was a hoarse rasp.

"I don't want to wait anymore." Her eyes glittered darkly at him in the dim light.

Her words made him want to shout in happiness. Instead, he leaned over the side of the hammock and rustled in the pocket of his slacks for the condom he'd put in there earlier. At the time it had seemed like wishful thinking. Now he was grateful for the preparation.

She watched him as he pulled his boxer-briefs off and tossed them aside. Her gaze devoured him as he rolled the condom over his cock. And when he bent to her, and began easing the silky black panties down her silky thighs, a shudder ran through her body.

"You're beautiful," he said, his chest tightening as he looked at the bared bottom half of her body. A narrow strip of hair crowned her pubis, dark curls laid out like a welcome mat for him. He splayed his hand on her lower belly, and her hips lifted to him as if begging him to take his touch lower, deeper.

He understood how she felt completely.

"Will you take off your bra for me?"

She nodded and reached for the front clasp of her strapless black bra. A quick motion of her hands and the lacy cups fell away.

He was on her a moment later, his mouth worshiping the softness of her breasts. Her fingers tangled in his hair as she held him closer as if begging him to deepen his kiss. He sucked her nipple into his mouth, his tongue teasing and manipulating her turgid tip.

Her breaths became pants, her writhing against him more and more frantic.

"Chandler—please. I—I want . . ."

"I know," he said, positioning himself between her legs. The hammock swayed with his movements, the soft creaking mixing with the crash of the waves on the shore. He looked down at her as he braced himself on his hands on either side of her shoulders.

"Say you want this," he said, the blunt head of his erection nestling against her hot, wet folds. As much as he wanted to sink straight into her welcoming heat, he needed to hear her ask for it. "Tell me."

"Chandler, oh God, please fuck me!"

He didn't wait any longer. With a smooth thrust he entered her, and both of them moaned aloud. Chandler gritted his teeth, his hips trembling as he fought to keep them still. She was tight around him, her body a warm, wet fist pulsing around his cock.

He wanted to pump and pump until he couldn't remember his own name, but he forced himself to be patient. She was tight, and he wanted to know she wasn't hurting.

Her pelvis rotated, lifting and sinking, forcing the hammock to sway. Her breath came in pants, her eyes wild as her hands clutched at him.

She was ready, and he didn't have to wait anymore.

Gripping the cotton netting of the hammock in his hands, Chandler withdrew, then thrust forward, slowly at first. He closed his eyes, his body setting the pace for them both. Eliza's nipples were pebbled against his chest, her legs wrapped around his hips, her pelvis following the rhythm, too. Her inner muscles gripped his cock, and he grew even harder inside her.

She was so hot, so slick around him, that even through the barrier of the condom he felt as if his skin was burning. It was a good burn, like the sun was contained within her body and he was seeing it for the first time.

Their movements became more frantic, Eliza's body lifting harder and higher against him. He gathered her to his chest and kissed her deeply, his tongue mimicking the movements of his cock within her. She cried out against his mouth, panting moans becoming desperate calls of pleasure.

The hammock rocked them back and forth as their bodies each strained to reach that elusive peak. Eliza's nails dug into Chandler's back, the sweet pain almost wrenching his orgasm from him, but he pulled it back just in time. No. He had to wait for her.

And when it seemed like she'd plateaued, he reached between their bodies and parted her upper folds, his fingers finding the pulsing heat of her clit.

"Come for me," he whispered against her mouth, thrusting hard into her. His fingers pressed gently against her clit. "Come now, Eliza."

As if she'd been waiting for his command, she arched her

back and cried out. Gripping her breasts, she moved her mouth wordlessly. Her inner walls spasmed and contracted around his erection, and the sensation was too much for him. As she took him deep, deeper than he'd been before, he let go.

His lower back tensed, his balls aching, and he surged forward and back, his orgasm bursting from him. He held her close and moved slowly, more sporadically, deep into her as the cum poured from his body.

Their breaths were loud in the cabana, bodies sweating and trembling.

Chandler let his weight fall beside Eliza, and she snuggled up close to his side. They didn't speak for a long while after that, the hammock swinging softly from side to side, the waves crashing rhythmically only a few yards away.

He rested his cheek against the top of her head, breathing in her scent.

This was unexpected, for sure. He'd hoped that they could get together, but he hadn't dreamed that it would be this good. Even though he'd just orgasmed so hard he'd had to check to make sure he hadn't blown his damn cock off, just the thought of sinking into Eliza's body again had his depleted erection considering the idea.

Enough of her would be a hard thing to get.

"Was it good?"

Her soft-voiced question made him laugh. But when he looked down into her face, and saw the frown knitted between her brows, he shut up quick.

"Sorry. Absolutely, yeah. I would have thought you could tell I enjoyed it. Did you?"

Her expression relaxed, and she snuggled close again. "Very much so."

As much as he wanted to spend the night there in the cabana with her, naked and snuggling and hopefully, in an hour or two, fucking, it probably wasn't the wisest decision. So, with a regretful sigh, he carefully moved to the edge of the hammock and stood.

"It's getting late. Did you want to go back to the party? They might still be drinking and dancing."

Eliza shook her head as she pulled herself into a sitting position. "I don't think I want to be around anyone else but you tonight."

He bent and scooped their clothes from the sandy floor. Turning the idea over in his head, he waited. Could he invite her back to his room? Would she come? Or despite her statement, was this just supposed to be a onetime deal?

God, he hoped not. After that encounter, he wanted to make sure that they could do this again, at least a couple of times before this trip was done.

He handed her clothes over, and the two of them dressed in silence. She kept glancing his way, and he wondered if she was thinking the same way he was.

Only one way to find out.

"Come back to my room with me."

He'd meant to phrase it as a question, he really had, but it had come out like a command. He hoped that wouldn't piss her off.

She stood by the front flap of the cabana door, bare toes curling in the sand. She bit her lip and glanced away from him. His heart sank imperceptibly.

"Stay the night with me. Please?"

After a moment, she nodded. He didn't bother to stop his grin as she slipped her hand into his.

This would be a night to remember. What had he done to get this lucky?

He sure as hell didn't know, but he was willing to take it anyway.

Eliza blinked into the darkness, the unfamiliar scent of hotel sheets strange in her nose. What? Oh yeah, that was right. She was in Hawaii for Bree's wedding. And last night—last night she'd—

A gasp escaped her as she turned her head on the pillow. He was there, sprawled out on the king-sized bed. A sheet came to his waist, the faint gray of the dawn light spilling through the crack in the blackout drapes.

Chandler. She'd slept with him. Twice.

Burying her face in the pillow, she stilled. Damn. Last night had been incredible. Sex in the hammock with the ocean only yards away, their private cabana shielding them from any prying eyes. And then he'd led her here, to his hotel room, where they'd spent another hour just talking and cuddling. But then she'd wanted him again, and he'd been more than happy to comply.

Her sex-kitten act had worked like a charm. But the light of the morning made things look a little different. She didn't know him. He was a total stranger. At least he'd used a condom both times. She hadn't even asked him to, but he'd done it anyway. That meant he was a good guy, right?

She snorted inwardly. Her ex had used condoms, too, and he was a total asshole. She'd have to base her opinion of Chandler on something much more concrete than that.

The red numbers of the alarm clock declared it to be five thirty. Eliza bit her lip, considering.

What would Eliza the bombshell do? Probably leave with a kiss and a wave, laughing as she did.

So that's what she'd do. Even though the thought of waking him up with kisses and then getting some more of him was tempting, it wasn't the way she wanted to play this. Fun, free, easy, and careless. That's who this Eliza was.

Easing from the bed, Eliza held her breath. *Quiet, now. Don't want to wake him.*

Chandler turned over, putting his back to her side of the room. Good. That meant he wasn't facing the door anymore.

Scooping her dress and shoes into her arms, Eliza ducked into the bathroom. Shutting the door with a soft *click,* she flipped the light on.

And then she groaned aloud.

Her dress was ruined—still wet with seawater and the hem was caked with sand. It had been awful to put it back on to get back to the hotel. And now, hours later? No way could she shimmy back into it. Well, a skilled dry cleaner might be able to resurrect it, but it was certainly unusable for her first Hawaii walk of shame. Hardly the tousled sex goddess she'd imagined.

Crap. What was she supposed to do now?

Her gaze lit on the plush white robe on the back of the bathroom door. Cliché, maybe, but it would have to do.

After shoving the dress and pumps into a plastic laundry bag, Eliza shrugged into the robe. Fortunately it was nice and big, so she could wrap it securely around her. Knotting the belt at her waist, she glanced in the mirror.

Her hair was everywhere, what makeup was left on her face was smudged, and her lips were swollen and reddened from the long makeout session they'd had last night.

If she ran into anyone, they'd have zero doubts as to what she'd been up to over the last eight hours or so. But this Eliza didn't care about that. She pinned a bright smile to her face and ran her fingers through her tousled mane.

Tucking the bag with her clothes in it beneath her arm, she flipped off the light and carefully turned the handle to the bathroom door.

Chandler's soft snores greeted her ears. She smiled to herself at the sound. Even asleep, he was adorable.

No, shut up. It was a one-night stand. That's all. You're wild and free this trip, not tied down to any man.

Her inner voice might have had a point, but Eliza didn't really care for it very much. Having another round with Chandler seemed like an incredibly fun idea.

As quietly as she could, she eased open the hallway door and tiptoed out. She didn't breathe until the bolt clicked home again.

She waited a moment, just to be sure that Chandler wasn't going to pop out of the room and ask her where she was going. He didn't, so she carefully padded down the hall. Trying not to be grossed out by the fact she was walking barefoot on the hotel's carpeted hallway, Eliza distracted herself by thinking about the day ahead.

The wedding was the day after tomorrow, so there was sure to be planning and decorating to do. After she grabbed a shower and found some breakfast, she'd get in touch with Bree and offer to help with whatever she could. Surely there was something she could do. If she didn't keep busy, she might find herself looking for Chandler.

And tempting as that was, it probably wasn't a good idea.

At the elevators, she punched the Down button and waited. Chandler was staying a couple of floors above her. That was probably a good thing. There was still a great possibility she'd run into him in the elevator or the lobby, but at least she wouldn't be tempted to knock on his bedroom door in the middle of the night.

Well, she would, but the distance made it less likely that she'd succumb to the temptation.

As the elevator doors whooshed open, Eliza stepped forward. But then she looked up. Gregory, the groom, was standing in the corner of the elevator, his brows hiked high as he took in the sight of Eliza's outfit.

"Good morning," she said cheerfully, trying to play it off as best she could.

"Floor?" he said simply as the doors closed behind her.

"Five, please."

The elevator whooshed to life, and Eliza began to pray silently to whoever would listen. Surely she hadn't done anything bad enough to warrant the groom getting such a bad impression of her the second time she'd ever met the man. Bree was her dear friend, and she couldn't take the thought of her new husband hating her.

"Great morning for a workout," Eliza said, nodding at Gregory's athletic shoes. "Heading to the gym?" Surely a little friendly conversation would convince him she was on the up-and-up.

"Yeah," Gregory said with a small, tight smile. "Got to get in my morning run."

"It should be a nice day."

"Yeah, it should."

Good grief, this elevator was taking forever. It seemed like it had been years since they'd been stuck in that tiny metal box together when it finally slowed to a stop.

The doors clicked and then opened. Eliza stepped forward, carried on a wave of pure relief.

"Eliza," Gregory said, punching the Door Open button and holding it.

Her breath froze in her throat as she turned. "Yeah?"

Gregory's face was a cold, solid mask. "I don't know what game you're playing, but don't play it with my cousin. I don't trust you."

She almost fell backward. "Excuse me?"

"You heard what I said. You're Bree's friend, so I don't have a problem with you now. But if you screw over Chandler for some reason, that will change. And you won't like me very much then."

Eliza stood frozen as the elevator doors closed slowly, removing Gregory's face from view.

What the fuck was that about?

The considerable afterglow of her evening with Chandler had been completely ruined by that cryptic warning. She wrapped her arms over her middle as she made her way back to her room.

It seemed like her past might have followed her here after all.

7

Chandler frowned without opening his eyes and shivered. Damn, it was cold in here. Andrea had always insisted it be much too warm, and ever since the divorce he'd taken great pleasure in cranking the AC up as high as he could. But he might have overdone it this time.

He drew a deep breath in through his nose, and a faint feminine scent greeted him. He smiled. Eliza. She must be cold, too. Well, a little snuggling would keep them both warm.

He reached for her, but his hand found cold sheets instead of a soft body.

"Fuck," he said aloud as he opened his eyes to the empty hotel room. The bathroom door stood open, and no one was inside. Looking over at the clock, he sighed. Not even eight in the morning, and she'd already hauled ass out of his room.

Well, what had he expected? Breakfast in bed with sex for dessert? If he was being honest with himself, well, yes, he'd have liked the hell out of that, but it wasn't to be.

With a heavy sigh, Chandler pulled himself out of bed and

walked naked to the shower. She was intriguing, that was for sure. She'd surprised him yesterday more than once. But today he was going to get to know her much better. And hopefully the night would end as wonderfully as the previous one had.

The steamy shower chased some of the chill from his skin, and he hummed to himself as he shaved. A quick check of the weather on his smartphone revealed that the day would be beautiful—sunny and low seventies. He pulled on a pair of long khaki shorts and a light blue tee. He slid brown leather sandals onto his feet and ran a comb through his still-damp hair.

That'll work.

He wasn't dressed to kill, but he'd planned this as a vacation. Of course the vague hope that he'd get lucky had crossed his mind. After all, he was a man. But other than some condoms and a couple of nice outfits for the wedding events, he'd packed mostly casual attire.

Hopefully Eliza wouldn't mind that he was dressing for the beach. He wouldn't mind seeing her in a swimsuit. Or less, actually.

With the faint hope that he'd see her in the resort restaurant, Chandler left his room and made his way down to breakfast. His stomach rumbled loudly, making him glad that there was no one in the elevator with him.

He exited the lobby doors and followed the sidewalk around the left side. Fortunately there was no lack of signage pointing to the various attractions on the resort grounds. When the beach came into view, Chandler smiled at the row of blue-and-white cabanas along the shoreline. He'd never seen a hammock as a particularly sexy piece of lawn furniture, but now he knew he'd never be able to lie in one again without thinking of Eliza reclining, naked and wanting him.

With a mental shake of his head, he cleared the tantalizing image. Nothing he could do about that right now other than scan the restaurant for her. If she wasn't here, he'd play it cool. As much as he wanted to search the resort grounds for her, it wasn't a smart idea. Space. Time. Patience. They had most of the week. Which would have been much easier if he didn't know just how incredibly sexy she was.

"Good morning," said the dark-haired woman smiling behind the hostess stand. A large purple flower was pinned in her thick, dark hair. "How many?"

"Just one," Chandler said after scanning the tables he could see. Damn it, no Eliza. It had been a long shot anyway.

"Follow me, please."

Normally Chandler would have done a surreptitious cataloguing of the hostess's assets. But this time all he could do was look around for Eliza.

Holy crap. One night with the woman and she was already under his skin.

"Chandler! Over here, buddy. There's room."

He glanced to the left, and saw Gregory seated in the corner booth alone. After a quick word with the hostess, Chandler took the menu and sat across from his cousin.

"You're up early."

"You should talk." Chandler nodded toward the half-full plate in front of Greg. "What's got you up with the chickens?"

"Got up to get my running in. There's a nice track around the resort, four miles around. Ocean view at least half the way." Greg wiped his hands on the red linen napkin.

"Sounds nice. I'll have to do that later today."

After ordering a cup of coffee and a breakfast sandwich, Chandler turned his attention back to his cousin. "Are your nerves getting the best of you yet?"

Greg smirked. "My nerves have been vibrating ever since I agreed to this crazy-ass scheme."

"Agreed? You mean Bree proposed to you?" Chandler didn't

bother hiding his surprise. After all, his cousin had always been an alpha kind of guy. He'd never dreamed that Greg would let a significant other take the lead.

"Not exactly." Greg frowned down at his plate. "I misspoke. Sorry. Just . . . wedding nerves."

"I get it," Chandler said. And he did, at least a little. He'd been pretty young when he'd married Andrea. But Gregory was in his thirties now. Surely he knew what he was doing, right?

"You know, it's not too late to change your mind about all this. I know it's hard to think about, but—"

"I had an interesting conversation in the elevator this morning." Greg cut off Chandler's concern. "I didn't think I'd see the walk of shame this early into the trip."

"Oh really?" Chandler kept his tone cool.

"Really. It was that girl you were sitting with last night. Eliza. Looked like she'd been up three-quarters of the night and having a helluva time."

Well, Greg was right, but he didn't have to know that.

"You know, I've always heard it's impolite to gossip." Chandler smiled up at the waitress as she brought him a steaming cup of coffee, then took a sip of the bitter, black brew. "Damn, this is good coffee."

"It's local. All the guests are getting a bag at the reception. And it's not gossip if I'm looking out for you. You're more like my brother than my cousin. I don't want to see you get hurt."

Chandler leaned forward and pitched his voice low. "What the hell is with this Papa Bear crap? What did Eliza ever do to make you think she's bad for me? Jesus Christ, Greg, we just met. Yeah, we spent the night together, but that was just as much my decision as hers."

Greg blew a breath out toward the ceiling. "I was afraid of that."

"What? If you don't stop being so goddamn cryptic I'm going to beat your ass. And don't pretend that I can't, because we both know exactly how many seconds it takes me to put you in a figure four."

Gregory smiled as Chandler mimed one of their favorite wrestler's submission moves.

"It's been a long time since you busted my ass with a German suplex, Chandler. I think I could take you now."

"Want to test it out?"

Gregory shook his head, and some of the tension eased between them.

Chandler took another sip of his coffee, and the silence lengthened. He still hadn't gotten an answer from Greg, but he was willing to give the man a chance to collect his words. But before they left this table, he'd know exactly what Greg did. He deserved that much, didn't he?

"I just remember what it was like for you after Andrea pulled her shit."

Chandler shook his head. "This is completely different. I've learned my lesson now. And besides, I just met this girl."

"Hey, you didn't know you were sticking your dick in crazy at the time, man. But Eliza, well . . ." Greg trailed off, dropping his fork beside his plate with a *clink*. Rubbing a hand over his short hair, he tried again. "I just think maybe she's into things that aren't compatible with you."

"Like what?"

Gregory shook his head. "I can't go into more detail than that. All I know is her last relationship blew up because of her weird bedroom shit. I know you're not going to leave her alone because I asked you to, but I want you to know that she's, well, not normal."

Chandler just stared at Greg for a long moment.

"Your bacon and egg bagel, sir. Would you like anything else?"

"No thanks," Chandler replied to the waitress. "This is fine."

After she'd gone, Chandler looked at Greg.

"I don't know what happened with her last guy, but last night was good. Hell, it was incredible. So I'm sorry if I don't seem like your warning is appreciated. I'm not interested in a relationship; I just want to have fun on this trip. So whatever she's got going on doesn't really have a damn thing to do with me."

Greg frowned, but nodded.

Chandler really didn't taste his breakfast after that.

Eliza took much longer than usual to shower and wash her hair. She even triple-conditioned it, just because the first two times she wasn't sure she'd left it in long enough. But when her fingertips started to resemble raisins more than human skin, she conceded defeat and turned off the shower.

She stood there, naked, shivering. Even though she knew it was silly, she had just kind of wanted to wash away the feelings that Gregory's warning had stirred in her. Whether he meant to or not, he'd made her feel dirty. Wrong. Weird. Just like the people back home did. Logically she knew that the hot water and soap couldn't make her feel better, but that was all she had. All the scrubbing in the world couldn't take back that feeling, but that didn't stop her from trying.

She dried her hair and brushed it until it shone. A light application of makeup made her feel like she'd donned some armor. A light green sundress skimmed her thighs, strappy brown sandals crisscrossing over her feet. She frowned at her toes. The peach-colored polish didn't exactly match her outfit, but what the hell. It wasn't like she'd ever been concerned about toenail-coordination before, and she sure as crap wasn't going to start now.

Shrugging into a white cardigan, she examined herself in the mirror. Not bad. She didn't *look* like a sexual deviant, anyway.

With a mental "shut up" to her evil subconscious, she stuffed her room key into her bag and yanked open her bedroom door. She wasn't hungry, but the headache stirring behind her temples told her it was time to scout out some caffeine.

She glanced at the clock. Half-past eight. The restaurant was probably getting crowded by now, or at least it would be soon. She didn't really feel ready to face a crowd. In the lobby, she checked the giant map of the resort mounted on the wall.

"Perfect," she sighed to herself when she saw the coffee bar and ice cream shop across the resort from the restaurant. She could grab a scone or a muffin with her latte, and that would be a good breakfast. It wasn't likely she'd see anyone from the wedding party there, anyway.

A twinge of longing pierced her as she thought of him. *Chandler.* Was he disappointed that she'd left without a word? He couldn't be mad; it was just a one-night thing. He didn't have any hold over her.

But now she wished she'd stayed. That way she wouldn't have run into Gregory.

She looked at the sidewalk as she walked, not wanting to lift her gaze. These feelings shouldn't be here on this trip with her. The regret, the shame, they'd been her constant companions for months. But here in Hawaii was supposed to feel different. Nobody knew what had gone on back home. So why would Greg talk to her like that? What had she ever done to him?

He must know something about Tyler. And the only way he could was through Bree.

The thought of her friend telling her darkest secrets made Eliza's heart ache. Pressing her hand into her chest, Eliza walked faster. No. No way would Bree have spread rumors about her to her fiancé. That was completely impossible, and she refused to give it any more thought.

But Bree could ask Greg why he'd warned Eliza away from Chandler. And Eliza made up her mind to ask her friend the next time she saw her alone.

The light around her suddenly dimmed, and Eliza reluctantly looked up. A puffy white cloud had moved in front of the morning sun, turning the cheerful breeze a little cool. Eliza sighed as she pulled the strap of her purse higher on her shoulder.

It figured. Her personal clouds were even blocking out the tropical sun.

"Hey, Eliza! Good morning!"

A cheerful voice from behind Eliza drew her attention. She smiled and waited on the edge of the sidewalk.

"Hey, Stacey. Good to see you."

Stacey's cheeks were flushed red and she fanned herself with her palm as she stopped beside Eliza. "I was hustling to try to catch up with you. I wondered if I could get your help with something."

"I don't know how much help I'll be, but I'm willing to give it a shot. I was heading to the coffee shop for a bite. Want to join me?"

Stacey nodded and the pair fell into step together.

Eliza shot her companion a quick look out of the corner of her eye. Stacey was really breathing hard. Eliza could sympathize. She wasn't exactly in the peak of physical fitness herself, but it looked like Stacey was really struggling. It couldn't be easy to be related to someone as effortlessly beautiful as Bree, especially when you struggled with weight.

"So," Stacey said once she'd regained some of her breath, "the help thing. I know Bree had a little bachelorette party back home before she left, but Gregory's having a bachelor party tonight. So I was wondering if you'd mind helping me put together a small last-minute thing. I thought it'd be nice to go out so she doesn't have to worry about what the guys are up to."

The thought of Chandler going out with the rest of Gregory's friends and getting a lap dance sent a lick of jealousy up Eliza's spine. *Ugh, seriously? You just met the guy. One-night stand, remember? If he wants to go do a stripper, that's really none of your business.*

"Sure," Eliza said with a brightness she didn't really feel. "What did you have in mind?"

"I wanted to pick your brain about that."

They'd arrived at the coffee shop, so Eliza held the door and then followed Stacey in. A blast of air-conditioning made her shiver beneath her cardigan.

"Hey, let me get yours. You're doing me a favor, after all."

"That's really nice of you," Eliza said, arching her brows at Stacey. "Are you sure?"

Stacey nodded, setting her strawberry-blond hair to swinging. "Absolutely."

They placed their order at the counter and Stacey paid. Making up her mind to buy Stacey a drink at the bachelorette party made Eliza feel less guilty as she accepted her hazelnut latte and blueberry muffin from the barista. Stacey's sugar-free iced mocha took a minute longer to make, and then the two of them made their way through the maze of armchairs and tables to a small booth in the corner. The rest of the shop seemed to be occupied by resort staff and the occasional unfamiliar tourist, no one else from the wedding party in sight.

"So," Stacey said, using her straw to stir her coffee, "how'd last night go? That guy was really nice."

Heat climbed into Eliza's cheeks and she hurriedly stuffed a chunk of muffin in her mouth to give her a chance to compose a coherent thought. Chandler. Good Lord, they'd fucked like teenagers in that cabana. But it wasn't enough. She wanted more. What would Chandler's reaction be if she asked him to tie her up and spank her? Stars exploded behind her eyes, and her sharp gasp sent a chunk of muffin straight down her windpipe.

Coughing and hacking, tears streaming down her face, Eliza finally managed to dislodge the blueberry death trap from her lungs. Stacey helpfully reached over and thwacked Eliza between the shoulder blades.

A gulp of steaming-hot latte soothed her raw throat.

"Sorry, I didn't realize you'd commit muffin hara-kiri if I asked about him." Stacey's concern was tinged with mirth.

"It's okay," Eliza said, her voice strained. "It went well. Too well, actually. That's not something I typically do."

Stacey nodded sagely. "I understand. But hey, if I'd had the chance I'd ride him like a cowgirl. He's hot. You should definitely hang on to him."

Hang on to him? Like, after the wedding was over? After this little vacation was done and she was back in her tiny hometown and people constantly snickered behind their hands about her? The thought was, strangely, not as dismaying as she'd thought.

But it was impossible. He'd become interested in the person she was pretending to be on this trip. The allure wouldn't last once the plane touched down in Ohio. Once he met the real her, the one who was plagued with doubts and fears and a crippling lack of confidence, he'd turn tail and run back to North Carolina. Eliza shook her head.

"That wouldn't work. But anyhow, this bachelorette party. Why don't we check out the different clubs in the area? You know how Bree loves to dance . . ."

Stacey seemed willing enough to drop the subject, and the rest of their breakfast was spent planning the evening's activities. Which was perfectly fine with Eliza.

She had to stop thinking of Chandler as anything more than a vacation fling. She had a feeling, if she didn't, she might be in danger of pursuing the idea Stacey had inadvertently placed in her head.

She and Chandler as a couple? Please. So not happening.

8

Once Eliza had managed to shove the thoughts of a future with Chandler to a dusty, cobweb-infested corner of her mind, breakfast with Stacey was actually kind of fun. They had a lot in common, and once they'd decided on fancy pedicures and then dinner, with a swanky club afterward, they spent the rest of the time chatting.

"I don't think I could stand living in such a small town," Stacey said, taking a swig from the bottle of water she'd procured once her mocha ran dry. "I'm a city girl all the way. Give me concrete or give me death."

Eliza laughed. "It's not so bad! Appledale is actually kind of pretty. And the people are ..." She trailed off, glancing away. She'd been about to say "nice," but that was a lie. They weren't nice. They were judgmental, gossipy, and she really didn't want to be associated with them anymore. But that was way more information than Stacey needed.

"Small towns aren't so bad."

Stacey wrinkled her nose, distorting the pale wrinkles found there. "I'll take your word for it. And you'll just have to come see me in Atlanta. Then I can show you the wonders of city life."

"Sounds like a plan," Eliza agreed warmly.

"I'd better get going," Stacey said, scooting to the edge of the booth. "I promised Bree I'd help her finalize the menu for the reception at eleven."

"Gosh, is it that late already?" Eliza glanced at her watch. Damn. She'd enjoyed the chat so much, hours had gone by without her notice.

"Yeah. Hey, do you want to come with? I mean, if you don't have any other plans."

"Sure," Eliza said, a smile breaking out across her face. Wow, she was easy if that was all it took to make her happy.

Together they left the coffee shop, skirting a jumble of kids who were descending on the counter and clamoring for ice cream.

"Just in the nick of time," Stacey said, glancing back at the swarm of preteens. "I've done enough babysitting in my life."

"You don't like kids?"

Stacey sighed, kicking at a small piece of gravel on the sidewalk. "It's not that I don't like them. It's just, well, kids can be really cruel."

Eliza nodded. "People in general can be cruel about a lot of things. I get it."

The sun was beaming down now, and the day was pleasantly warm. Eliza tilted her face to the sun as they walked. Back home things were turning cold, so this little dose of warmth was amazing. Did she really have to go back in six days? She didn't want to think about it.

"Here we go," Stacey said, holding open the door to the main building. "The catering department is located in here."

The lobby was more crowded than it had been when Eliza had seen it yesterday, and she and Stacey had to maneuver their way past a crowd of suitcase-bearing travelers. Probably checking out, Eliza mused. The reminder that this was only a temporary vacation wasn't a welcome one. Ugh, she had to stop being so damn depressed. Shaking off the mental blues, Eliza pasted on a smile and passed the door to the catering department that Stacey held open for her.

"Ooh, good, you brought Liza!" Bree stood and clapped her hands gleefully. "Oh, this is good. My best girls together to help me out."

Eliza accepted the hug that Bree gave her, and then Stacey did likewise. They sat at a long, white tablecloth–covered table, Bree in the middle and her attendants on either side.

"This is swanky," Stacey said, tracing the silver edge of the china place setting in front of her. "I love the silver with the blue."

Bree nodded happily. "Yeah, the colors are going to look amazing together. I was really glad this resort had an opening on such short notice. It's been one of my favorite places to visit in Hawaii for forever, it seems like."

The catering director entered then, and the next half hour was filled with tasting the dishes that Bree and Gregory had chosen for the reception. Everything was delicious, fresh and simple, flavors that evoked both the fall season and the tropical surroundings. It was just a formality, as the catering staff had already begun prep work for the menu, but Eliza thought it was nice of the staff to give the bride a preview anyway. Once the tasting was completed, and Bree thanked the catering director, the three walked from the catering office arm-in-arm.

"Oh gosh, I'm so stuffed," Bree said, sticking out her tongue. "If I keep eating like that I'll never fit into my dress."

"Oh, shut up," Stacey said, poking her cousin in the side. "I so much look at a Kit Kat and I gain three pounds. You could eat a six-course dinner and still look amazing."

"I love the compliments, but I wish you'd stop putting yourself down to give them."

Stacey didn't look abashed at Bree's chide.

"Easy, ladies, no sniping, or you'll ruin the fun tonight," Eliza said.

"Fun?" Bree's brows winged high as Stacey groaned.

"Now the cat's out of the bag."

"What cat? Oh gosh, was it a secret?" Eliza clapped a hand over her mouth. Crap, why couldn't she keep her trap shut?

"What's a secret? What are you planning?"

Stacey just shook her head and pulled her arm free to open the lobby doors. "Nope, you're not getting another word out of us. Just be ready to leave at five this afternoon. Ooh, and wear flip-flops, okay?"

"O-okay." Bree looked suspicious, but Stacey just waved her off.

"I've got some stuff to take care of now, but I'll see you in front of the elevators on the ground floor at five." Stacey blew a kiss in their direction and walked toward the main tower.

"I'm glad to see you and Stace hit it off," Bree said, smiling in Eliza's direction. "I thought you might."

"She's really nice." Eliza nodded. "You've got good taste in family."

Bree just snorted.

A sudden thought popped into Eliza's brain. That scene with Gregory earlier. Gosh, should she bring it up now? She didn't really want to worry Bree, but she needed to find out why Gregory would be so cold toward her when she'd never met him before. The only explanation was that he knew something about the ugliness back home. But how could Eliza ask Bree about it without coming off as an accusatory bitch?

"Is something bothering you?"

Damn Bree's Spidey senses.

"I ran into Gregory this morning on the elevator, and it was kind of weird," Eliza admitted in a rush. She told Bree the story, not bothering to cover up the fact that she'd spent the night with Chandler, a fact that made Bree squeal like a teenage girl. But when she got to the part about Gregory's warning, a thundercloud-dark look crossed Bree's face.

"That was a jerk move of Greg," Bree said, crossing her arms over her middle before flopping down into a patio chair. They'd stopped at a small circle of tables that was probably used as overflow seating for the nearby restaurant. Eliza sank into the chair opposite Bree as her friend continued. "I'm really sorry that he was so impolite."

"It's not that," Eliza protested, tucking her hair behind her ear. "It just made me worry that he thought bad things about me. I mean, you're my friend. I want your new husband to like me. It's going to be weird if we can't get along. Do you know why he'd be that way?"

Bree sighed, tugging at the hem of her shorts over her tanned legs. "Not for sure, no. But I do know that he and Chandler are really close. Gregory saved his life once. I think he's just protective of him."

"But why does he think I'm going to be bad for Chandler? I mean, he doesn't know anything about me, really. Does he?"

Bree shook her head vehemently. "No way! I've never told him a word about the whole shit with Tyler. I would never do that to you."

"I know you wouldn't." And she did. The fact that she'd doubted Bree for a minute made her feel like shit. Eliza pursed her lips and blew. "I'm sorry. I just don't know where that came from. It made me feel like I was back at home, surrounded by all that ugliness."

"I know. And I'm sorry."

Bree rounded the table and enveloped Eliza in a big hug.

"I'll talk to him, okay? He'll apologize."

"No, that's okay. I just—No. It's fine. I kind of want to forget it."

Bree frowned, but nodded. "Up to you."

"I should let you get back to Greg. Didn't you say you were meeting with the photographer this afternoon?"

"Oh gosh! You're right. I'll catch you tonight, though, okay?"

"Deal." Eliza smiled and waved at Bree's departing back.

Ugh. Well, that had gotten her no closer to an answer. Eliza looked around. A lush park was spread out to her right, with a sign that announced a nature trail.

There. She'd take a walk, check out the scenery, and clear her brain for a while. A kind of reset. And when her walk was over, she'd go back to her room, take a nap, and get ready to party her ass off with the rest of the girls tonight.

There was still plenty of time to enjoy this trip. And one weird occurrence wasn't going to stop her.

Gregory had invited Chandler to a round of golf, but he'd declined. It wasn't really his favorite sport anyway, though normally he'd have gone along for the ride. But things were still odd between them because of Greg's insistence that Eliza was no good for Chandler.

It was too weird. There wasn't any clear indication where Gregory had gotten his information, but Chandler assumed it was Sabrina. She and Eliza were friends, so there might be a connection. Chandler sighed as he punched the Down button on the elevator. He'd spent a little while reading in his room, but the urge to get out and move around had chased him from the solitude. He'd put his flip-flops on, intending to walk along the surf.

Besides, he couldn't accidentally run into Eliza by hiding in his room.

"Afternoon," he said with a nod as he entered the elevator. Leonard and his female companion were already inside.

"Hello there. You disappeared much too early last night."
The woman winked at Chandler. "I had planned to ask you to
dance."

"I guess I'll have to make up for that at the reception,"
Chandler said with a polite smile.

"If you dance with Gladys you might be taking your life in
your hands. She's got two left feet."

"Leonard!" Gladys accompanied this exclamation with a
thwack to Leonard's shoulder. He winced good-naturedly.
"Don't listen to this old windbag. I'm a terrific dancer."

"I'm sure," Chandler said, relieved as the elevator doors
whooshed open. "Excuse me."

He walked through the lobby and turned right toward the
beach. But a moment later a gale of laughter turned his head.
Leonard and Gladys seemed to be following him.

Great. As nice as the old couple was, he didn't want to spend
his afternoon flirting with Gladys and defending Leonard.

But if he didn't walk along the beach, where else should
he go?

He thought back to that morning with Gregory. There was
that running trail, but flip-flops weren't exactly the best gear to
run in. Going back up to change shoes seemed like a waste of
beautiful daylight. But he had looked out the window of the
restaurant that morning. Wasn't there a nature trail past the
outdoor seating area? It was a nice day; maybe he should kill
some time walking through the woods.

His mind made up, he turned left at the fork. To his relief,
the pair of septuagenarians turned toward the beach.

With his tail finally lost, Chandler began to enjoy the solitude. It really was a beautiful piece of earth. He lived near the
beach, but for some reason the water here was completely different from the blue-gray of the Atlantic Coast. It was almost
too bright, too sunshiny. A wry smile crossed Chandler's face.
Trust him to be on vacation on one of the most beautiful islands

on earth and all he could think about was the blustery Outer Banks.

He had to get out of his own head. And the best way to do that was to look around and enjoy the present.

The trailhead wasn't far from the restaurant, and gravel crunched underneath his sandals as he crossed to the sign announcing the trail. He felt good, actually, energized and ready to move. Even though he hadn't slept much the night before, it seemed that the nocturnal activity had rejuvenated him.

He gave a wry grin. If only he could see her again, maybe some of the confusion tumbling through his brain would be cleared up. It was worth a shot, anyway.

The vegetation around him was much too cultivated to call what he was on a true nature trail, but he enjoyed it nonetheless. Thick-trunked trees lined the path, smaller bushes and vibrant flowers nestling at their bases. A squirrel chittered at him from a lower branch, and Chandler waved. Cute little bastard.

A voice from ahead stopped him dead in his tracks. The hairs on the back of his neck prickled in awareness.

Hey, chill out. There's no reason to think that you'd be alone on this trail.

But despite his brain's logical argument, he still couldn't shake the feeling that dogged him. So he walked closer to the source of the sound, being careful to stay quiet.

The trail rounded toward the beach ahead. That made sense. Hau'oli Resort was on a sort of peninsula, surrounded on three sides by coastline. The trail could only go so far before bending back on itself or running into the ocean.

As he neared the bend, he recognized the voice. Female. He'd heard it before, in fact, last night as she'd called out his name.

Eliza.

"... don't know why you would think that." She paused, and Chandler waited behind the trunk of a palm. Yeah, it was a dick move to eavesdrop, but Eliza sounded upset. He'd only stay a minute, and then he could decide whether to press on and talk to her or leave her to her privacy.

"Tyler, that's really unprofessional. Our relationship happened before you even worked for Quality. I didn't do anything wrong, and for you to keep spreading these stories around makes you look petty and immature. I'm not even in the state right now, I'm on vacation. Send me an e-mail, and I'll deal with whatever the problem is when I get back."

Ah. Ex-boyfriend and current coworker, or even boss? That spelled bad news for sure.

"That's it, Tyler. Don't call me again. I'll be back at work next Thursday. 'Bye."

Silence fell along the trail then. Damn it. He'd waited too long. Should he walk forward and chance pissing her off? Or turn tail and get out of there like a coward?

Nope. He was a man, and he'd 'fess up to his mistakes.

He walked around the bend, shoulders back and a friendly expression on his face.

"Well, hey there," he said, calling out a bit too loud for their proximity. Eliza's head jerked upward, eyelids wide. "I guess this nature trail holds more beauty than I'd anticipated."

"Ha-ha," Eliza said, rolling her eyes as she stuffed her phone into her bag.

"I'm not interrupting you, am I?"

"No, it's fine. Just a work phone call." Her tone went sour, and he immediately changed the subject. He wasn't about to bring up uncomfortable things between them now. Although he did wonder for a minute if the things that had Greg so worried were the things she'd accused her coworker of spreading around. The PI in him wanted to follow that lead to its end, but the decent guy in him had made a vow never to use his job to check up on a girl he was interested in.

Even though it was really damn tempting.

"This is really serene," Chandler said, reaching out and threading his fingers through hers. She jumped, but didn't pull away. "It's nice and quiet out here. Private."

"It is, I guess." Eliza's glance darted around them with renewed interest. "I like how cool it is. It even smells green."

He closed his eyes and breathed in for a moment. She was right. "It does. Walk with me?"

She nodded, and together they continued down the path.

For a moment they said nothing, and Chandler just enjoyed the fact that he was out here with her, all alone in the woods, holding her hand like they were on a date. That was a delicious thought, a date with her. Fancy dinner, dancing, then discarding their clothes on their way to the bedroom. Or maybe the shower. A hot tub? The hammock again? Hell, he was really making himself uncomfortable here. His shorts were becoming awkwardly tight in the crotch region.

Eliza's fingers tightened on his. He glanced down at her, lust shooting through his veins when he saw the pink tip of her tongue dart out to wet her lips.

"Liza?"

She looked up in response to his question, tilting her chin up to him as if asking for his kiss.

Who was he to say no to a beautiful woman?

9

She should have been surprised by his kiss, but somehow, she'd asked for it without saying a word. As if he could read her mind, he bent down and pressed his lips to hers.

Her body took over from her beleaguered mind. Tyler's phone call had forced bile into her throat, turning her stomach into an acidic whirlpool. She'd felt shaky, panicked, almost hunted. And then he'd come into view, taken her hand, and suddenly things were better.

He was like the best anxiety pill on the planet, and she was about to become addicted.

Her purse fell from her shoulder to the soft green grass below her feet, but she didn't care. Her arms wound around his neck as his tongue pressed past her parted lips to taste her. Mmm, he tasted of mint. Gum? Candy? Didn't matter. He was delicious, and she wanted more.

Her body pressed against his, her breasts flattening against his hard body. Her nipples tightened and peaked, the sensitive flesh rubbing against the confines of her bra as she writhed against him. He reached down and cupped her ass, bringing her onto her toes. *God, he's so hard already. It's like we didn't do anything last night.* The feel of his erection brought a smile to her face, even though they were still kissing.

Her hands crept upward to tangle in his tousled hair. Her toe cramped, but it didn't matter. Chandler had taken all her weight, leaving her free to wrap her legs around his waist. Without lifting his mouth from hers, he walked backward until they were pressed against the smooth trunk of a tree. Eliza moaned aloud as one of his hands ran up her side to cup her breast.

"Liza," Chandler whispered as he pressed soft kisses to her throat. The tender touch sent tight heat to her core. "I want you."

"I want you, too," she gasped against his hair.

He pulled the hem of her sundress higher, and she took a moment to thank the powers that be that she'd worn such an easy-access garment. He spread his stance wide to keep her weight on his thighs, bracing his back against the tree. The maneuver freed up one of his hands to run beneath her silky panties, and she moaned aloud when his finger parted her, running down across the slick folds.

Her hips rocked as she begged him to enter her. She didn't need to say a word. He knew what he was building within her. But something inside her wanted more. And she couldn't be silent about what she needed forever.

"Chandler," she said, trying like hell to keep her mind clear enough to have this conversation, "do you like to talk dirty?"

"Does that get you off? Want me to talk about your beautiful pussy, how I want to sink my cock deep inside it?" He timed his words with a couple of flicks to her clit, and she bit her lip.

"Yesssss," she drew out the word as he rubbed up and down. "What about other stuff?"

"Like what? Like fucking you out in the middle of a nature trail where anyone can walk by and see us?"

God, he was good. The thrill of someone discovering them roared to the front of her brain, and she tried to quiet her breathing. It didn't do a damn bit of good, because Chandler chose that moment to reach between them and loosen his shorts, freeing his hot, swollen cock.

The brush of that silky head against her nearly had her singing, but she had to wait. Had to get this out. She'd lose her nerve if she wasn't this turned on, so she had to tell him what she wanted now before her brain came back online.

"God, Chandler, please. Tie me up. Spank me. Fuck me in the ass, in the mouth, however you want to."

He set her down then, and she almost cried out at the loss of his strong body against hers. Her pussy was swollen and throbbing, and empty want screamed out from between her thighs. She stared at him for a moment, completely lost in shock.

Had she fucked everything up? Did he hate her now?

The doubts didn't have long to take over her brain, because Chandler reached into his pocket for a foil packet. He looked down the trail, and then back, and Eliza followed his gaze. No one was there. It was exactly why she'd chosen this path to take her phone call. The solitude was perfect.

"Here," he said, leading her into the foliage a bit. Another smooth-trunked tree stood just behind the bend in the trail. Anticipation sapped her strength, and she sagged against the tree trunk as he ripped the square open and stretched the condom over his erection.

"Liza," he said, a predatory look in his eyes that thrilled her from her aching breasts to her throbbing clit, "take off your panties."

She hesitated for a split second, but then her body took over where her brain misfired. The pale yellow panties whispered down her thighs and she stepped out of them, tossing them atop her purse.

"Turn around, and pull up your dress."

His tone was low and authoritative, but it was more the sight of his hand on his cock that made her turn. There was something about a strong guy with the confidence and virility to pleasure themselves in front of a woman. Maybe she was crazy for liking it that much, but she didn't care.

Another time she'd ask him to masturbate while she watched. But for now she wanted him too bad.

She turned her back to him and pulled up the hem of her dress, resting it atop the flare of her hips. Bending over slightly, she gripped a low-hanging branch of the tree. The position was almost too perfect. Well, it would be if Chandler could tie her wrists there and spend about two hours teasing orgasms out of her.

"Please." Her whisper seemed loud to her, but she knew it was almost undetectable. "I want you so fucking bad."

He was behind her only a second later, his big, warm body pressing up against her bared bottom. The cold metal of his zipper grazed against her sensitive flesh, the difference in sensation enough to send shivers of anticipation up her spine. It felt good, that soft little pain, but she wasn't so sure it'd continue to feel good.

"Can you take off your shorts? Your zipper . . ."

She didn't have to say more. He disappeared for a second, fabric rustled, then he was back, all soft hot skin against her ass and sensitive pussy. Her nails dug into the bark of the tree as she pressed backward against him, her clit throbbing and aching as he teased her inner lips with the blunt tip of his hardness.

"You're a wonder, Liza. You're so damn beautiful it makes me hard just to look at you. And this ass, my God, why did I not spend all last night worshiping it?"

A palm lightly landed on her bottom, and she yelped in surprise. But oh, it was good. She wanted more. Harder. She wanted him to bend her over his lap and let his hand fall over and over, palm cupped to make a louder sound, a gentle shake after each stroke to ease the sting. Moisture flooded her as he bent down and pressed his lips to the spot he'd spanked.

"Later I promise that I'll spend enough time dedicated to this beautiful part of you. But for now, it feels like you want something more."

His hand slicked across her, fingers entering her so slowly she almost screamed. Two fingers. Not enough. It wasn't his cock, so it wasn't enough. But she rocked against his hand anyway, the stretch and heat of his fingers feeling good. So good, but not good enough.

"Please, Chandler. I'm ready."

He added a third finger and she cried out. Oh God, so good. Not enough.

"I want your cock. Please, please, fuck me."

Never had he been so happy to fulfill a request.

He was so hard it hurt. Eliza's ass pressed against him tightly, her wetness slicking against the length of his cock. Her breaths were pants, moaning cries that seemed to wrap around his balls and yank.

He'd give both of them what they wanted now. But first . . . He looked toward the trail again. Still silent, still empty. Thank God. The thought of stopping now was enough to give him balls bluer than the tropical sea. With another light smack on her ass, he positioned himself at her entrance. She arched her back in supplication, and he slid home.

Damn.

Sliding the hem of her dress higher, he gripped her hips and began thrusting. God, she was slick, so wet, horny as hell. She met every one of his thrusts, forcing him harder and deeper inside her body. The heat was incredible, the scent of her arousal mingling with the green scent of the forest surrounding them, a heady and tantalizing mixture. It was like Gaia, or Diana, the scent of a goddess in the wilderness.

Chandler wondered if he'd lost his mind. And then she reached back and gripped his ass, and he was certain he had. But he really didn't give a good damn. If this was insanity, it was sweet, and he didn't want to be in his right mind ever again.

The tiny, wet sounds of their fucking, Eliza's quiet cries, his heavy breaths, they mingled into a sweet serenade. As much as he enjoyed watching her soft ass bounce against him, he closed his eyes just to savor the feeling of her hot body enveloping him, gripping him, urging him faster and deeper into her. His heart was thundering in his ears, his blood roaring through his veins as he moved faster, harder.

Eliza's sounds became louder, more frantic. A momentary worry broke his rhythm, and Chandler glanced both ways. No one was visible on the path, but they'd better wrap this up, despite how good it was. The forbidden excitement of discovery spurred him on, and he reached between her legs to fondle her clit.

"Come for me," he said.

Her legs clamped tight on his hand, forcing him to press harder against that throbbing nubbin.

"Oh God!" Her movements became uneven, shuddering. She slammed back against him, forcing him deep. And then her inner walls convulsed around him, and he was gone. He spilled every last drop, encouraged by the grip of her body.

They didn't move for several minutes, mostly because Chandler doubted that either of them would be able to walk very steadily for a moment or two. Reluctantly, he withdrew, keeping his hands on Eliza's hips to steady her.

"Am I dead?"

Her question startled a laugh from him.

"I don't think so. Not unless I'm dead, too, and heaven looks a lot like Hawaii."

Eliza smiled, running a hand through her tousled hair. "I guess heaven's kind of nice after all, if you're here."

The statement was oddly tender, and his chest gave a funny little twist. They looked at one another for a long moment.

"Then I hope we can visit heaven again and again," Chandler said.

Eliza's smile thinned, but she nodded. "Yeah, for a few more days."

The reminder that this trip was short wasn't exactly welcome, but she was right. Silence fell between them and Eliza looked away.

"Gosh, I dumped my purse all over the ground." She knelt by the mess and began gathering her things.

Chandler glanced downward and grimaced. Um, that was one inconvenience he hadn't considered before embarking on sex al fresco. "Hey, Liza, do you have a tissue?"

She glanced upward. "Yes, why, do you need one?"

Chandler nodded toward his flagging erection, still sheathed in latex. "I need to dispose of some evidence."

"Huh? Oh God, the condom. Yeah. Hang on."

Her cheeks colored prettily as she raked through the grass to grab the small packet. Jerking a couple of white tissues free of the plastic rectangle, she passed them over without really looking at him.

"Thanks," he said. He hadn't expected things to feel awkward between them. After all, this wasn't the first time they'd had sex. But for some reason he was unsure what to say, what to do next.

Once the condom was safely wrapped in some tissues, and they'd both righted their clothing, they walked toward the trailhead again. Eliza was quiet, holding her purse over her middle like it was some kind of shield.

She was a puzzle, that was for sure. Maybe she was still worried about that work call. Yeah, that was probably it. He'd distracted her, but now reality was making her worry again. Or maybe she was self-conscious about what she'd asked him for during sex.

The dirty talk had been exciting, for sure. She'd asked him to tie her up and spank her, among other things. Maybe those were things she hadn't had the courage to ask about before. Or maybe she had, and it hadn't turned out well. Either way, it was Chandler's job to reassure her. Well, he was making it his job.

"I meant what I said, you know."

She bit her lip. "What do you mean?"

He speared her with a direct look. "Tying you up. Spanking you. Talking dirty. I'll do it."

He'd thought her cheeks had been pink before, but he'd been wrong. The shade they'd gone now put some of the tropical flowers surrounding them to shame.

"You mean it? You don't have to."

"I want to. I'll admit, I haven't done a ton of kinky stuff, but I think I can manage to get pretty good at it, if that's what you're into."

They emerged from the trail, and Chandler glanced toward the restaurant. Two servers were out there, setting the patio tables for the upcoming dinner service.

"Wow. I hadn't thought—well, maybe we should talk about it later. It's not exactly private here." She nodded toward the sidewalk. Chandler looked ahead. There were couples, families, random tourists sprinkled along the walk. Damn it, she was right. But he didn't want to let her get away without making some kind of plan to see one another again, and soon. Once they reached the concrete, he'd lose any chance to talk about this.

He had to move fast.

"Hey, listen. I like you. I want to get to know you better,

maybe spend some time talking, instead, well, not instead of, but maybe before and after, sleeping with you."

Eliza tilted her head in question. "We can just have some fun. I'm not really looking for anything more right now."

"Okay, I get that. But that's no reason we can't hang out and chat, right?"

"Um, yeah, I guess. Maybe later." Eliza walked a little faster. "Sorry to run out on you, but I've got to get ready for the bachelorette party tonight."

"It's still early. Why don't we take a walk down on the beach?"

"I can't. I just—right now I need some time alone to think."

"About Tyler?"

His desperate gamble paid off only six feet from the sidewalk. Eliza stopped dead, almost like a remote control car whose batteries had just been disconnected. She turned slowly, her lips parted and brows knitted.

"What do you mean? What do you know about Tyler?"

He opted for the truth. "I heard you talking to him when I was walking down the trail. I'm guessing he's your ex, right? Did he hurt you? Listen, I'm not going to tell you that I'm perfect, but I am interested in you. And I'm not—"

"I can't talk about my ex with you. I'm sorry." She walked away from him then, and he couldn't be certain, but he thought he saw the telltale shine of tears on her cheek.

Shit. He'd definitely pressed her on the wrong issue. He tossed the crumpled tissues into a trash can and jammed his hands in his pockets.

Maybe Greg had been right. Maybe she wasn't good for him. But despite his assertions that all he'd wanted was some fun on vacation, he really didn't have any intention of leaving her alone afterward.

Aw, hell, who was he kidding. He was going to keep chasing

her. She'd gotten under his skin, and he couldn't scrub her away. Didn't want to.

Maybe it was for the best. A little chase added spice, right?

He gave a small smile as he entered the main hotel building and headed toward his room. Tomorrow was another day, and she couldn't stay mad at him forever.

10

When Eliza's hotel room door shut behind her, she finally let herself breathe.

What had she been thinking? God, there could have been kids on that trail. There were families at this resort, after all. But her libido had overcome her good sense, and then her worries had flown like water over a falls.

She pressed her palms against her heaving chest. She'd done it this time. Asking him to tie her up? Spank her? Had she learned nothing from fucking up with Tyler?

"Suck it up, Jackson." Her voice sounded loud in the empty room. "You've got to get ready for Bree's party."

Shedding her dress and still-damp panties, she made her way to the bathroom. Turning the knob all the way to cold was an exercise in self-flagellation. A small shriek escaped her as she stepped into the icy spray. Her teeth chattered as she soaped up quickly.

Even though the cold was distracting, it still wasn't enough to keep her brain from reviewing the last hour. Tyler's phone call had rocked her, that was for sure. Ever since they'd broken up, he'd gone out of his way to avoid her at work, a fact for which she was grateful. His dad owned the company, and Tyler had only joined up after his Internet start-up had bit the dust. Never really interested in chemistry, Tyler held a managerial position that had nothing to do with his abilities and everything to do with the fact he was a spoiled brat. Of course, she reported to him. If not for the fact that she loved her job, and Quality was the only company within an hour's drive that would allow her to do the work she loved best, she'd have quit a long time ago.

She sniffed. The cold was making her nose run. Better rinse off quickly and get out.

Wincing as the cold water hit her sensitive nether regions, she shivered. Her escapades with Chandler came to mind. He'd heard some of what she'd said to Tyler. He'd snooped, basically, and come way too close to the truth. That was unacceptable. Of course, she hadn't known that when she basically asked him to treat her as his personal sex slave. Would it have mattered?

The faucet squeaked as she killed the flow. Probably. Maybe not, though. Her sex drive had a habit of wrecking her common sense. Thus, the whole issue with Tyler.

Her hands shook with cold as she reached for the fluffy white towel on the rack above the toilet. She'd always thought that you were supposed to communicate with your lover, tell them what you liked, what you were into. That was the way to have good sex, right?

It had backfired majorly with Tyler. Oh, he'd been okay with it at first. The tamer stuff, at least. The dirty talk, spanking, those things he was fine with. But when she'd really opened up to him, he'd looked at her like she had two heads. He'd been her first real relationship, and it had blown up in her face. But apparently she hadn't learned her lesson enough, because she was making the same mistakes with Chandler.

"Nope. This is just a sexy vacation fling. Nothing more," she said as she pulled the closet's trifold door open.

Maybe tonight at the bachelorette party, she'd find someone else to have fun with. Maybe that was the answer—get Chandler off her mind. He'd been sweet to her, but that was no reason to become overly attached.

She dressed in black shorts and a sparkly silver tank. Black flip-flops with rhinestone straps would allow her newly painted toes to dry during dinner. Her makeup didn't take long since she didn't wear much. Stacey had made the reservations this afternoon, so all she had to do was show up downstairs.

It was a little too early to go down, but what could she do? Standing there and staring into the mirror was starting to make her crazy.

She flipped through the TV channels, but nothing caught her interest. She'd been stuck on her current level of Candy Crush for the last two weeks, and she wasn't really into the idea of trying and failing five more times. The book she'd brought had lost her interest.

"It's not that early," she reasoned, tucking her ID, credit card, and some cash into her front pocket. "I can take a walk on the beach if nobody's waiting yet."

The thought that she might run into Chandler made her pause, but just for a second. There must be hundreds of people staying in this building. The chances of running into him had to be slim, right? And she couldn't spend the rest of her vacation avoiding him, not with them both in the wedding.

The door clicked shut behind her and she took a steadying breath as she walked to the elevators. She'd be fine. There was nothing to be afraid of. Embarrassed? Okay, maybe a little, but fear? No way.

He was big, strong, and sexy, but not scary.

A family of five was crowded into the elevator that stopped on her floor, and Eliza smiled and waved them on.

"I'll wait for the next one," she said. "I'm a little claustro-phobic."

The tall man near the door laughed, and pushed the Door Close button. Once the elevator was on its way down, she pushed the button again. One of the six had to be nearby. And hell, it wasn't like she was in a hurry anyway.

She had plenty of time to regret her decision, though, be-cause the elevator that stopped next had Chandler, Gregory, and two other groomsmen inside it.

Shit.

"It's okay, I'll grab the next one," she said with a nervous wave. "I'm a little claustrophobic."

"It's okay, there's plenty of room," Chandler said, scooting Gregory over to the side. Now close to half the elevator was empty. "Come on in."

"No, it's fine," she protested, but it didn't do any good. Chandler held the door open with a broad palm, waiting for her to get on.

"Bossy," she muttered beneath her breath as she entered and stood in the cleared space. Which just happened to be next to Chandler.

He poked her in the side, a gentle, teasing poke. Obviously he'd heard her. She didn't give a damn. He was being bossy.

But you told him you liked that. You wanted him to tie you up and spank you and tell you what to do.

If she could kick her subconscious in the teeth she would have, but she settled for biting the inside of her lip and staring at the elevator's tiny black screen as the floors counted down.

"You look nice," Gregory observed from the corner behind her. Startled, she gave him a small smile.

"Thanks."

"Hot date tonight?"

Chandler made a strangled noise at Gregory's question, but Eliza didn't bat an eye.

"Yup. Bree and I picked up some surfers on the beach this morning. They're taking us out for drinks and wild monkey sex."

The younger of the two groomsmen, Sabrina's brother Brent, laughed aloud. "Is that before or after they take you wind-surfing?"

"We're going kiteboarding instead. More upper body strength required."

Brent snorted. "Good one, Liza."

"Thanks, Brent. If you'll excuse me." The doors thankfully hissed open, and she exited with her head held high.

She halfway hoped that Chandler believed she was going out with some other guy. And a slightly bigger half hoped that he'd be jealous as fuck.

So much for her fling idea. She really was a petty bitch when she thought about it.

"Hey, Eliza, over here."

She'd never been so happy to see a familiar face in her life. At least if she was with Stacey, Chandler couldn't follow her and try to confuse her again.

It really was for the best that they stay away from one another. Really. And if she said it to herself enough times, maybe she'd start to believe it.

Stacey was seated on a long, plush bench beneath the map of the resort. She was wearing a dress with sleeves that came down to her elbows. It was actually a much more flattering cut than the one she'd worn last night.

"You look nice," Eliza said, sinking onto the bench next to her.

"Aw, thanks. I doubt anyone will look twice at me tonight. I mean, check you out." Stacey mimed drawing an hourglass fig-ure in the air and whistled.

"Thanks, but I bet Bree will put us both to shame."

"You're probably right." Stacey's sigh was a little more dejected than the situation warranted, but before Eliza could ask her about it, a guy cleared his throat in front of them.

"Hey, can I talk to you for a minute?"

Chandler. She just couldn't get rid of the guy. And she was trying. Really. Sort of.

He'd been following the others out to the parking lot, but something had stopped him in his tracks. Well, not something. Someone. Eliza had looked so fucking hot, her legs tanned and long in those shorts, those silver spangles making her skin glow. He was 99 percent sure she was teasing about meeting up with surfers, but his testosterone overrode his good sense and he couldn't stop the thought from gnawing at his frontal lobe like a Doberman with a rib eye.

"I'll catch up with you guys in a minute," Chandler said, patting his pocket. "Forgot my wallet, got to run back upstairs and get it."

"Want us to walk with you?" Greg said, arching a brow at Chandler.

"No, really. Grab the car, I'll be right there."

Chandler walked away before anyone else could volunteer to walk him to his room. She couldn't have gotten far; in fact, he didn't even think she'd exited the building behind them.

"Jackpot," he whispered before pushing open the glass doors. She was sitting with that girl who'd been at the table with them last night, Bree's maid of honor. They looked to be deep in conversation.

Oh well. He didn't have the time to be especially polite. He cleared his throat, and she looked up.

"Hey, can I talk to you for a minute?"

He wasn't sure if her expression was excited or exasperated, it changed so quickly. In the end, though, her mouth settled into a flat line and her eyes went curiously blank.

"Sure, go ahead." Her voice was a little cool. Okay, that stung.

"I can give you guys some privacy," Eliza's companion said, her light blue gaze darting from Chandler to Eliza and back again.

"No, it's okay, you don't have to go," Eliza interjected quickly, grabbing the girl's arm before she could rise from the bench.

"Yeah," Chandler said, fighting the urge to put his hands in his pockets. What was he, a damn teenager? "I just wondered what you were doing later tonight. Maybe you and I could go get a drink after dinner."

"Sorry, I think we're going to be out pretty late." Eliza tightened her grip on her friend's arm, who winced like she was in pain. Actually, maybe she was. Eliza's nails seemed to be digging too sharply into her friend's skin.

"Well, hey, let me get your phone number, and maybe we can meet up tomorrow."

"The rehearsal's tomorrow. I'll be helping decorate and stuff most of the day."

Disappointment flooded him, but before he could say so, she broke in again.

"But maybe I'll see you at the rehearsal dinner?" As she said it, her gaze raked over him as it had last night.

It was a tiny rope Eliza threw him, but he'd take it. And besides, the unwilling third wheel of their conversation looked like she'd rather be sinking into the floor. Out of deference to her—he'd been stuck as wingman for Gregory a lot in his lifetime, so he knew what it was like—he'd let the nebulous promise of the rehearsal dinner see him through the night.

"Okay," he said with a smile. "I guess I'll see you tomorrow night then, if not before. And I'm sorry, I didn't get your name?" He spoke to the girl next to Eliza, who'd extricated her arm and was rubbing the tiny marks Eliza's nails had made in the pale skin of her forearm.

"Who me? Oh, I'm Stacey. Stacey Hough, Sabrina's cousin." She talked fast, in a high-pitched nervous tone.

"It's good to meet you," Chandler said, hoping his smile was warm and comforting. "See you tomorrow?"

"S . . . sure," Stacey stammered, looking over at Eliza as if questioning.

With a casual wave, Chandler turned and sauntered toward the door. A stinging, burning sensation bloomed in his back, as if Eliza's hungry stare was boring a hole in him.

God, he wished he could blow off the bachelor party and take her upstairs. But Greg was counting on him tonight. Damn it.

But he'd take care of Eliza later. Things between them were too delicious to ignore.

"That was quick," Gregory said when Chandler reached the car. He gave his friend an odd look. "You went all the way back to your room?"

"The elevator was still there," Chandler lied smoothly. "No waiting. So, guys, you ready to head out?"

Brent tossed him the keys to the rental car he'd acquired that afternoon. They'd discussed just grabbing a cab, but with the four of them there, it had seemed more reasonable to drive on their own. Especially since Brent didn't drink. Something about weak kidneys, if Chandler remembered correctly.

"You show me where we're going, and I'll be able to get back no problem."

"Sure, my GPS will get us there," Chandler said as he opened the driver's side door to the silver BMW. "Pretty nice wheels here, B."

"They gave me a free upgrade when they heard we were going out on a bachelor party night. I'd asked for the shittiest minivan they had."

"You would," Greg said, giving his soon-to-be brother-in-law a good-natured punch to the shoulder. "Asshole."

"Easy, guys," Randy, the last groomsman, said. "The night is young. I don't want to have to turn you in to the cops so soon."

The ignition turned smoothly, a soft dinging sounding through the sleek interior. Chandler cut his eyes in the rearview mirror at Randy. "If anyone gets called, it'll be your ass first. I told you, I'm not interested in whatever it is you're doing back there."

Randy had a past with drugs, despite his longtime friendship with Gregory. So the idea that there were narcotics in the car wasn't really that far-fetched.

"Ease off him, Chandler. I told you, he'll behave himself," Greg said, flattening his palm on the center console. "Come on, it's my last night of freedom. Let's grab a beer before I come to my senses and hop the first plane out of here."

A chorus of cheers met Greg's statement, and Chandler steered the car onto the street in front of the resort.

The restaurant they'd chosen was about ten minutes away, a Brazilian steakhouse. After that, they'd take in a movie, because as Brent had said, there was no need to hit the strip club before 11 p.m. Their table was reserved until one, and if they felt like it after that, there was a dance club just next door to the strip joint.

All in all, it should be an excellent evening. For Gregory and the rest of the guys, it probably would be. And if Chandler could stop thinking about how gorgeous Eliza had looked in those short-shorts and sparkly tank, he'd probably have a good time, too.

But the thought of stuffing dollar bills in a stranger's G-string didn't have the appeal it normally would. And he was fairly certain he knew why.

"It's too quiet in here," Brent said, leaning up between the front seats. "Greg, put on some tunes."

"Sure," said the man of the evening, grinning as he punched the Power button.

Fortunately, with the deep bass surrounding them, Chandler could let his memory wander where it wanted. Which just happened to be straight back to that private trail through the greenery.

Damn. She'd been upset when he'd found her, and it seemed that every bit of that emotion had turned to lust when he bent close to her. He wasn't complaining, not at all. She'd been more open and honest with him while they were in the midst of making love than she'd ever been with him. But why did she shy away from spending time with him outside of the bedroom? Well, hammock, or bedroom, or even semi-secluded jungle trail. It was like sex released her, let her loose and made her free. Once it was done, it was like someone pulled the plug on the light that belonged inside her. She withdrew from him, hid herself away.

When they had sex, she was even more beautiful than normal. Sex really did showcase the beauty she was, the honest, passionate woman who lived behind the mask. Why hide all that?

"Hey, Chandler, wasn't that the restaurant?" Brent tapped him on the shoulder.

"Oh shit, yeah. Sorry, I'll make a U-turn at the next light."

Damn it. This was Greg's night. He had to pull his head out of his ass so his cousin could enjoy tonight.

His confusion could wait.

11

_____

The music was so loud Eliza swore she could taste it. Or was that the fourth cosmopolitan she'd had since arriving at this club? She wasn't sure. Either way it seemed to be a sharp, exciting taste. Like possibilities, or future lovers, or even making up for past mistakes. She hadn't thought of Chandler more than six times in the past hour. Which was a much better average than she'd had during bridal party pedicures, or dinner, or the first club they'd been to.

"Hey, Stace, need a refill?" Bree yelled to be heard over the newest club beat. She held up her empty cocktail glass, the gold and white "Single today, Bride tomorrow" sash glinting as she wiggled to the music. "I'm buying!"

"Seriously, stop it. Between you and Eliza, I'm going to be completely hammered." Stacey laughed, her eyes sparkling in the glow of the black lights above. "I've already had enough. Just a water for me."

Bree pouted. "You sure? I've just got you two to celebrate with, you know, since Rachel's pregnant. My bridesmaid posse is incomplete. I won't even get to see her until the rehearsal to-morrow."

Rachel, who'd been Bree's roommate after college, had been married for two years. It was kind of a miracle she'd agreed to be in the wedding, since her doctor wasn't too happy with her traveling so late in her pregnancy. They'd compromised with a three-day trip, so the stress wouldn't be as hard on Rachel.

Stacey shook her head. "I'll have another later." Her smile faded as her gaze fixed on something behind them.

"Fine." Bree rolled her eyes. "Liza, another cosmo?"

Eliza shook her head vehemently, and the room swam a bit. She stepped backward to regain her balance and stumbled into a large guy with a buzz cut and too many chains around his neck.

"Oh gosh, I'm sorry," she stammered, regaining her balance quickly. "I didn't mean to hit you."

"No worries," he said, a wide, eager smile spreading across his face. "I was coming over here to talk to you anyway. Here, I talked to the bartender, and she said you liked cosmos." He held out a pink cocktail to her.

Eliza blinked. Really? Well, that was unexpected. A little flattering, or at least it would have been if the guy was anything approaching attractive. But he wasn't her type. The cloud of cologne around him was actually a little hard to see through, let alone breathe with. And she wasn't born yesterday. She knew not to take a drink from a stranger like that.

"No, that's okay. Thanks anyway."

Eliza turned back to Stacey and Bree, but a large hand fell on her shoulder.

"Hey, I'm talking to you. Don't be such a bitch."

Her heart leapt into her throat, and she knocked his hand away, whirling to face him again. Bree grabbed Eliza's arm and pulled her back, which she was glad for, because anxiety had thickened her tongue. She wanted to tell him he was a dick, and he should leave them alone, but the anger in his face made her feel small. Like Tyler had. The sneer across the stranger's face was too familiar, too frightening.

"What's the matter? Pussy got your tongue?" He laughed at his stupid joke, the sound carrying far in the break between songs.

"She said she doesn't want a drink, you fucktard. Leave her alone."

Suddenly there was a body in between Eliza's and the stranger's. *Wait, Stacey?* She held her arms out to the sides as if she was a wall.

"I was talking to your friend, you fat ugly cunt. Fuck off." The guy walked forward, muscling her out of his path. He shoved as he moved by, and Stacey hit the ground hard.

"Stace!" Bree cried out, reaching for her cousin. But Eliza couldn't let her go, because Buzz Cut was standing right in front of them now, using his height to intimidate. Was it cowardly of her? Maybe. But right now, the alcoholic haze that had been so pleasant before felt like quicksand around her brain. She couldn't think fast enough. What to do?

"Why do you have to be so stuck-up? Are you too good for me? Is your pussy gold-plated?" His breath blew across her face, thick with the scent of beer.

Beer.

That was it.

He wasn't just an asshole, he was a *drunk* asshole.

"Help Stacey," Eliza said over her shoulder in Bree's direction.

"What? I'm not leaving you with—"

"Go. I'll be fine."

Bree glared at Eliza, but went over to Stacey, who was holding the side of her head. She must have hit it on the floor when she fell. A small crowd had gathered around them now, and a thick-necked guy with dark skin and a mean stare was heading across the dance floor over to them. Thank God, it was the bouncer who'd let them in. He'd looked them over and pronounced them to be the hottest three who'd walked into the club that night. Bree had slipped him a generous tip.

He'd back Eliza up. She knew it.

"You didn't answer my question, saggy tits. I said, is your cunt gold-plated?"

"Nope. But you sure as hell better hope your balls are armored." She didn't give him a chance to figure out what she meant, she just kicked upward as high and hard as she could.

The top of her foot connected with his crotch with tremendous force. Eliza's pained curse and Buzz Cut's strangled cry mingled with the upbeat dance remix currently blasting through the speakers.

Eliza hopped backward on the foot that wasn't throbbing as Buzz Cut fell to his knees. The cosmo fell with him, spilling over the dance floor.

"You fucking bi—"

"Get the hell out of here before I call the cops." The bouncer reached down and grabbed Buzz Cut by the neck of his stupid blue tank top. "Unless the lady wants to press charges?"

Eliza shook her head while Buzz Cut squawked.

"Her press charges? She fucking kicked me for no goddamn reason!"

"Oh really? Because from where I'm standing, it looked like you tried to give her a drink you just screwed with."

Shit. Eliza stared at the puddle on the floor. She hadn't really thought he would try that; she was just being ultra-careful when she'd refused the drink.

Bree had helped Stacey to her feet. The two of them watched as the bouncer talked to Eliza about what he'd seen.

A minute later, Eliza nodded. "Yeah, we probably should."

She didn't want to ruin Bree's night, but she didn't want this guy to get away with this ever again, either.

"It's okay," the bouncer said. "I can give a statement, and the cameras might have caught him doing it anyway. Just give me your number in case they want to get in touch with you tomorrow."

Eliza scribbled her number on a scrap of paper from the bouncer's pocket, and he and Buzz Cut left the room through a back door together, Buzz Cut still whining about his sore balls. Good. She hoped she'd ruptured one, because her foot still throbbed.

"Are you okay, Stacey?" She hobbled back to her two companions. "I'm so sorry."

"It's not your fault." Stacey sniffed, her full lower lip trembling as she dashed away tears. "He was just an ass."

"You didn't deserve any of those awful things he said or did," Bree wailed, hugging Stacey tight. Their height difference put poor Stacey's face right in Bree's cleavage. "You're so beautiful, and brave for doing that! You aren't fat, and I—"

"That's enough, Sabrina," Eliza said, pulling the now-sobbing Stacey away from Bree's embrace. "Really, she's okay."

Eliza rubbed Stacey's back, wishing she could fix the night. God, it seemed like everything went to shit when she was around. Such great things fell apart with Eliza's "magic" touch, it seemed. Everything had been so great, and now?

Now nobody felt like dancing.

"Hey, let's go to another club," Bree said, frowning as she crossed her arms tightly. "This one's kind of lame."

"I think I need to go home. I mean, back to the hotel." Stacey sniffed. "But you guys keep having fun. I'll just hail a cab."

Eliza wanted to protest, but she looked at Bree, who was already nodding.

"That's okay, Stace. Your head hurts, right? I don't blame you for wanting to lie down. Do you need us to come with you?"

"No, don't cut your big night short. I'm fine, really."

But Stacey didn't look either of them in the eye.

Eliza bit her lip, glancing from one Hough to the other. As grateful as she was to Stacey, and as awful as she felt for what had happened, she couldn't let a drunk Bree run around the island alone.

"Okay. Let's go outside, and we'll wait for the cab with you."

It didn't take long. The street held several nightclubs and a strip joint, so cabbies were camped out waiting for clients. They packed Stacey into a waiting blue cab, and waved her off.

Arm-in-arm, Eliza and Bree walked down the street, Eliza trying like hell to pretend the night hadn't been completely ruined.

If only she could believe that.

Chandler wondered if he'd made the right decisions at the bachelor party. But now it was kind of moot, wasn't it? It was the next morning, and a pounding headache kept him company while he shaved.

He hadn't really drunk that much the night before. His symptoms were more the result of trying to keep Randy out of trouble. Dumbass didn't realize when the stripper put the dollar bill in his teeth that he wasn't supposed to lick her cleavage.

Chandler shook his head as he rinsed the razor under warm water. Fortunately, the stripper had calmed down after a hefty tip, and they scooted out to the club next door. But they'd only been there for half an hour when Brent had tapped his shoulder. "Hey look, Sabrina and Eliza are here."

His first reaction was excitement, but he'd stuffed it down quickly and frowned in the direction Brent indicated. On the upper dance floor, near the mirrored columns, Sabrina and Eliza were dancing.

God, she was beautiful. Her movements were loose, flowing, her hair wild, small strands sticking to her cheek. There was a ring of guys around them, most of them keeping their hungry eyes on Sabrina, but there were at least two that had looked at Eliza like she was a double-decker sundae and they'd forgotten their spoons. He'd tightened his fists at his sides, rounded up the guys, and left the club.

"Hey, what's this for?"

Chandler had forced a light note into his voice. "You can't have a bachelor sendoff with your fiancée watching, can you? We're just going to move our party next door."

So they'd gone to a smaller club across the street, staying until last call forced them out.

Chandler put his razor on the edge of the sink and splashed his cheeks clean. He'd have to hurry if he was going to meet Gregory for lunch like he'd promised.

He padded out of the bathroom, the towel still tucked around his hips. Shit, what was he supposed to wear to this rehearsal thing? He'd better check with the groom so he didn't embarrass himself.

But for now, he satisfied himself with some khaki shorts and a golf polo. He didn't play, but he liked the silky, breathable fabric. He'd figure out what else he'd need later that night.

Wonder what Eliza will wear?

The thought popped into his mind unbidden. Damn it. He wasn't going to get her out of his head that easily, it seemed. He'd gotten a lap dance last night that hadn't even made his cock twitch. Eliza had fucked him in the head, that was for sure. Imagine asking someone to tie you up and spank you and then, ten minutes later, telling them to get lost?

Too much. She was jerking him around, and even though he didn't have any reason to expect anything from her, he was getting fed up. It was too close to the kind of shit Andrea used to pull with him.

Get over yourself, Morse. Go meet your cousin, get him

hitched, and get your ass back to North Carolina before you get stuck with another crazy woman.

Sound advice, but it didn't improve his mood, or his still-thundering headache.

Before leaving the room, he swallowed two Tylenol dry. They stuck in his throat.

He didn't meet her in the elevator, or in the lobby of the tower. There was no sign of her on the semi-crowded sidewalk as the weekend travelers arrived. When he got to the restaurant, he scanned the tables, but he didn't see her there, either.

A sigh escaped him.

"What's with you?"

Chandler turned at the amused tone.

"Greg, sorry I'm late."

"You look like hell." Greg clapped him on the shoulder and steered him to the booth in the corner. "I thought you could hold your liquor."

"I can. I can't, however, keep running interference between your buddy Randy and the various employees of Bottoms Up Gentleman's Club."

Greg laughed aloud. "Damn, he should have gotten his ass kicked for that."

Chandler shook his head as he sank into the booth. "He almost did. When Security didn't do it I was tempted to do the job myself."

Greg smiled as he picked up the little roll of silverware in front of him. "Hell, he deserves it. Just wait until after the ceremony tomorrow, okay? I don't need him to worry Bree. She's already had a panic attack this morning because of Stacey."

"Stacey?" Chandler frowned. Now that he thought about it, he hadn't seen her with the other two last night. "What's wrong?"

"Some drunk jerk apparently decided to hit on Eliza, and he wouldn't take no for an answer. Stacey stood between them, trying to make him leave them alone, and he knocked her down. She hit her head pretty hard, apparently."

A red haze started climbing through Chandler's vision, and he fought to keep himself calm enough to listen.

"Is Stacey okay?"

"Bree told me that when Stacey got back to the hotel she started getting dizzy, so she went to the hospital. They said it was just a minor concussion, she should be fine. Of course, when Bree found out her maid of honor spent most of the night in the ER, she lost her mind. And then Eliza had to go to the police station, and she wasn't sure if she'd be back in time for the rehearsal."

"Police station?" Fuck, he was about to run out of there after her without enough information. *Calm down. Breathe. Get the facts, then react.*

"The guy who was hitting on Eliza tried to pass her a drugged drink. Seems he's got a record of sexual assault, and they needed to get her statement. She's back now, though."

The adrenaline pumped through Chandler's system, and he gritted his teeth against it. All he wanted was for that asshole to be in front of him so he could throttle the shit out of him.

"You'll be happy to know that Eliza kicked him in the balls."

That startled a laugh out of Chandler. He was shocked that he was capable of such a sound right then, but the mental image did give him a sense of relief.

"Good. He deserved worse, but I'm glad he got that much."

Chandler smiled his thanks at the waitress as she dropped off two waters for them. The cool liquid cleared the full feeling in his throat, and finally his headache began to fade. His stomach was in knots, though. It probably wouldn't relax until he'd seen Eliza and made sure she was okay. Damn it, no. She wasn't his responsibility.

"So how's Stacey today?"

There. That should prove to himself that he was altruistic and his motives were pure. Either that or he was chasing Stacey instead. Which wasn't that bad of an idea, really. Well, it wouldn't have been before he'd spent time with Eliza. It was probably going to be a while before any other woman looked as attractive to him again.

Damn it.

"She's okay, I think. We brought her some flowers this morning. Looked like hell, but that's probably because she was exhausted. They ran a bunch of tests on her last night, so it's not like she got a lot of sleep." Gregory stared down at the table. "I think she took that hard. She was really depressed this morning."

Chandler sighed. If things were different, he'd try to do something to help her feel better. And to help Eliza cope with the knowledge that something bad had almost happened to her last night. To talk to the bride-to-be, who was assuredly panicking that her big day was less than twenty-four hours away and people were being hospitalized and incarcerated left and right.

But he was a single guy, with no relationship to any of the women. He'd best keep his nose firmly in his own business.

"A toast."

"With water? For what?" Greg arched a brow but raised his glass to Chandler's anyway.

"To beautiful women. May they be worth it."

Greg snorted. "Dude, they're never worth it."

They both drank, though Chandler was sure Greg was wrong.

There was someone worth it. And Chandler had a hunch that he might have sat next to her on the plane a couple of days ago.

12

Eliza slammed the car door behind her and waved to the police officer as he drove away.

Pressing her hands into the knot at the small of her back, she leaned backward and tried to ease the tension. God, that seemed to take forever, but it was really only about two hours. It would have been much shorter if Buzz Cut, whom she'd learned carried the unfortunate name of Mortimer Dewey, hadn't been so set on pressing charges for her totally deserved kick to his balls.

Fortunately for her, the bouncer and the security footage both had her back. It was a clear case of self-defense. That hadn't stopped Sabrina from freaking out when the policeman had showed up at the resort this morning, though.

"Gosh, Bree." The thought weighed on Eliza and she started walking toward the event hall where the reception would be held. She was supposed to be helping decorate, and instead she'd sipped instant coffee while trying not to roll her eyes at Buzz Cut's outrageous lies.

A cloud covered the sun, and a breeze seemed to calm the

heat that had become oppressive during her walk. She squinted up at the sky. Hopefully it'd be a little cooler for the ceremony tomorrow afternoon. And once the wedding was out of the way, she could start to relax and really enjoy this trip.

Maybe. If she could forget Chandler, that was.

Damn it, she shouldn't have allowed his name to pop into her head. Now there was his face, that wide, boyish smile, that beautiful slight drawl, those muscles, his abs, his—

Before her memory could soar into his pants, the man himself called her name.

"Eliza!"

She thought about pretending not to hear him, but damn it, she'd had a rough twelve hours or so and she just wanted to see a friendly face. Even if that face was too handsome for her own good. It'd be hard to keep up the charade of confident, carefree bombshell now, but she wasn't sure she cared at that point.

"Hey," she said, offering a lame smile in a bit of penance. She watched as he jogged toward her.

"Are you okay? Gregory told me about what happened last night." His expression was sincerely concerned. Damn it, that shouldn't touch her, but it did. It made her warm inside, like the cloud had just moved away from the sun and the rays touched inside her chest.

"I'm fine. It was just a drunk asshole. I'm not in any trouble."

"Good," Chandler said, and the two of them started walking together. As they proceeded down the walk, Eliza's hand bumped into Chandler's. Without even thinking, she reached out with a pinkie and caught his. The touch, so simple, rocketed up her arm and curled around her brain, which was purring like a kitten. Why did that feel so good?

Chandler didn't try to grab her hand, he just kept his pinkie linked with hers.

She bit her lip and didn't look at him. If he'd have tried to deepen their touch, she could pull away. But she'd initiated this. How could she back out without making it weird?

Shit. What was she doing? She'd told Chandler that she just wanted to have fun. But now she was leaning on him like he was a friend, or something more. This wasn't smart, not at all. But she couldn't stop herself—didn't want to.

"I guess you're headed over here to help out with decorations, too, right? Greg roped me into it this morning. He said that you guys were kind of short-staffed with Rachel being pregnant and Stacey feeling bad."

"Oh God, Stacey. I haven't heard how she was since I got back from the station. Is she okay? Do I need to take her anything?" Eliza's concerned glance flew back to the main tower, where all their rooms were.

Chandler used her distraction to lace his fingers through hers and squeeze, palm to palm. "She's fine. I took her a coffee a little while ago. She just needs some rest."

Eliza shot him a doubting glance. His voice had been a little too comforting, too bright. He was hiding something.

"Maybe I should go see her myself. I mean, she might want some company."

Chandler shook his head. "She's resting, and besides, we've got to get the decorations finished before the rehearsal tonight. Bree's about to have a nervous breakdown, and you're the only healthy and able bridesmaid left. Come on, she needs you."

"You're right." He was, but she didn't have to like it.

Together they pushed through the doors to the event hall. The entryway held a large round table with a huge floral centerpiece. Three hallways spoked from the foyer, and on the leftmost branch was a sign with an arrow. "Wedding Reception."

"I guess we go this way?"

Eliza swallowed, but her mouth was dry. "I'd say just follow the sounds of the hysterical yelling?"

Oh Lord, she'd been afraid of this.

"Mom, I told you, you can't switch the place cards around. They're in those spots for a reason, I set up the seating chart myself." Bree held both hands out to her mother, whose arms were flapping around like a frantic chicken's wings.

"The Childresses are some of our oldest friends. How can you think to seat them with the Ballards? Don't you remember what happened in ninety-seven when we were invited to that cocktail party? Evian Childress spilled her drink all over Bonnie Ballard's exquisite hand-woven rug. Imported from Turkey, it was, and then ruined."

"Evian was four. She spilled her Kool-Aid. It happens." Bree's temper was beginning to show, but her mother was having none of it.

"It will be a disaster. And Lance Yarvey next to Francesca Ramone? Darling, please, they've been having a secret affair for the last ten years!"

"Then they'll have a lot to talk about," Bree snapped, slamming a handful of place cards down on the white tablecloth. "I can do this without you."

"My God, what have I done to have such an embarrassment for a daughter?" The tears were flowing now.

As nice as it would have been to stay by Chandler's side and avoid the confrontation, Eliza knew what she had to do. She rushed to their side.

"Hey, Mrs. Hough! Oh gosh, you're so gorgeous today! That color lipstick looks amazing on you. You've got to tell me what shade it is."

"Hello, Eliza," Bree's mother sniffed, dabbing ineffectually at her tears. Bree rolled her eyes as her mother continued, "Thank you. It's Canterbury Coral."

Drawing the woman's arm through hers, Eliza kept up a stream of questions and compliments. Moving toward the corner of the room, she caught Bree's eye. A sad, but grateful smile graced the bride-to-be's face. She resumed setting out the name cards in the appropriate places, more than likely having to check over her previous work to make sure her mother hadn't wrecked everything.

Chandler moved to her side and placed a friendly hand on her upper back. Eliza snapped her gaze forward.

Mrs. Hough craned her neck to see what was going on behind her. "What is it? Has Sabrina done—"

"No, no, I just have a little headache. I didn't sleep well last night." Eliza said as she held open the door of the event hall for Mrs. Hough.

"Well, I expect not. Gladys told me about that policeman coming to get you this morning. You girls were up to no good last night. I've told Sabrina time and again that she can't pretend to be a teenager anymore. Why, she's twenty-six! How she can possibly keep dancing and drinking like that and expect to be seen in a positive light, well, I—"

Eliza just smiled, nodded, and walked Mrs. Hough as far as she could from the event hall. She'd find someone else for the woman to glom onto, and then circle back to help with the decorations.

She'd thought she wanted to stop holding Chandler's hand, but not like this. Her fingers felt empty without his.

Chandler watched as Eliza skillfully drew Sabrina's mother away from the confrontation. For a moment, he just stood, almost in awe of what he'd seen. She'd taken what was a pretty volatile situation and completely defused it. Even skilled mediators weren't always as successful.

She was good. But then again, he'd known that before this had happened.

"Are you okay?" He moved to Sabrina's side, patting her back. "I know how family can get sometimes."

"Yeah," Sabrina said with a weak smile. "She's always like this. I didn't really want her to come, but Greg reminded me of how much worse she'd be if she missed it, especially if Daddy came. I agreed, but now I'm wondering if it could be any worse than this."

Chandler followed Sabrina's gaze over to the departing couple. Eliza held the door open for Mrs. Hough, but before they exited, he caught Eliza's eye. A small smile passed between them, and a warm feeling took up residence in Chandler's chest.

"You like her, don't you?"

The quick change of subject took him aback. "Who?"

"Eliza." Sabrina straightened a place card and stepped back to study her diagram. "The two of you look great together, you know."

"Really? Well, she's incredible. She'd look great standing next to anyone." He wasn't trying to butter up the best friend, he was just being honest. Eliza could stand next to a hobo and make him look good.

"It's more than that. I think you scare her, but in a good way. You should keep it up."

"Scare her?" This was getting more and more weird. Wasn't he supposed to be calming Sabrina down and helping decorate? How'd he end up getting a crash course in Eliza Jackson 101?

Sabrina sighed as she made her way to the stage at the far end of the patio. Bags of decorations were there, left by the wedding planner before she'd taken a team to prepare the area for the ceremony.

"Eliza's a little different. She's coming out of her shell here, and that's awesome. But it's a big change for her. You see, at home she's become pretty introverted, because her . . ." Sabrina trailed off as Chandler took a heavy candle stand away from her. He started walking it in the direction she pointed, but she didn't continue her sentence.

"Eliza doesn't seem that introverted to me." Well, she had a couple of times, if you didn't count the few minutes she'd told him in explicit detail what she wanted to happen between them in the bedroom. He counted them, over and over again.

"It doesn't matter why she's that way at home. What does matter is that she has a good time here and now, and I think you're good for her. If you want to be, that is. So she might kick up a fight, but that's fine. Let her. But don't let her push you away."

Chandler grunted as he put the wrought-iron stand down near a grouping of tables along the wall. "I don't intend to."

"Good." Sabrina put white pillar candles atop the stand. She glanced backward as the door to the patio squeaked open. "Now's your chance to stick around. Why don't the two of you start winding the tulle around the backs of the chairs? I need to scoot over to the beach and make sure Greg's doing okay with the ceremony decorations."

Without waiting for an answer, Sabrina waved to Eliza and hurried off in the direction of the beach where the ceremony would take place.

"Where's Bree heading off to?" Eliza frowned at her friend's departing back.

"She's going to check up on Greg and the wedding planner. I don't know why she hired a planner. She seems to be micromanaging everything herself."

Eliza shrugged a narrow shoulder. "That's Bree. She's pretty particular."

Chandler bent and picked up a bag of white netting. "She left us with instructions. Is this tulle?"

"Yes." Eliza laughed. "Your face when you asked that . . . It's not poison, you know."

So what if he'd exaggerated his ignorance? It got him that adorable laugh, so the slight deception had been totally worth it.

"We're supposed to wrap this around the chairs. I guess like that one."

Together they examined the two chairs that had already been done, by Sabrina or the wedding planner earlier, Chandler guessed, and then they started at the head table. Gregory and Sabrina's chairs first. Chandler held the bolt of tulle and un-wrapped it while Eliza took the end and guided it through the slats of the painted-black chairs. Finishing at the back of the seat with a poufy white bow, Eliza snipped the tail with a pair of scissors.

"That's close enough, right?"

Chandler stepped back and took a critical eye. One side of the bow was at least double the size of the other, and the whole contraption leaned sharply to the left. The tails were uneven, and the extra tulle sagged at the back of the seat. Well, to be per-fectly honest, it looked like shit. Biting his lip, he glanced back at the dark-haired, scowling woman.

"You're right. It's awful. You want to wind?"

"I didn't say it was awful," Chandler protested lamely.

"You didn't have to. I have eyes. Here, switch with me. I told you I'm not super girly."

She hadn't said anything of the kind, but Chandler didn't point that out. He just grabbed the end of the tulle that Eliza passed him, and between the two of them they unwrapped the mangled mess that she'd made of it.

Chandler began wrapping while Eliza held the extra bulk of the material. A comfortable silence fell between them as Chan-dler tied an expert knot at the back of the chair.

"You're pretty good at that."

"Thanks." Chandler grinned as he started on the next chair.

"I guess those summers I spent working on my dad's fishing boat were enough to teach me a couple of knots."

"Your dad's a captain?"

"Was. He owned a commercial fishing boat for a few years while I was a teenager. It was hard work, but I enjoyed it."

"That's great." Eliza cut the end of the tulle as he held it out for her. Tucking the scissors back into her waistband, she moved around the table after Chandler as they prepared to wrap the next set of chairs. "It must have been great bonding time for you and him."

She was more right than she knew. Those memories were some of the most precious ones he had. Chandler set his jaw as he knelt down to get a better angle on the next chair.

"Why did you quit?"

He didn't want to say, but he wanted to know her more, and that street went both ways. He took a deep breath before answering.

"I didn't exactly quit. Right after my senior year of high school my parents were both killed in a car accident, and the boat was sold to pay off their remaining debts."

The bolt of fabric clattered to the floor, and Chandler turned at the noise. Eliza was kneeling down and wrapping the extra fabric around her arm.

"Sorry about that, I guess I'm kind of klutzy."

"No, it's okay. Let me help."

He reached for the bolt of fabric, but her fingers fumbled again and she dropped it. They both reached for it at the same time, hands touching beneath the silky white netting.

He didn't think, he just took her hand and squeezed. She squeezed back.

"I'm sorry that happened to them, and to you," she whispered. The sun was peeking through the vines in the pergola above them, throwing sunny spots on the top of her hair, making it look like shiny, melted chocolate.

"It's not your fault," he whispered back, leaning closer.

"I know. But I can still be sorry."

His hand found her cheek, his thumb rubbing across the soft skin. Her eyelids fluttered shut, and his thumb continued to caress her face.

"Don't be sorry for me, Liza. Just let me kiss you."

She nodded, and so he did.

13

Eliza knew she shouldn't have let him kiss her. It was too much like caring. This didn't have anything to do with a vacation fling, with a sexy stranger getting physical just for the fun of it. This was too close. But damn it, he felt good. And she'd wanted to help heal the pain she saw in his eyes when he'd mentioned his parents' deaths.

The kiss was soft at first, gentle, lips and breath mingling, Chandler's hand holding hers inside an envelope of flowing white fabric. But before she could lose her head and open her mouth to him, he pulled away.

"Thank you," he said simply, and resumed wrapping the tulle around the chair.

She didn't move for a moment, because she wasn't sure what to do. Grab him and kiss him again? Touch that warm, beautiful body of his, so tantalizingly close to her? Stretch out on the table and fuck him like a horny teenager?

Maybe not that last one, because a group of voices was coming near. Scrambling, Eliza gathered the tulle and stood, hoping what had just happened wasn't written plainly all over her face.

"That looks great," Bree said with a smile. Gregory stood beside her, holding her hand. There was an odd look on his face, as if he was trying to hold back anger. It was a tight, drawn, closed expression. Eliza stepped nearer to Chandler, and Greg's eyes narrowed a bit further.

"Chandler is much better at this than I am," Eliza said with a nervous laugh. "You should have seen the chair I did."

"Eliza's not the girliest girl you'll ever meet," Sabrina said, poking Gregory in the side and getting a halfhearted smile in return. "When we went out to the clubs together in college I always had to dress her first. If not she'd have worn jeans and a ratty T-shirt on the dance floor."

"I think she's doing a good job on her own now," Chandler said, eyeing the outfit that Eliza had worn to the police station. It was a pair of Bermuda shorts with a flowing turquoise tank. Simple but comfortable and it fit well. In any case, hearing it from Chandler was nice.

"Do you want us to finish this, or do we need to do something else?" Eliza didn't know what else to say. She certainly wasn't going to comment on her newly acquired fashion sense, that was for sure.

"Oh no, it looks wonderful, doesn't it, Greg? We were getting in the planner's way, so she sent us off. Actually, we're going to go over our vows." Bree looked down, a shy smile on her face. It was an unusual expression for her. Normally Bree was so vivacious and bubbly, not really mushy or sentimental. But seeing how her friend felt about Greg made Eliza a bit less nervous about the angry-looking man.

"Okay. I'll see you at the rehearsal then?"

Bree nodded, Greg waved to Chandler, and then the happy couple walked away together. Eliza watched them go, gripping the tulle a little tighter when she saw Gregory's shoulders tighten in response to Bree cuddling his arm close.

"I worry about her."

"Who, Sabrina?"

Eliza blinked. She hadn't realized that she'd voiced her concern aloud until Chandler responded. Whoops.

"Sorry, that was an inside thought."

Chandler put the finishing touches on the last bow of that table. "For what it's worth, I think Sabrina is perfect for Gregory."

"But what if he's not right for her? He seems really uptight and irritable."

Chandler frowned slightly, taking the end of the fabric she handed him at the last set of tables.

"Gregory's been through a lot. He and I both have, really. But he's one of the best men I know. He saved my life eight years ago. I'm sure Sabrina will be safe and taken care of with Gregory."

"Saved your life? How did that happen?"

Chandler closed his eyes, and Eliza wondered if she'd pressed too hard. So far, Chandler had revealed a lot more of himself to her than she had. His honesty and transparency was pretty refreshing, actually, and was part of the reason her passion-soaked brain had been comfortable enough with him to ask for some kinky favors in the future. Of course, tying up and spanking were pretty tame compared to what she'd asked Tyler to participate in, the whole reason her hometown thought she was a freak. She shuddered, but then Chandler spoke and she was able to shove her bitter thoughts down.

"It was a case of wrong place, wrong time, really. About a year after my parents died I was in downtown Charlotte, visiting Greg and his parents, my aunt and uncle. We'd gone out to a restaurant together, but I had parked in the wrong deck. It was only about four blocks away from the restaurant, but it was through a rough part of town. I got mugged and the guy pulled a gun."

Eliza's stomach dropped and she covered her mouth with her free hand. "Oh no."

Chandler didn't lift his gaze from the motion of the tulle in his hands. Over and under the slat, between the next, pass through, repeating the motions until the slats were covered in twists of gauzy white fabric.

"The guy pulled the trigger, but I ran and his shot went wide. Gregory had driven around the block to make sure I didn't lose my way. He saw the guy chasing me, gunned the motor of his pickup, and knocked him down. The mugger was injured, but not seriously."

Tears were tracking down Eliza's cheeks, but she didn't move to wipe them away. Her heart was pounding as if the danger to Chandler was real, at that moment, instead of years in the past.

"Gregory was tied up in court for a while after that, but eventually the charges against him were dropped. I wondered, for a while, why that bullet didn't hit me. My parents were dead, and my cousin's life was being ruined because he'd protected me. It was hard to remember that being alive was a good thing. But eventually, things got better. Somehow they always do."

Chandler stood, having finished the last bow. His face was blank, and the sight was somehow more upsetting than the hurt Eliza was trying like hell to smother.

"There. I think that looks good, don't you?"

Eliza didn't answer, she just put the last remnants of the bolt of tulle on the closest table. Taking a deep, steadying breath, she closed her eyes for a moment.

She'd been so certain that this trip was about her. That she could become the person she wanted to be, shed her past and make a whole new start, just for a few days. But she hadn't, for even a second, considered she might meet someone who made her care.

Though she hadn't known Chandler long, she felt for him.

She hurt that he'd lost his family, that his cousin had been forced to defend his actions in court when all he'd been doing was saving Chandler's life. Was it more than she'd have felt for a complete stranger? Yes. Was it something more than simple empathy? No, not yet, but she had a feeling if she wasn't very, very careful, she'd end up feeling much too much for this man.

The consequences were real, but for now, she'd ignore them.

"Thank you for telling me," she said, closing the distance between them. She wrapped her arms around his waist and rested her head on his warm, hard chest. "I'm sure you're right. Gregory and Bree will be just fine."

Chandler's arms wrapped around her, and his chin rested atop her head. She closed her eyes and breathed him in. He was strong, he smelled so good, and she wanted to reach within him and heal the wounds that still must twinge whenever he thought of the past. She'd never understand, but she wanted to help him heal. Leaning her head back, she looked up into his eyes. He didn't move to kiss her, but she reached up and wound her arms around his neck to pull him down to her.

She kissed him, her tongue rubbing along his bottom lip, tasting him. He parted his lips and she eagerly delved between them, tasting the edge of his teeth, his tongue, the deep warmth of his mouth. He groaned then, pressing his hips forward to let her feel his growing erection.

Her fevered brain ran through the nearby possibilities. There was a bathroom just inside the event hall there, or maybe a dressing room with a lockable door, and they could—

But Chandler pulled away when she reached down to rub his ass.

"What's wrong?" The rejection stung, even when she saw the shuttered want in his eyes.

"Nothing. It's just getting late, and we've got to be at the rehearsal in twenty minutes."

"Oh." Eliza glanced at her watch. He was right. "Shit."

Chandler scratched the back of his head, looking toward the floor as he did so. The motion made him look like a wistful kid. "Sorry I made you sit through my life story."

"No, no, I was glad to listen. I mean, I'm sorry that you had to go through all that."

"We'd better get over to the rehearsal."

Eliza bit her lip. Should she be brave? Chandler had been in telling her all that. What the hell, roll the dice. "But if you're up for it, I'd love a rain check for after the rehearsal dinner."

He gave her a smile and waved as he walked away.

Hope flared in Eliza's chest. Another night with Chandler sounded like a dream come true. Especially if he remembered the promises he'd made in the woods. Just the idea sent a delicious shiver between her legs.

This rehearsal was going to last forever.

Chandler really had intended to make good on the promises he'd made on the trail to Eliza, especially since whatever reservations she'd been having had seemed to be taken care of. But somehow his unburdening to Eliza had reminded him of how he'd first met Andrea.

In his freshman year of college he'd spent a lot of time drinking and generally behaving like an idiot. He was mad at the world and didn't really give a shit about the consequences. But then Andrea had invited him to a party, and her free-spirited lifestyle seemed like the perfect antidote to his apathy. She'd listened to him cry, and had offered him comfort. He mistook that for love, for passion. It wasn't, and in the end he was alone.

He wanted to make sure he wasn't repeating the same mistakes with Eliza. So he needed a little bit of time to get his head back on straight.

Hopefully she'd understand.

As the best man, it was Chandler's responsibility to walk down the aisle next to Stacey. They stood on the beach near sunset, just the time of day that the ceremony would be tomorrow. The red glow of the dying sun made the ocean look like it was burning. Rows of white chairs faced the shore, and a beautiful white stage complete with columns, flowers, and billowing fabric was positioned in the front. It was a sort of fairy-tale setup, actually.

"I heard you were a hero last night," Chandler whispered to Stacey as Mrs. Hough and Sabrina started to argue about the order of the processional.

Stacey snorted. "Hardly. I barely slowed that jackass down. Whoops." She blushed as she glanced toward the priest at the altar while Chandler tried to stifle his laughter.

"It's not a church. You're allowed to say 'jackass' on the beach."

Stacey cracked a small smile at that, but it didn't quite reach her eyes. "I guess you're right."

"How's the head?"

"It's a lot better. A bit of a headache, but not too bad." Stacey gingerly patted her hair just behind her right temple. "I fell the wrong way, that's all."

"Well, if you need to lean on me, feel free. I'll catch you if you fall." Chandler patted her hand in a friendly way.

Stacey gave him a sideways glance. "Don't worry, I'll be fine. Besides, I'd hate for you to get a hernia right before the ceremony." She gave a laugh to prove she was kidding, but Chandler frowned slightly.

He started to say something about her self-deprecating humor when the wedding planner clapped her hands to get everyone's attention.

"Okay, that's settled now. Everyone has a list of the order, and that's what we'll be using. Remember, I'll be standing at the back of the seating area to let you all know when to process.

Gregory and Sabrina want to thank you for coming here to be a part of this important day. And I've been told to inform you that after the rehearsal, there'll be a barbecue and pool party at the honeymoon villa across the resort. So let's get this done, grab your bikinis, and we'll party!"

Cheers went up from most of the wedding party, but beside Chandler, Stacey had gone ghost-white. She clutched his arm like she was drowning and he was her only anchor to dry land.

"Are you okay? Feeling sick?"

Stacey shook her head, looking straight down at the white runner beneath their feet. "No, no, it's not that, it's just, I didn't realize that, well, I should have known. Bree's always planning something. It's just, swimming, I—"

The wedding planner rushed over to them, a large binder stuffed full in her arms. "Yes, maid of honor, Stacey, is it? Right, good, and here we have Mr. Chandler. Oh yes, nice and tall you are. There, wait for the last bridesmaid to take her place, and then the groomsman. Now, you two go!"

An insistent hand planted between Chandler's shoulder blades and shoved. They walked slowly up the aisle, and it was hard not to notice how Stacey's hand shook as they moved.

When they stopped at the front, and Chandler released Stacey's arm, Eliza caught Chandler's eye.

"Is Stacey okay?"

She mouthed the words, but he caught them instantly. A slight shake of his head gave her all the information she needed, and her frown became more pronounced.

Chandler moved into his position and clasped his hands behind his back. It was obvious why Stacey would be uncomfortable. Gregory had told him what the guy at the club had said last night. Of course she'd be self-conscious. Hopefully Eliza could make her feel better, and then the two of them could enjoy a swim together.

And after that? Well, he needed time to think. But his body

wasn't exactly on the same boat as his mind. Anticipation rumbled through him as he imagined keeping every one of his promises to Eliza.

The rehearsal went smoothly once a tall glass of wine had been handed to Mrs. Hough to make her a bit easier to get along with. The priest went through the motions, cracked a few jokes, then they were dismissed to get ready for the rehearsal dinner.

"Eliza," Chandler called, trotting to catch up to her and Stacey. Eliza glanced back, but Stacey kept her gaze glued firmly to the ground. "Is Stacey feeling okay? Will I see you guys at the dinner?"

"Her head's hurting pretty bad." Eliza's lie was pretty transparent, but Chandler wasn't about to tell her so. "I'm going to walk her to her room and keep an eye on her for a while."

He couldn't help being disappointed, but he knew it was for the best. He'd hoped he would get the chance to just talk with Eliza at dinner, see if he could organize his thoughts and feelings about her. Stacey had been through an ordeal, and since she'd experienced it while trying to protect Eliza, of course Eliza felt partially responsible. It was admirable, really. Just not the best timing for him.

"Of course. Can I do anything for you guys? I'd be happy to bring you some dinner, or something."

Eliza bent to Stacey's ear, but her strawberry-blond head shook vehemently. Eliza looked a little disappointed as she answered Chandler.

"No, sorry. She's not hungry."

"You go with him," Stacey said, her hollow glance landing on Chandler. "Seriously, don't worry about me, I'm fine. I don't want to ruin your night."

"You're not," Eliza said as the two of them slowly walked toward the main hotel tower. "I'm not that interested in a barbeque anyway. And swimming? Pfft, no. I'm miserable at it."

"I doubt that." Stacey's voice had a tiny trace of mirth.

"Nope, seriously. I suck. One time when I was a kid . . ."

They were too far away now, and Chandler cursed softly. Damn it. He wanted to hear the rest of that story.

"Hey, man, you need to hurry up. The steaks will be gone by the time you get there." Gregory clapped Chandler on the back.

"I doubt that. It looks like the party's missing a few members." Chandler nodded to Eliza and Stacey as they walked down the sidewalk, far away now.

Gregory put his hands on his hips. "Huh. Wonder what's going on between them?"

Chandler's hackles raised, and he couldn't exactly pinpoint why. "What do you mean? Stacey's feeling terrible because she got concussed last night, and Eliza's a nice person. She's helping her get back to her room and making sure she doesn't sit alone and cry all evening."

"Whoa, there, ease up. I'm not trying to piss you off, man." Gregory put his palms out to Chandler in a supplicating gesture.

Chandler raked a hand through his hair. "It's okay. You just phrased that weirdly. Anyway, I've got to go to my room and grab my trunks."

"Sure, man. No problem."

As Chandler walked away from his cousin, he wondered what he could do to save this night. Hire someone to sit with Stacey? Maybe have Brent ask Stacey out? No, they were related, that wouldn't work.

"Get your ass upstairs, change, and eat your goddamn steak."

It was a plan. Not a good plan, but a plan nonetheless. All he had to do was make it through twenty-four more hours. Then the ceremony would be over, their responsibilities as wedding party members would be done, and they'd have several days of uninterrupted time to get to know one another.

Chandler allowed himself a small smile. He'd get to see Eliza in a swimsuit after all. At least, he would if he was lucky.

All the way back to the hotel he scanned the grassy areas for a four-leaf clover.

14

The next day was a complete blur for Eliza. She got up early, her eyes bleary from lack of sleep. After the rehearsal dinner and pool party, Bree and Rachel had come up to Stacey's room, and they'd talked late into the night.

Well, everyone but Stacey had talked. Stacey nodded and laughed, and gave one-word answers every time Eliza tried to draw her out of her shell. She wished she knew what to do to help Stacey feel better, but she didn't. So she just did the best she could to be there and make her laugh. Hopefully that would be enough.

After stumbling through the shower in which she tried really hard not to get her hair wet, Eliza threw on a maxi dress and flip-flops and hurried to Bree's room.

It was chaos.

Mrs. Hough was there, already arguing about the hairstyle Bree had chosen. Rachel was sitting on the bed, wide-eyed, staring at the ordeal in front of her. Stacey was there, too, trying like hell to keep the Houghs from killing one another.

"Great, everyone's here!" Bree chirped, clapping her hands

and forcing a big smile. "Okay, girls, we're out of here! Mom, sorry, but we've got to go. My makeup appointment is in thirty minutes, and after that we've got to get to the hair salon. Four updos are going to take a while."

Mrs. Hough stood and clutched her designer purse to her chest. "I'll come with you, dear. After all, it's only right, I am your mother. I should speak with the stylist and make sure that your appearance is—"

"Mom, seriously. No. Go find Uncle Robert and have a nice breakfast. I promise I'll see you before the ceremony."

Mrs. Hough didn't like this idea, it was obvious, but there wasn't a lot she could do. This was Bree's day, and when Bree made up her mind almost nobody could stop her. Not even her crazy mother.

Eliza snapped pictures while Bree got all dolled up. Rachel tickled Stacey and Eliza managed to get a shot of her smiling. She hoped it wouldn't be the only picture that Bree's maid of honor looked happy in, but it just might be.

After a few hours of curlers and hair spray and enough bobby pins to make a half-scale model of the *Titanic,* the four of them left the salon and made their way back to the hotel. There was food at some point and a tense couple of hours when Mrs. Hough arrived to "help" them get ready, but eventually they were all dressed and ready for the ceremony. With a few minutes to spare, too.

"Just breathe, Bree. Come on, everything's going to be fine." Eliza was in the bathroom of Bree's hotel room, rubbing the back of a nearly hysterical Bree.

"I'm going to kill her. She's ruining this day, and I'm going to literally strangle the woman. What do I do?"

"Just ignore her. Let me and the others run interference, okay? If she comes up to you, grab one of us, and we'll distract her so you can make your escape."

"Oh man, why didn't I hire a hit man when I had the chance?"

Eliza laughed at Bree's groan, but she wondered exactly how much truth was in those words. She'd had a contentious relationship with her mother for as long as Eliza had known her.

A knock on the bathroom door drew their attention.

"Bree? Are you okay? We need to start heading down to the ceremony. There's only five minutes to go."

Panic filled Bree's eyes, and she gripped Eliza's shoulders. "Am I doing the right thing? I'm not, am I? I can't believe this. How could I have let it get this far? I'm the one pushing for this, Greg didn't even want to get married. But we love each other, it's the right thing to do, isn't it?"

"Whoa, whoa, whoa," Eliza said, shaking her head. "There is not enough time here to go through all that. What do you mean, Greg didn't want to get married?"

"I asked him." Tears threatened to ruin Bree's eye makeup, so Eliza grabbed a tissue and started dabbing maniacally. "I proposed to him, and he said no at first, but then he said yes and I was just so happy I didn't question it. But I know it's been fast, I just haven't ever felt like this for someone before, and I—"

"Sssh." Eliza hugged Bree hard. "He said yes. You're amazing, and from what I hear about Gregory, he's a great person, too. Did you know that he saved Chandler's life?"

Bree sniffed and nodded.

"See? Greg's a hero. And in about three minutes he's going to be your hero. But not if we don't head down to that beach so you can get married, okay?"

A tremulous breath blew between Bree's lips. "Okay. You're right. If Gregory didn't want to do this he'd have told me a month ago when we got engaged."

Eliza inwardly blanched at the timeline, but she didn't say a word. Who was she to judge? It seemed that the two of them were truly in love. So what did it matter if they'd been engaged for a month or a year?

"Right. He said yes, and he meant it, so let's go get you hitched!"

Bree laughed at Eliza's exaggerated version of Gregory and Chandler's accents. "You're cute with a drawl."

"I try. Now come on."

Together they left the bathroom. Rachel looked relieved, and Stacey was trying her damndest to pretend she was happy. It wasn't exactly convincing, though.

"I sent Aunt Beatrice down already," Stacey said, passing Bree's bouquet of Asiatic lilies to her. "That way she can be seated and you don't have to deal with her all the way down there."

"You're my favorite," Bree said, planting a kiss on Stacey's cheek. "Okay, girls, you look fabulous. Are we ready to do this?"

They put their bouquets in the middle of their group as if they were a soccer team about to do their warm-up cheer. Relief filled Eliza when she saw Bree's eyes sparkle with their usual vivacity.

"You're my best girls, and I can't imagine anyone else standing beside me today. Thank you."

"Aw, shucks." Rachel giggled. "Let's hurry before your groom thinks you're a runaway bride!"

With a cheer, the four of them dashed from the hotel room. Eliza hung back a moment to make sure Stacey was coming. She moved a little slower than the rest of them. *Still having a headache?* Eliza wondered.

"You look gorgeous," Eliza whispered to Stacey as they waited for the elevator.

Stacey opened her mouth, then closed it, and settled for a

small smile. "Thank you." She crossed her arms over her stomach, one hand rubbing her upper arm.

Damn it, Bree, why couldn't she have had a shawl? She's so self-conscious. . . .

But the elevator got there and Eliza followed the other girls without saying anything. It was too late for a wardrobe change anyway. Stacey looked fine, but Eliza knew what it was like to want to hide beneath clothing. After all, she'd been doing the same thing for a while herself, until this trip.

The strains of the string quartet could be heard from the sidewalk as they approached the wedding pavilion. Eliza's throat closed up a bit, the music was so beautiful. The sunset was even more beautiful than it had been the previous night, making the ocean look like a lake of fire. The gold-red rays silhouetted the priest and Gregory as they stood at the front of the crowd.

"It's showtime," the wedding planner whispered with a bright smile as they stopped at the back of the crowd. Eliza caught Chandler's eye, and he winked.

God, her stomach was turning somersaults. After last night, she'd wondered if he was mad at her. But if she was reading his hungry gaze right, that rain check was still on the table.

Rachel reached the end of the aisle, and the wedding planner tapped Eliza on the shoulder. "Go."

Gripping her bouquet in front of her, Eliza stepped forward.

He'd intended to watch Gregory's face for his first glimpse of the bride, but Chandler couldn't take his own eyes off the second bridesmaid to walk down the aisle.

She was sexy as hell in that icy blue dress, spaghetti straps showing off her shoulders and collarbone. He'd like to nibble that exposed skin, kiss and lick and peel that dress all the way down her beautiful thighs. . . .

But she turned left at the front of the aisle and went to stand beside Rachel, then it was his and Stacey's turn to walk down the aisle. Once they'd reached their places, the crowd stood and turned as the music swelled and shifted into a beautiful rendition of "La Vie En Rose." A collective gasp escaped them as Sabrina appeared at the end of the aisle.

Her smile was huge, bright, almost magnetic. She walked down the aisle alongside her father, almost seeming to float instead of step. She was a magnificent bride, but was it wrong of him to think that Eliza was even more attractive? He made a mental note to keep that observation to himself. He didn't want Greg to kill him after he'd gone through all that trouble to save his ass.

As the audience was seated, Chandler took advantage of their distraction to step out just a hair. Just enough so he could see past the happy couple and glue his gaze to a dark-haired goddess. Nobody else might agree with him, but for some reason, the piles of curls atop her head, the gauzy blue fabric of her short dress, the tasteful, light makeup she'd applied, all of it combined to make her look more elegant than he'd ever seen a woman before.

Even Andrea, on their own wedding day, hadn't been as attractive to him as Eliza was right now.

"Dearly beloved," the priest began, the words socking Chandler in the stomach.

Why'd he have to think of his ex right now? Of course, it was probably just the wedding. He hadn't been to another since his own had happened, several years ago now. It was only natural that Andrea pop into his memory at a time like this. It didn't mean he had to like it, though.

But then, Eliza caught him staring, and an incredulous smile spread across her beautiful face. Her white teeth flashed, then she put on a mock scowl.

Pursing his lips, Chandler glanced away, as if completely

bored. Out of the corner of his eye, he saw Eliza lift her bouquet to cover her slight giggle.

Good. She was thinking of him now, too.

The beginning of the ceremony passed without major incident, Chandler exchanging glances with Eliza whenever he could. He was in the middle of a rather long staring contest when someone touched his shoulder.

Chandler blinked. It was Greg.

"Rings, man?"

"Oh right." Chandler fumbled in his pocket as the audience tittered. He produced them with little fanfare, and his major task was over. Everyone looked happy, well, except for the mother of the bride. That one never looked happy until she was inside her third bottle of wine.

The rings were exchanged, the vows were said, and everyone clapped and cheered as Gregory pressed a long, lingering kiss on his new bride's lips.

The string quartet started a cheerful tune, and Chandler held out his elbow to Stacey. Her cheeks were blotchy, as if she'd been crying. It was actually pretty sweet. He hadn't figured she was the type to get emotional at weddings.

"You look beautiful," he said in a low voice as they walked together up the aisle.

Her breath caught, as if she was trying to choke down a sob. "Thank you. You look great, too."

When they reached the event hall, Stacey pulled free, claiming she wanted to visit the ladies' room and touch up her makeup. Chandler nodded and waved her off.

Finally, the ceremony was done. And he had definite plans for the reception.

The wedding guests sat at the chairs he and Eliza had carefully wrapped the day before, and even Chandler had to admit the decorations looked great. It was almost like a fluffy white dream, with a four-tier wedding cake serving as the centerpiece of the dance floor. Of course, once they cut the cake they'd wheel it out of the way so everyone could dance the night away. It was the part of the day he was most looking forward to.

"Chandler, darling, can you get me a glass of wine?"

"Of course, Mrs. Hough. Red or white?"

Sabrina's mother shuddered. "Red, darling, I can't abide white. Too sweet for my tastes."

"You've got it." Chandler debated just bringing the bottle and leaving it at the table, but maybe that would be a bit too obvious. So he settled for a large glass. He was just setting it on the table in front of Mrs. Hough when the wedding planner tapped on the microphone.

"Your attention, please," the woman said with a huge smile. "Allow me to present the new Mr. and Mrs. Trailwick!"

The room erupted in cheers from everyone except Mrs. Hough. Chandler glanced down at the woman beside him, but her face was a mask of irritation.

"Are you okay?"

She jumped as if startled. "Of course! Why wouldn't I be?" A fake laugh escaped her, and she grabbed her glass of wine as if she'd been waiting for it instead of glaring at her daughter and her new husband.

Weird. There were a lot of things he didn't understand about this wedding, and that was really starting to irritate him. Chandler forced himself to clap and smile as Sabrina and Gregory made their way through the crowd to the head table. Maybe he'd start asking some questions, figure out what was gumming up the relationships around here. Greg was still a little off, the new in-laws seemed less than pleased, poor Stacey had looked like someone ran over her puppy ever since the bachelorette party. . . .

He stopped cataloguing the things that didn't add up just

then, because Eliza was suddenly there. His misgivings from earlier seemed further away now. To hell with Andrea, this was different.

Without bothering to say good-bye to Mrs. Hough, Chandler made his way directly to Eliza's side.

"Hello, beautiful."

She glanced away as if embarrassed at his frank compliment. "Hi, yourself."

"Allow me to escort you to your seat?" Chandler held out his elbow, and she tucked her hand through. It was cold, and he pressed it close to his side to warm it.

"Thanks."

They walked through the crowd and Chandler's imagination started running wild. Her skirt was short; maybe during dinner he could put a hand on her knee and see what she thought about that. Warming up during the reception was a good idea, right? And after massaging her thigh, he'd feed her a bit of his slice of cake. Imagining her sucking the sweet icing off his fingertips sent a bolt of lust that wrapped straight around his cock.

Then they'd get out on the dance floor. Brushing bodies, moving closer, Eliza would turn and press her ass against him, shaking to the beat.

"Hey look, you're sitting on the other side of the table from me."

Chandler's plans fell to the ground and smashed at their feet. He frowned as he stared at the place cards. Yup, sure enough, Eliza was seated next to Randy, and Chandler was next to Stacey. Shit.

He pulled out Eliza's chair for her while trying to figure out how to fix this. He couldn't just swap place cards; that would be rude, wouldn't it? Maybe he could ask Randy to switch seats with him. But then he remembered the argument Mrs. Hough and Sabrina had had the day before about the seating arrangements. The last thing he wanted was to cause waves for the happy couple.

Double shit.

"I guess I'll see you later?" Eliza glanced over her shoulder at Chandler. Was it a bad thing that he was a little happy to see the disappointment in her eyes? Nah, it wasn't. They felt the same.

He bent over and pressed his lips close to her ear. "Save a dance for me."

She shivered as he kissed the delicate curve of her ear, then nodded.

Chandler walked away, satisfied enough for the moment.

The night was young, and they'd both get what they wanted eventually.

He could be patient for a little while longer.

15

The dinner was delicious, but Eliza didn't taste much of it. She was torn between laughing at Randy's lame jokes and keeping an eye on Chandler, who sat at the other end of the table. Stacey's chair had remained curiously empty, but when Eliza had asked Rachel about it, she'd just waved off Eliza's concern.

"She told me she had a headache and was going up to her room. I asked her if she wanted me to go with her, and she said no. She's fine."

Eliza wasn't sure, but she let it go. Stacey was an adult, and if she wanted to be alone, that was up to her.

Bree and Gregory cut the cake, with the predictable smashing in Gregory's face, and a slightly more sedate dab of icing put on Bree's nose. It was sweet, but Eliza couldn't help but wish they'd hurry up.

She drank a glass of wine, but her anticipation of the night to come was much stronger than any buzz alcohol could give her. She switched to water after that. No reason to dull her senses when what she really wanted was to be able to remember absolutely everything that happened tonight.

As the wait staff rolled the remaining cake to the opposite side of the dance floor, Eliza wiped her suddenly damp palms on her skirt.

Why was she nervous? Nothing had really changed between them. Well, except for the way she'd started seeing Chandler as a person instead of just a fun sexual partner. She couldn't think of him as just a fling now, no matter how many times she promised herself she would. Knowing him, even just the brief flashes she'd seen, had ruined that forever, and she couldn't help but be glad she knew more of the man he was.

But even if she thought of him as a good person, a likeable person, they could still have fun. After all, this whole—whatever it was—would be over the moment they left Hawaii.

The wedding planner waved to the head table and grabbed the mic again. "It's time for the first dance! Everyone, Mr. and Mrs. Trailwick!"

Eliza watched as Gregory and Bree took to the floor. Gregory's face was a little serious, but Bree looked radiantly happy. Maybe that was just Greg's personality. If so, that was okay. Bree had enough positive, bubbly energy to make up for the fact that Greg was kind of a sourpuss.

A warm hand landed on Eliza's bare shoulder, making her jump.

"Hey there."

She smiled at the familiar voice. "Hi."

"I got lonely over there, so I thought I'd come by." Chandler dropped into the seat that Randy had recently vacated, something about having a smoke break. "How was your dinner?"

"It was good, but I'm glad it's over."

An evil grin spread across Chandler's face. "Seems like you might be looking forward to something other than dessert?"

She nodded as her stomach flipped. His eyes were dark with want, and his gaze raked from her face to her bared neckline, down to where the hem of her dress skimmed the tops of her thighs.

"Come on," Chandler said, standing. He held his hand out to her. "Let's dance."

Eliza looked over at the dance floor, somewhat surprised when she realized that Bree and Gregory's first dance was over, and couples were crowding onto the floor. Finally. "Okay."

He squeezed her hand and the two of them ran onto the floor like kids at their first prom. The song was bouncy and up-beat, really fun. Lights hung from the rafters above them, throwing scattered beams across the polished floor that had been laid just that morning. Eliza laughed, swinging her arms above her head as Chandler put his hands on her hips.

One song became two, and then two became three, different tempos and beats causing them to change the way they moved. Eliza lost count after a while, because one sexy song bled into another, and a slow ballad gave the perfect opportunity for their bodies to align, so close that not even a whisper could move between them.

"You're incredibly sexy," Chandler whispered close to her ear, one of his hands rubbing down the small of her back to rest just atop the curve of her buttocks. He squeezed lightly, and she fought the urge to press harder into his growing erection. "I haven't forgotten my promises."

Shivers went down her spine, and her skin tingled as goose bumps raced across her exposed skin. "You haven't?"

"Nope. And if you follow me up to my room, I can prove it."

God, the temptation was too much for any one woman to have to bear, wasn't it? Eliza wrapped her arms tighter around him, but looked across the dance floor.

Sabrina was dancing with her brother, and Gregory was camped out in the corner talking to Randy. Mrs. Hough was holding court in the center of the tables, at least three wine bottles standing by her untouched wedding cake. Mr. Hough was nowhere to be seen. Rachel and her husband were dancing, both of them holding her belly. Other couples looked to be at least as interested in one another as Eliza and Chandler were.

"Isn't it bad luck or something to leave before the bride and groom?"

Chandler pulled back a bit and looked toward Bree. "I don't know, really. We can stay if you think we should." He leaned close again, whispering so as not to be heard above the music. "Just keep in mind that I intend to keep you to myself for the rest of the trip. We've got some catching up to do. I'm a man of my word, after all."

Eliza bit her lip as her nipples pebbled painfully. He had a sexy voice normally, but when he pitched it low like that, his breath blowing across her ear, his scent tickling her nostrils as his body heat bled into hers—

She had no choice. Not really.

"Let's sneak away. Nobody's watching. But we probably should leave separately, otherwise people might get suspicious."

She was a little surprised by her initiative, but Chandler seemed to take it in stride. He pressed a tiny kiss just below her earlobe and stepped back. The evening breeze played between them, ruffling the hem of Eliza's dress and chilling her more than it should have. Or was that just the excitement of the night that was to come? She wasn't sure. She'd have to wait to find out.

"Okay. Let's do this. You go on ahead, and I'll say good night to Gregory. I'll follow you up in about five minutes so it doesn't look odd. You remember my room number, right?"

A plastic key appeared in Eliza's hand, and she tucked it into her strapless bra as quickly as she could. "Okay. Got it."

She walked away quickly, trying like hell to look completely innocent. It was hard, because her heart was thumping like she'd just run a marathon. It seemed like everyone was looking at her as she passed by, like there was a blinking neon sign on her forehead that read "about to have wild, kinky monkey sex. Please point and laugh."

That was ridiculous. She was ridiculous. Nobody knew where she was going.

But there was one thing she had to do before she left. She wouldn't forgive herself if she didn't. Wheeling around, she made her way back to the dance floor.

Tapping Brent on the shoulder, she smiled. "Can I cut in?"

Brent blinked, but stepped aside. Sabrina just laughed and linked her hands behind Eliza's neck. They swayed to the music for a moment.

"You're beautiful, you know," Eliza said as they twirled on the floor. "Everything went perfectly."

"Thanks to you. I thought Mother would be much more of a pain than she was." Bree sighed as she looked over at Gregory. Relief rippled through Eliza as the groom's face lit up in a smile.

"You deserve to be happy." Eliza hugged Bree, then stepped back. "I just want you to remember that."

"Oh Liza, so do you. And you will be just as happy, I know it."

The song ended, the friends embraced, and Eliza told a quick fib about needing to run to the ladies' room.

As she passed Chandler, she didn't say a word, just gave him a wink.

The elevator seemed to take forever. She didn't want to wait any longer. Chandler was a man of his word, after all, and she wanted to know exactly how he intended to keep his promises.

Chandler watched Eliza go. She was as beautiful going as she was coming. He grinned. He'd see her coming again very soon.

"Hey, man, I'm heading to the bar. You want anything?" Randy said with a loose smile. It looked like he'd been to the bar quite a bit already this evening.

"No thanks, I'm good. I'm going to say good night to Gregory and head upstairs."

"Oh really?" Randy looked around, tugging at the sagging bow tie at his throat. "Is there a party upstairs?"

A better party than you know. But sorry, bud, you're not invited. Chandler just shook his head.

"Okay then." Randy looked disappointed, but he wandered off in the direction of the bar.

Chandler made his way through the thinning crowd to where Gregory was seated in the corner. He glanced around before plopping down in the chair next to his cousin.

"The man of the hour and you're not surrounded with well-wishers?"

Gregory spun the glass in front of him, causing droplets to dampen the white tablecloth. "I've been surrounded with them all night. I just needed a breather."

As much as Chandler wanted to say a quick good night and run upstairs to where Eliza waited for him, he knew he had to do his duty as best man first.

"Are you good?"

Gregory arched a brow at him. "What do you mean?"

Propping his forearms on the table, Chandler leaned closer to his cousin. "I mean, you look like you just got sentenced to prison instead of married. What's the deal, man?"

"There is no deal. Everything's good. I'm just glad it's done now."

"I didn't figure you'd be so nervous about a wedding."

Gregory just shook his head, and lifted the glass to his lips. "It's no biggie." Draining the rest of his water, he sighed and put the empty glass back down in the center of the damp ring the condensation had left. He tilted his head toward the door, cutting his eyes toward the exit. "So, you're following her upstairs?"

Chandler tightened his jaw. "Is that a problem?"

"No, man. Go have fun. We've all got to make our own mistakes, right?" Gregory slumped back in his chair, his gaze far away.

"If it wasn't your fucking wedding night, I'd cram those words down your damn throat. But as it is, I'll let you slide. Sabrina would murder me if I caused a scene."

Greg sighed, looking down at his lap. "Sorry, man. I'm being a dick. Go, have fun."

Chandler stared at his cousin for a moment, wondering. There wasn't a lot to do, though. He'd given Greg plenty of opportunities to talk about whatever was bothering him. *You can't force someone to share their problems.*

It was a lesson he'd learned well over the course of his own failed marriage.

"It was a great wedding. Have a good night, man." Chandler patted Greg on the shoulder as he stood.

"You, too."

A nagging feeling dogged Chandler all the way to the door of the event hall. He passed through the air-conditioned foyer and then to the sidewalk outside. The main hotel tower rose in front of him, the promise of the night to come looming large in his mind.

Other people could take care of their own problems. He couldn't force anyone to accept his help. What he could do, though, was keep his promises. And he intended to.

There weren't as many people milling around the resort at this time of night. Chandler glanced at the screen of his phone as he waited for the elevator to ascend. Nearly eleven. It was a little surprising that Gregory and Sabrina hadn't left yet. Of course, their honeymoon was taking place in a villa on the other side of the resort, so it wasn't like they had a very long way to go.

Not his problem anyway. But he really did hope that Gregory would be happy with Sabrina. She seemed like the type of woman who'd be really good for him.

The elevator dinged and he grinned like a kid who'd just seen his Pop-Tart spring out of the toaster. He'd thought about tonight a lot during the day. Hell, he'd even planned for it. He couldn't wait to see Eliza's reaction to the way he'd left his hotel room.

A TV was blaring loudly somewhere down the hall, and he was kind of glad for it. Someone else must be covering up the sounds of their own type of late-night fun. Not a bad idea, actually.

At his door, he stood still a moment, closed his eyes, and took a deep breath. Why was he nervous? Was it because Eliza had done a really good job of convincing him that she didn't want anything else to do with him after that little encounter on the nature trail? Or was it performance anxiety of some kind?

He'd done his research. He wasn't sure how much into this type of thing Eliza was, so he wanted to make sure they were on the same page. He'd found a really nice online community who'd welcomed his questions with open arms. They'd collectively patted him on the back for taking the steps to educate himself in the lifestyle.

So, all that was left was to open the door and see if Eliza had bolted or not.

He patted his pocket, then stared at the ceiling with a laugh. She had his only room key. Rapping against the door with a knuckle, he waited.

"Hello?"

"It's me," he said, his hand lying against the door. "Can I come in?"

"I'm not sure. I think I might have come into the wrong room."

There was a note of laughter in her voice, or was it anticipation? He jammed his hands in his pockets.

"Oh really? That's weird. Maybe I should come in and take a look. See if someone has tampered with the room."

"Shouldn't I call Hotel Security instead?" Her innocent tone was way too over-the-top to be believed at all. "I mean, there's some seriously disturbing sights in here. It's actually turning me on."

"In that case I definitely need to see what's happening in there."

Only a heartbeat later, the door squeaked open. Eliza stood there, barefoot but still dressed in her blue bridesmaid's gown, her eyes sparkling.

"Hi there." She leaned against the door frame.

"Hi yourself. Gonna let me in?"

"I guess you do need to see the damage, huh?" She shook her head sadly and stepped aside to let him in. "It's a shame what some people get up to in hotel rooms. You know, just because they aren't at home they feel like they can take a perfectly nice room and turn it into an adult amusement park."

Chandler made his way into the room, pleased to see that his setup still looked like he'd left it. Fortunately, Brent had lent him the rental car, and an adult store was only fifteen minutes from the resort. His purchases were spread out on the desk, and the bed already bore the under-mattress restraints he'd picked up. One of the cuffs was open, as if it had been recently tested.

The thought made his cock twitch with interest.

"An amusement park, huh? Which ride is your favorite?" he asked as he pulled her body close. Mmm, she was soft, warm, rubbing up against him like a kitten.

"Do you really need to ask?"

Her hand fell on his pec, then traced downward, over his

abs. She bent down and then kneeled in front of him, her hand massaging his groin through the dark fabric of the tuxedo pants he wore. Her fingertips traced his shaft, then lower, her palm cupping his balls and squeezing ever so slightly. He watched as she stared at him, her mouth working as she massaged him erotically.

"Well, if you want to get on, all you have to do is say so."

She grinned, lowering his zipper. "Didn't you know? The longer you wait in line, the better the roller-coaster ride is."

16

The shock she'd felt when she'd seen what he'd done to the hotel room had quickly turned into interest. No, *interest* wasn't the right word. *Lust. Passion. Want. Hunger.* Her body went hot, then shivered, pulses fluttering through her breasts and belly as she examined each item he'd left for her.

Paddles. Floggers. A blindfold. Cuffs already prepped and ready. Massage oil that was scented like suntan lotion. He'd thought of everything.

She wanted to show him just how grateful she was. He could have taken the information she'd given him and spread it around, made other people think she was a freak. He hadn't. He'd kept his promise.

His zipper rasped softly as she lowered it. Acutely aware of his gaze on her, Eliza moved slowly, much more slowly than she truly wanted. With agonizing care, she delved into the flap of his boxer-briefs, her fingers curling around his hot, hard length. His throat worked as she gripped tighter, maneuvering the head free of the cottony confines.

"You've got a beautiful cock." She let her words blow breath over the swollen head, smiling when a crystal drop appeared at the slit.

"Thank you for the compliment."

"I think I can do better than compliment, though." Rising a bit higher, she opened her mouth and took him in. The warm, salty taste of that drop slid over her tongue. His hips jerked slightly as she took him deeper. Her fingers curled around the base of him, and when she started a rhythm, her mouth and hand worked in tandem to please him.

His knees bent, his breathing becoming deeper and more ragged as she sucked him. Eliza closed her eyes and concentrated on the taste, the feel of him. His cock was silky, thick, and just the right length for her. He liked it when she took him deep, swallowing and compressing the head of him with her throat. His moans told her that. But she didn't know just how close he was until he gently gripped her hair and stepped back.

"That's too good, you've got to stop."

Eliza ran a thumb across her lower lip. It was wet, a little swollen. Nice.

"If you don't want me to keep going, then what do you want to do?"

He pulled her to her feet and turned her around wordlessly. The zipper of her dress stuck at the ruched waist, and Chandler cursed as he fumbled with it. But eventually he won against the zipper, and her dress fell to the floor around her bare feet. The air-conditioned breeze made her shiver, but his warm hands made her shake with something much more powerful than a chill.

He massaged her waist, then brushed higher until he was cupping her breasts. Eliza arched her back and bit her lip as he pinched and rolled her nipples through the strapless bra she still wore. It was good, but his touch on her skin would be so much better. As if he was reading her mind, he unfastened the front clasp of her bra. It fell atop the blue chiffon puddle of her dress.

Wearing nothing but a thong now, Eliza stepped forward as Chandler led her over to the bed. There was a cuff on either side of the pillows, and another on each side of the foot of the mattress. The black straps disappeared beneath the mattress.

"Sit down," Chandler said, and she did. "Lie on your stomach."

Her nerves tensed with anticipation, but she did as she was told. Spreading her arms and legs out in an X, she waited for him to cuff her. She knew it was coming, it was obvious. But what she didn't know was just how much she was looking forward to it. She'd dreamed of doing stuff like this for a very long time. Her fantasies were so well-developed that she'd even confessed her most private ones to Tyler. But he'd never been interested in doing anything like this. So when the Velcro made a ripping sound as it opened, rustling slightly as Chandler placed the cuff on her wrist, Eliza's moan was real.

"Are you okay? Is it too tight?"

She shook her head vehemently. "No, it's good."

He repeated the operation on her other wrist, and now she was bound. Logically, she knew it wouldn't be that difficult to remove the Velcro and free herself if she really needed to, but that wasn't the point. The fact that she was now Chandler's prisoner, and he held total control of her for the moment, by her own choice, made her shake with need.

"Now bring your knees beneath you. I want you on your hands and knees when I spank you. I'll cuff your ankles later. Understood?"

"Yes," Eliza said as she began to move. But a sudden light smack on her bottom startled her, and she yelped.

"That's 'yes, sir' to me for now."

"Yes, sir." Her voice was small, but the light, stinging feeling on her bared ass cheek was incredible. Her pussy set up a steady, hungry throb as she waited for him, facedown, on her knees.

Would he use a flogger first? A paddle? His bare hand? God, she wasn't sure which she wanted more. She wanted it all. His hands pulling her hair, the sound her ass would make as he struck it, the gentle exploration of her body when he was ready. Not when she wanted it, but when he wanted to give it to her.

She wiggled her ass in the air as if she could beg him to move faster. To start this delicious punishment already. She'd waited so long, longer than he knew. Surely he could tell how much she wanted this.

"Eliza. I will give you what you want. But if it's too much, then you have to tell me. If you don't agree to this, then it stops now. Do you understand?"

"Yes, sir." She turned her head to look at him. He'd removed his shirt and tuxedo pants, standing there only in his black boxer-briefs. He'd tucked his erection back into them. That was a shame. But the black cotton didn't exactly hide his generous size. The memory of how he'd felt thrusting into her distracted her for a moment. Then she looked back up at his face, and realized he was speaking.

"I'm sorry. What did you say?"

He just smiled. "I said if it's too much, just say red. Like a stoplight. If you're starting to get uncomfortable, but you want to keep trying just softer, then say yellow. Otherwise, I'll assume we're on green. Do you understand and agree?"

His instructions were oddly formal, but it fit with the scenario they were partaking in, so Eliza didn't mention it.

"Yes, sir. Now may I please have my spanking?"

"You may." His palm landed briskly on her left cheek, staying there and massaging the sensitive skin after the blow. Eliza gripped the covers beneath her hands, pulling slightly at the cuffs. The sting seemed to leave her ass and pool straight in her pussy, kicking the throb there into high gear.

A tickling feeling began at the backs of her knees, soft kisses of touch. She pushed her hips backward, trying to figure out what that feeling was. It sent a spear of want straight into her chest. The tickle raised higher, across the backs of her thighs, then disappeared for a moment. She didn't have a long time to be disappointed about it, because then the tickle became a light sting across her cheeks.

Slowly at first, left cheek, then right, rhythmic, over and over and then she realized what was happening. That flogger. He was twirling it like an expert, like the ones she'd seen in videos when she was desperate for some sexual satisfaction and the only way she could get it was Internet porn and a vibrator. Over and under, back and forth, the pressure varying as he maneuvered it.

With each smack, she breathed. Wetness flooded her body, begging for him to take her. Her hips moved on their own, back and forth, meeting each of his strokes as if it was his cock and not a small flogger.

Her body was in his control, and it was thrilling.

But then the flogger dropped lower, strands tickling her pussy through the damp silk thong. Her breath caught in her throat, her eyes wide as she stared at the covers beneath her.

"Would you like me to spank you here?" A gentle flick of the flogger against her nether lips wrenched a cry from Eliza. Her brain was a fog of red, of want and hunger and an almost animalistic urge to bring him inside her. But on the other hand, that felt amazing.

It wasn't a choice.

"Spank my pussy, sir. Please."

He couldn't deny that he'd wondered how this would go. If he'd enjoy it, or if he'd just do it because it was something she wanted. But now? With her ass pointed directly at him, her moans and cries coming like soft morning rain over him, the scent of her arousal wrapping around his cock and drawing him closer?

Now he knew exactly how this would go. It'd be amazing for them both.

"Please spank my pussy, sir," she repeated herself because he hadn't moved since she answered. Spreading her thighs wider apart, she moaned.

Chandler's free hand dropped to his groin, palming his painfully hard cock. The other hand held the flogger, and he used it to tease the darkened silk between her thighs.

She was so wet for him. Because he'd cuffed her, and spanked her, and made her call him sir.

He wanted to plunge inside her right then and there, but he'd wait. They hadn't made it through the line to the roller-coaster ride yet.

"I'm going to take your panties off."

He waited a moment, but she said nothing, so he ran his fingers beneath her waistband and rolled the fabric down. With no warning, he pressed a kiss to her bare pussy. She gasped.

"You're beautiful," he said, then licked the seam of her, collecting her honey on his tongue. She was sweet, heady, and she tasted like woman.

Tossing her panties aside, he then removed his own underwear. He picked up the flogger and examined his target. A single strip of hair crowned her, but her lips were smooth, either shaved or waxed. Beautiful. He put his thumbs on either side and spread her wide to his gaze.

"What—What are you doing?" Her voice was halting.

"I'm looking at you."

"Why? Is something wrong?"

Chandler fought the urge to laugh, sure that she'd take the

sound the wrong way. "No. I think you're incredible. And I'm going to spank you now, because you asked for it."

"Thank you, sir."

Those three words moved him into action. He picked up the flogger, his other hand keeping her labia spread. He wanted to see her clit. Each flick would tease her, make her want him more.

The first gentle strike of the flogger on her sensitive skin had her bucking against the cuffs. The second drew a strangled scream from somewhere deep in her throat. By the third, she was almost crying, begging him for more. Her pussy was swelling, glistening with her response right before his eyes. It was mesmerizing, incredible. He wanted to feel her heat as he sank into her there, deeply, her soft, wet heat welcoming him in.

"Please," Eliza sobbed as he flicked her clit over and over with the flogger. "It hurts, it's so good, I can't—I—God, Chandler, please—"

"Tell me what you want," Chandler said, flicking just a little harder, careful not to go over the line of intolerable pain. He wanted to keep her in that space, that safe space that felt dangerous, that dark threshold of pain and pleasure. He was beginning to understand this now. The feeling of control, the exchange of power, the trust. She trusted him to give her pleasure. It was a feeling that intoxicated him.

"I want more of this. I want you to blindfold me, to fuck me in the ass, to let me tie you up and ride you until you come. I want to force you to suck my clit, I want you to worship me, I want to worship you. I want it all, don't you see?" Her voice pitched high, and he dropped the flogger and began a steady massage of her damp, sensitive skin.

"But right now? Right now I want to feel your hard cock inside me. Please, sir, don't make me wait." The begging in her voice made his dick twitch.

He slipped a finger inside her, groaning aloud at the sweet feeling of her flesh surrounding him. Adding a second finger, be began a slow, swirling motion. In and out, wide and narrow, stretching her inner walls, feeling her clench around him.

"I want to see your breasts." Chandler reached up and freed her right hand. She wasted no time in freeing her left. His fingers withdrew, and she rolled onto her back, her legs splayed apart, her chest heaving as she breathed.

He was on her in a moment, spreading her thighs wide, his mouth seeking and finding her hardened nipple. She gripped his hair, pulling him closer, forcing him into harder contact with her.

"Bite, please. More. Rougher."

He grazed his teeth over her taut nipple, and she shrieked her pleasure. Sucking, laving it with his tongue, he spent long moments buried in her breasts. Alternating often, his hand taking over when his mouth was otherwise occupied.

She moved, always moving, her hips lifting to him, her back arching, her lips kissing wherever she could reach. She grabbed the hand that had been buried between her legs only moments ago and sucked his still-damp fingers into her mouth.

She's tasting herself. She's sucking her own moisture from me.

The thought made his balls go high and tight, tingling in desire. It was more than he could handle. The line was done; it was time for the coaster.

He pulled away and stood, looking down at her. She was splayed across the bed, naked and trembling. The desire was written across her face, and she reached a hand up to him.

Condom.

The only clear thought to pop into his head at that moment was protection. Fortunately he'd left several packets atop the desk with the other implements he'd purchased earlier that day. Ripping the silver-blue pouch open, he slid the lubricated sheath over his hard dick.

It had taken mere seconds to put on the condom, but when

Chandler turned back to Eliza, one hand was between her thighs, rubbing her clit. The other was covering one breast, forefinger and thumb pinching and rolling her beautifully dusky nipple. Her mouth was parted, her touch becoming faster, more frantic.

"Wait for me," Chandler said. No, he didn't really say it; he commanded it.

He crawled across the bed and grabbed her hand, pulling it away from her pussy. "Not yet."

"Then hurry," Eliza said, scooting lower on the bed and raising her hips to him. "Come inside me, please."

With a quick move, he rolled them until she was atop him. Lifting her hips above his groin, he positioned herself at her entrance.

"Ride me, Eliza."

Her hands braced on his chest, and she looked down at him. Her hair was tumbling down now, their activity too much for the pins that had held the mass up. It was beautiful, falling on either side of her face.

But then he couldn't think anymore, because her hips slid down, down, covering him, taking him deep into the tight heat of her body.

Chandler groaned as Eliza brought her knees in closer to his sides. And then she began to move.

Up and down, over and over, slowly at first, then rocking, swiveling her hips like a belly dancer. She took him so deep, so good. He braced his feet on the bed and matched her thrust for thrust, his balls smacking her ass lightly with each stroke. She settled on a rhythm and her fingertips dug into his chest. It was good, so good. She tightened around his cock, faster, harder, deeper, taking him over and over, her hair tickling his chest as she bent down. He captured her mouth in a quick kiss, his tongue touching hers before she sat up and arched her back again.

"Oh God," she moaned to the ceiling as Chandler reached up and gripped her breast. He pinched her nipple as he'd seen her do before, and with the other hand he found her swollen, throbbing clit.

With each of their thrusts, he rubbed her clit. Frantic cries came from her, her breasts bouncing as they fucked. Too much, it was too much. His lower back was tightening in preparation; he couldn't hold back this orgasm much longer.

He pinched her clit gently. She screamed, her inner muscles shuddering around him. She sank down hard, taking his cock so deep into the well of her body. The depth, the heat, the grip of her inner walls combined and he lost his mind, pouring his orgasm deep inside her body. Rocking back and forth, slowly, gently, she coaxed every drop from him.

Slumping forward, she laid her forehead on his chest.

Chandler stared at the ceiling, trying to decide if the tip of his cock had blown off. Honestly, he didn't care. That was incredible.

He hoped she'd want to do it again. But in a few hours, maybe. Or sooner.

Even if it killed him, Eliza was incredible. And he wanted more.

17

The sand was warm beneath Eliza, and she reached over from her beach blanket to rub her fingers through it. Beneath the surface it was cooler. Waves crashed not far away, the rhythmic sound encouraging her to close her eyes and just relax.

She breathed deep through her nose, the salty scent making her smile.

Maybe a quick nap wouldn't be a bad thing. After all, neither she nor Chandler had gotten much sleep over the past two days. In fact, ever since the night of the wedding, they'd done more fucking than sleeping.

After that incredible session with the flogger, they'd snuggled close to one another, talking until late in the night. She'd asked Chandler about his friends, and he'd told her. He had asked Eliza about her parents, and she reluctantly began to share little bits of her life with him. It was easier as she went along, Chandler's gentle responses encouraging her to share more. He never judged, or seemed to be put off by the things she shared. He'd just listened. He really seemed to care. Which was probably why she'd screwed up in the first place. But then he'd asked a question that startled her out of her memories.

"So you've been in a relationship before, right? What ended it, if you don't mind my asking?"

Eliza had sat up, suddenly cold. The question made sense; after all, Chandler had just told her he'd gotten divorced because his wife was more interested in her career than in a relationship. But she couldn't tell him. Not yet. Maybe not ever, really.

"I need to go to the bathroom," Eliza had said without looking at him. She'd just grabbed his shirt off the floor, shrugging into it as she walked.

A few minutes of the water running and a few brisk splashes on her face had convinced her that she was right. It wasn't worth it. They were just vacation fuckbuddies. If things got too weird, the fun would be over. They didn't have a future together by virtue of geography, but Eliza wasn't willing to sacrifice the next few days because of Chandler's curiosity.

She didn't need to share the past with him, because they didn't have a future together.

Fortunately, when she'd returned to bed, he hadn't said a word about her sudden disappearance. He'd just taken her in his arms and kissed her, gently, then more insistently, until they'd had sex again. Afterward, when she pillowed her head against his chest, she'd wondered what life would be like with a man like Chandler.

She hadn't been able to adequately picture just how good it could be.

Footsteps on the sand drew her bleary eyes open.

Chandler was rubbing a towel over his wet hair, smiling as he sank down onto the blanket beside her.

"You should have come for a swim with me. The water feels great today."

"Mmm," Eliza grunted as she rolled onto her back, squinting behind her sunglasses. "The beach feels greater. And dryer."

"You'll change your mind when everyone leaves and I drag you into the surf to take advantage of you."

She quirked a smile up at him. "Is that a promise, sir?"

"It is." He winked, then lay back onto the blanket beside her.

Eliza shivered as his wet arm brushed her, giving her a chill. For a minute they were quiet, just soaking up the sun's rays, Chandler drying while Eliza thought. It had been so wonderful, just her and Chandler, that the whole wedding seemed far away. They'd run into a couple of guests, but it seemed a large number of them had left already, even some who were scheduled to stay longer.

"I wonder why Stacey scooted out so early?" The question came unbidden from Eliza's mouth. "I mean, I didn't see her at all after the wedding. Didn't get to say good-bye or anything."

"I don't know," Chandler said, rolling to his side and propping his cheek on one hand. "It might just have been her head; maybe she wanted to go see a doctor back home."

"Ugh," Eliza said, throwing her arm over her sunglasses. "I still feel awful about that. It's my fault she got knocked down."

"Hey," Chandler said, threading his fingers through Eliza's. "It's not your fault Stacey got hurt, just like it's not Stacey's fault that that jackass decided to pick on you. Whatever she's going through, she's got to do it on her own."

Eliza knew he was right, but she didn't have to like it. She pulled her shades off, tossed them on the blanket, and stood. Linking her hands, she stretched her arms above her head. Chandler's gaze was full of lustful appreciation.

"Have I mentioned how much I love you in that pink bikini?"

Eliza propped her hands on her hips and looked down at the fuchsia two-piece. "You can thank Bree for this. I'd never buy anything like it. And I doubt I'll wear it ever again once this trip is over. In fact, you can have it as a memento if you want."

Chandler came to his feet beside her. "I hope I get more to take home with me than a bikini. Like, maybe a phone number, address, permission to visit . . ."

Eliza just laughed and ran toward the surf. Mostly because she didn't know what to say.

More? This wouldn't go any further than the resort. A few magical days with a sexy stranger, and then they'd both go back to their lives.

Knee-deep in the waves, Eliza stopped cold.

Why? Why did she have to go back to her life the way it was? Life back home sucked. It sucked hard. But that was her reality, right? There wasn't any way to get away from her past, unless she moved across the country. But she liked her job, she liked her town, despite the hell it had been recently. Why should she let anyone chase her away from her home?

"Hey, wait for me!" Chandler was on her heels now.

So she didn't have to speak, she dove beneath the water. Salt stung her eyes, bubbles burst around her, and she swam straight out to sea. Far away from the past, from the feelings that Chandler had started within her. She didn't understand any of this, and she was tired of trying.

She had two more days here in this tropical paradise. Two more days to figure out exactly what she wanted when she wasn't Eliza the bombshell anymore, when Eliza the chemist with a misunderstood reputation was back to stay.

Would Chandler like that girl?

She wasn't sure she wanted to find out. If the answer was no, well . . .

Rejection was something she didn't think she'd ever really get used to.

Breaking the surface in a rush, Eliza shook her head to clear her ears. Treading water, she turned around and looked for Chandler. Where was he? He had to be able to swim faster than she could. She was pretty slow. But she didn't see him. Worry started knotting in the back of her throat, and she started paddling back toward shore. Maybe he'd turned a different way?

A hand wrapped around her ankle and pulled. She had just enough time to grab a quick gulp of air before her head dipped below the waves.

"Ch . . . Chandler!" She sputtered and cursed when she broke the surface, kicking as his grip moved higher on her body. He surfaced and yelped good-naturedly when her kick connected with his shin. "What the crap, are you trying to drown me?"

He laughed. "No, I'm not. I'm just keeping my promise."

She scowled, rubbing water from her eyes. "What do you mean?"

Nodding toward the shore, he brought her body into full contact with his. "You see anyone on the beach there?"

Understanding dawned. "No."

He grinned. "Any objections?"

She shook her head. Once again, her heart thumped in anticipation of his touch. He dove below the surface and began to run his hands up her legs. She moaned.

This place was turning her into a sex-crazed fiend. But she couldn't find it in herself to be really upset about that.

Later that night, after Chandler had showered and changed, he knocked on Eliza's hotel room door. He felt a little silly, actually.

"Hey," Eliza said as she pulled open the door. Her hair was damp, and she was holding the ends in a towel. "Come on in."

"When I said we should share a room for the rest of the trip, I was really talking about mine." The wheels of Chandler's suitcase clacked over the bump in the threshold.

"Yeah, well, does your room have a whirlpool tub?"

"Yours has a whirlpool?" Chandler stuck his head in the bathroom. "Well, I'll be damned."

Eliza's giggle warmed him through. She thwacked him with her towel on the way by. "Move out of my way, or I won't be ready in time for our dinner reservation. You said seven thirty, right?"

"Right," Chandler called back as he put his suitcase atop the rack beside hers. He smiled down at it. He remembered this case. He'd grabbed it for her in the airport when she was a stranger who'd been a bit more than curt to him.

Damn, that seemed like it had happened forever ago. Well, it sort of was. They were both changed from who they'd been then, at least a little. He could tell just by looking at Eliza that she was more comfortable in her own skin. It suited her. He'd liked what he saw in the airport, but now? He couldn't get enough.

The whir of the hair dryer drew his attention to the bathroom. Knowing he'd be in the way, he sank down on the room's single king-sized bed. It was odd being in a room with feminine things scattered around it. There was a makeup case on the desk, its contents spilling over the side. A lingerie bag was lying atop her suitcase, a lacy bra and panty set laid atop it like they were being put on later. Or maybe taken off? Hey, a guy could hope.

Crossing his arms over his middle, Chandler sank back against the pillows. Just to breathe. He hadn't been with anyone since Andrea, and he'd wondered if he could ever relax around a woman again. Andrea's change had hurt him deeply, and part of him had worried that he'd never be the same again.

And now he knew. He couldn't be the same again. He could be better.

The hair dryer stopped suddenly, the room feeling more quiet than it was in the absence of the loud sound. Brushing noises then. Chandler watched in the mirror in front of the bed. If his head was at the right angle, he could catch glimpses of her shiny brown-black hair as she brushed it.

She was beautiful. He wanted her, and for more than just the next two nights. But every time he brought up going home, or staying in contact, or anything like that, Eliza ran off, or shut down, or changed the subject.

He wasn't stupid. Fear of commitment was easy to understand, hell, he felt it himself. But he'd be crazy not to know that Eliza was special, and he wanted to continue their relationship even when this trip was over.

So tonight he'd begin to try to get her to understand. He'd show her he was empathetic, he'd try to help her see that a past failed relationship didn't mean that her future was doomed. It had killed him not to research her past, but so far he'd stuck to his vow and hadn't looked. He'd wait for her to share with him, no matter how long it took.

If only the calendar didn't march forward quite so quickly.

"Sorry, I'm almost ready," Eliza called from the bathroom. "Just a minute and we can go."

"No rush," Chandler said, putting his laced-together fingers atop his head. "Your bed is comfortable. Want to order room service?"

"Again? I don't think so."

Chandler grinned and stood. They were both a little tired of the resort restaurant at this point. The indoor entertainment had been much more interesting than leaving to find sustenance had been, but after their little rendezvous in the surf, Eliza had declared she was starving. And as a gentleman, he had to make sure she didn't dry up and float away.

So reservations were made, and unless they left within the next minute or two, they'd miss them entirely.

"Okay, room key, purse, wallet, phone, I'm good!" Eliza smiled at him, patting her bag on her side. "Sorry again."

"Stop apologizing." He dropped a kiss on her nose. "Let's go before you start gnawing my leg."

"I am hungry. I think it was the swimming. I always get hungry when I go swimming."

"You are hungry for sure, but I think it was the fucking. You always get hungry when you go fucking."

She punched him, even though his mimicry had been perfect. So he grunted in apology, and was apparently forgiven, because she didn't pull away when he grabbed her hand at the elevators.

The cab he'd called was waiting in front of the hotel towers, and as Chandler gave the cabbie directions, Eliza started to dig through her purse for her ringing cell. Chandler looked over as the cab pulled forward. Eliza frowned at the screen, hit Decline, and dropped the phone back into her purse.

"Everything okay?"

"Yeah," Eliza said, sounding tired. "Just crap from home, that's all. Sorry. I'll turn it off."

"Whatever makes you more comfortable," Chandler said, keeping his tone even, and put an arm around her shoulders. She snuggled next to him, sighing with pleasure as he massaged her scalp.

They stayed quiet on the drive to the restaurant, the radio playing a low-key tune in the front seat, the cabbie humming along. Drawing circles on Eliza's arm, Chandler kept his brain moving forward.

He had to draw her out, had to prove himself trustworthy to her. Time was running out, and if he didn't pull this off she'd run away and he wouldn't get this chance again. He had to be careful, but move decisively.

He wasn't going to lose her because of carelessness.

"Here we go," said the cabbie as he pulled to a stop in front of a brick building with a black awning in front.

Eliza waited while Chandler paid the guy, and together they walked hand in hand to the hostess stand. Eliza squeezed his fingers tightly when he asked for a private booth. Hopefully she approved.

After the appetizer plates had been cleared away, and their entrées had arrived, Chandler saw his chance and he struck.

"So, you're from the Midwest, huh? I've been out there several times for different jobs and things. Some really pretty areas out there. Small towns, that kind of thing?" He arched a brow as he broke off a piece of bread.

"Yeah, it is. Well, it can be. My town used to be one of my favorite places in the world." A nostalgic smile lit her face, and Chandler stared.

"There's this little main street that's lined with these cute mom-and-pop stores. You know, art galleries and jewelry shops and a hardware store that still sells the same bolts they had in 1920. And in the summer they open up the stage in the town square to local bands. People spread out blankets and just listen to music on the grass. I grew up there. So it's home."

But one word had stuck out to him, so he asked.

"You said it *used* to be. What changed?"

Her smile disappeared, and was replaced with a dark look.

"The way people looked at me changed. I guess they thought they knew who I was, and when I turned out to be a little bit different they treated me like an outsider. And now, even though I live there, I don't think I can ever feel at home there again."

18

She knew she'd said the wrong thing because the look of concern on Chandler's face made her want to cry. She stared down at her pasta, wondering what to do now. Damn it, this wasn't supposed to happen this way.

"I don't know why you feel the way you do, but I know what it is to feel like everyone has betrayed you."

Thankful for the conversational safety line, Eliza grabbed it. "What do you mean?"

Chandler gave a wry grin as he wiped his fingers on his napkin. "Well, I told you about my ex-wife, Andrea."

"Right."

"We met in college, and we shared a lot of mutual friends. So when we split, the friends split, too. A lot of them sided with Andrea."

"That's awful," Eliza said, setting her glass down. "But I thought you'd said she broke it off."

"She did. So a lot of our friends had heard her complaining, and they thought I was a bad guy because things didn't work out." Chandler stared down into his plate as if he could understand the universe if he looked long enough. "For a while there, I'd go out to the same restaurants and bars that I always had, and I'd get the cold shoulder."

Somewhere inside Eliza's chest, a little glow began to flutter. She pressed a hand against her sternum to keep it from moving too much.

"I know how you feel. When Tyler and I broke up, my whole life changed. No place felt the same; no people looked at me the same way. It was as if someone had ripped the mask off of me and everyone could see the monster beneath."

The words sailed out of her, leaving her breathless when they'd gone. She wanted Chandler to know he wasn't alone. She got that feeling, she really did. She'd experienced that hell, was still living it at home. He wasn't alone, and he wasn't bad. She had to let him know that.

Reaching across the table, she caught his fingers with hers and squeezed. Just to let him feel that she was there, and she understood.

He flashed her a small smile. "I'm sorry that you went through that. So Tyler started telling people you were an awful person, too?"

"I—Well, I don't—"

She stopped talking, and pulled her hand free. Her palms were sweaty now. She rubbed them on the napkin in her lap.

The background noise of the restaurant seemed suddenly loud. Distraction. She had to change the subject, or do something, or get away from this dangerous precipice somehow. Telling Chandler would be too hard, too pointless. Why rip the bandage off with him now? They only had a little time together anyway, no need to sully it with ugly memories.

"Liza?"

Her gaze fluttered upward.

Chandler was looking at her intently, his brows lowered slightly in concern. His hand was stretched out to her, palm-up. An offering.

"You aren't a monster. You're an incredible person. And the more I know about you, the more I want to know. Please, won't you let me get to know you better?"

The *yes* popped into her brain immediately, but her mouth refused to release the word. She stared at him, and the glow in her chest intensified. The glow compressed her lungs, making it harder and harder to breathe. What was that feeling? She'd been attracted to him from the moment she'd first seen him, but this was more than that. This was that choked-up feeling she'd gotten when her dad had surprised her with a puppy on her eighth birthday. This was that terrifying and overwhelming feeling she'd gotten when Tyler had been at his most charming.

This was the beginning of something special, and it terrified the pants off of her.

"I need to use the restroom," she said, and scraped her chair back. Her napkin fell to the floor, but she didn't waste the time to pick it up. She just bolted for the sanctuary of the ladies' room.

It was empty, and she thanked her lucky stars for that. Inside the first stall, she slumped against the closed door and counted her breaths to slow them.

This was worse than she'd imagined. God, why did nothing ever go like she planned? Chandler was just supposed to be some guy. Some stranger who wanted to fuck her, and then after a couple of days of passion they'd both be on their merry way. Him to North Carolina, her back to her small-town hell.

She sniffed, and it echoed against the tiles. Thumping her head on the door behind her, she stared at the drop-tile ceiling.

"I really didn't think this through."

She hadn't at all. This trip was supposed to help her come to grips with who she was, and allow her to be someone different than she had been. But then what? She'd changed here, at least a bit. She dressed nicer, had managed to be more outgoing, she'd even started to get feelings for someone.

Oh shit.

The glow had flared in her chest the second she'd thought that. Feelings. For Chandler. Like, a connection, a want within her for more than his body. For his caring smile, for the way he seemed to put her at ease. God, how could she go back home and face everything being the same when inside her, things were so very different?

The door to the restroom opened then, and footsteps echoed as the second stall became occupied.

Eliza flushed quickly, and jerked open the door. She spent too long washing her hands, just because she wasn't quite ready to face him yet.

She looked in the mirror. How could she look so much the same? It seemed like a different person should be staring out at her.

Well, if she was different, then she could make different decisions, right? She nodded and turned off the tap.

When she got home, she'd figure out a way to squash those rumors. Tyler couldn't run her out of her own hometown. Her parents might not live there anymore, but Eliza felt a connection to that place.

And even if it was shitty, she'd stay there. No one could tell her how to live her life.

Could they?

She walked out of the bathroom and wound her way through the restaurant. Chandler was sitting there and fiddling with his phone. But he looked up and smiled when she pulled her chair back.

"Sorry about that," she said with a smile. "Just had too much water."

"It's okay," Chandler said, returning her expression. "I've got all night to spend with you. There's no rush."

Well, there was, a little. This trip would be over eventually, and decisions would have to be made. In fact, after tomorrow night, they'd be saying good-bye.

All the more reason to be enjoying tonight.

"I thought about the chocolate cake for dessert," Chandler was saying as he tapped the small dessert menu on the table.

"Sounds good to me. Two forks?"

He arched a brow at her playful tone. "Want to share?"

Leaning forward, she propped her chin on her hands. He really was a great guy. What would life be like if she could follow him back to his home? Would they have any kind of chance at a relationship? Or would he find out about the things she wanted and run just like Tyler had?

If things were different, she might be able to take that chance. But for now, her personal transformation was too important. Going home and taking control was her first priority. Maybe after that she could lead a different life.

But until then . . .

"Yes. I want to share your cake."

Chandler watched as Eliza closed her eyes in bliss. The tines of the fork dragged against her bottom lip, leaving a tiny line of chocolate there. Damn, he wanted to lick that spot.

"That was divine." She sighed and put down her fork. He couldn't help but be a little disappointed when she wiped her mouth with the napkin.

Oh well. Maybe they could pick up some chocolate sauce somewhere and put it to good use in the hotel room. Now that was a plan he could get behind.

"I'll take care of this whenever you're ready," the waitress said with a friendly smile as she placed the black folder on their table. Eliza reached for it, but Chandler was quicker.

"No, this is my treat." He tucked his credit card inside the holder and passed it back to the waitress.

Once she'd gone, Eliza shot him a look. "You didn't need to do that. This isn't a date."

"Oh really? Do you usually rub your foot up the leg of a guy that you split the bill with?"

Her foot disappeared and a flash of disappointment went through him. It was worth it, though. That irritated look on her face was adorable.

"I just mean that we aren't dating, so there's no reason for you to take care of the bill." She tucked her hair behind her ear, studiously avoiding looking him in the face. It would have been cute if her words weren't so depressing.

"No, we aren't dating," he agreed. Her surprised gaze shot to him. Was she expecting him to argue? "But I'm in the habit of treating people that I like to dinner when I can. So you'll have to just get over it."

"That's a little high-handed of you."

"I thought you liked it when I was high-handed."

"That's only in the bedroom." She sniffed and looked out the window to her right. "In real life it can get pretty irritating."

"Duly noted."

He really shouldn't tease her so much, but damn, it was fun. The waitress returned with his credit card, and as he filled out the tip amount and signed the receipt he could feel Eliza's eyes on him. It was only fair. She was driving him crazy with her on-again, off-again approach to whatever it was they were to one another, and he was running out of patience.

He wanted for this to last longer than the vacation did, but unless he moved fast, things wouldn't work out. So starting tonight, he'd have to kick it into high gear. Luckily for him, horny Eliza suggested things that normal Eliza wouldn't ever dream of saying out loud. For this to work, he'd have to implement some of horny Eliza's suggestions.

And fortunately, he had an excellent memory.

"Ready to go?" He held his hand out to her and she took it.

They walked to the door of the restaurant, Eliza calling thanks to their server as she passed.

At the curb, Chandler waved for a cab.

"Where are we heading?" Eliza asked as she got in the cab, thanking him as he held the door open for her.

"Back to the resort, unless there's somewhere else you wanted to go."

"Really, back already? It's kind of early."

Chandler glanced at his watch. It was nine thirty.

"It's late enough. Tomorrow's our last day in Hawaii, so we need to get our rest."

"That doesn't make much sense," Eliza grumbled, but she didn't say anything else.

Her hand lay on his thigh most of the way home. He didn't make a move to touch her, but she continued to keep physical contact with him anyway. It was a good sign.

The cab pulled up in front of the hotel tower, and Chandler paid the cab fare, pushing aside Eliza's cash when she tried to thrust it at the man. As the cab drove away, Eliza's face was a mask of pure irritation.

"You need to let me pay for something."

"You can pay for things when you get home."

Was she growling? That was actually sort of hot.

Eliza turned on her heel and stalked to the hotel doors. Chandler made sure to enjoy the view as she twitched away from him.

"Now I wish I hadn't let you move in with me." She punched the Up button beside the elevator doors and tapped her foot as she waited.

"That's a terrible thing to say." Chandler stood behind her and wrapped his arms around her waist. She stayed stiff in his embrace, but she didn't pull away. When he started kissing the side of her neck, though, she sighed and melted against him.

"Still angry?" The beep of the elevator's arrival mingled with his words.

"No. Just . . . Let me pay for some things tomorrow, okay?"

"If that's what you want." They stepped into the elevator together. Once the doors were shut behind them, Chandler pulled Eliza in close and began to kiss her.

She tasted faintly of the chocolate that she'd eaten. Sweet, dark, sinful. He groaned his approval as his hands wandered over her back and down to cup her ass. She opened to his tongue, and he tasted her more thoroughly.

They arrived on her floor much too fast. Another hour or so in that elevator alone with her would have suited him just fine.

"Come on," she said, pulling free of his embrace. With a sigh, he followed.

The hallway was quieter now, the weekend crowd having long-since departed. In just another day or so it'd be full again. Of course, by then they'd be gone—him to North Carolina, and her to—wait, she'd never even said what state she lived in.

She might live within driving distance. Now, that was a tempting thought.

"Sorry. The card fell to the bottom of my bag." Eliza propped her purse on her knee as she rifled through it. Chandler watched. She might be put together on the outside, but the inner workings of her purse were pure chaos. He smiled. It was kind of like getting a glimpse into Eliza's private life. She was gorgeous, but a little scattered. He liked that about her. Even though his inclinations were toward order, it seemed that a little disorganization suited Eliza to a tee.

Saying good-bye to her would kill him. But he didn't want to think about that now.

"Aha!" She pulled the plastic key card free and gave the lock on the door a swipe. It chirped, the light flashed green, and then they were inside.

"Boy," Chandler said, covering his mouth as he yawned. "I'm beat."

Eliza's pleasant expression fell, almost like she was a kid who'd been told they were going to miss the class field trip. "Really? Already?"

Inside, he was laughing like crazy, but he kept his expression bleary on the outside. "Yeah, I'm really done in. I guess it's all the late nights we've been having."

Scuffing her toe on the carpet, Eliza dropped her purse beside her suitcase. She stared at the lighter streak in the carpet while she spoke. "I thought you were enjoying the late nights."

"I was. I am," he corrected himself, falling backward on the bed. Spreading his arms and legs wide, he looked over at her. "I just don't think I've got the energy to tie you up and spank you tonight, Liza. I'm sorry."

She shook her head. "It's okay. Really. We can just sleep."

Rolling to his side, he clucked his tongue in a disapproving way. "I hadn't figured you to be so lazy."

"Lazy? What the crap do you mean?"

He'd sparked her temper. Good. He'd always liked playing with fire. Propping his cheek on one hand, he watched as she glared at him. She was gorgeous that way, her hands on her hips, her eyes glittering with anger.

"I mean I didn't know you were so passive in the bedroom. If I had more energy, then I could tie you up and fuck you seventeen ways to Sunday. And you'd scream my name, and beg me to do more, harder, deeper, but since I'm tired? Well, I guess we just can't have sex until I can dominate you again. It's a shame that it's the only thing you enjoy."

Understanding dawned, and a slow smile spread across Eliza's face. She took a step toward him.

"So you're tired, huh? What if I told you that I wasn't going to take no for an answer?"

He rolled to his back again, feigning a sigh. "I guess if it's what you want, I can try to muster up the strength."

She pinned his wrists to the mattress, her smile almost predatory. Lust fired in Chandler's blood as she gripped his skin harder.

She'd learned as much as he had, apparently.

"No, you lie there. Where are the cuffs?"

He grinned. "In my suitcase. Front pouch."

"Be right back."

19

Eliza's heart beat hard, her body covered in sweat. Her hand stung a bit, but it was a good sting, the kind that radiated up her arm and down to her throbbing core. Chandler lay spread-eagled on the bed, his beautiful body glistening, his chest heaving as hard as hers had been.

Pinkened strips of skin painted his legs, little gifts from the paddle he'd so thoughtfully purchased for them to use. He was hard, and she'd done that. She'd cuffed him to the bed, spanked him, and was now thinking of other ways to bend him to her will.

God, this had been such a good idea.

"I don't like that look on your face."

"What look?" She dialed the evil grin up to eleven. "I would think that this look would get you excited."

"It does. I just didn't know how diabolical you could be, madam. I'll remember that next time you ask me to tie you up."

Oh, she dearly hoped he would. Putting the paddle down, she walked across the room to kneel by his side. Not touching him, just close enough that she could feel his body heat.

"You look hungry."

"If I do, it's because you made me that way."

She traced a fingernail over his chest, reveling in the way his skin felt to her fingertip. He was so beautiful, his muscles firm, his skin smooth, that delicious trail of hair on his belly pointing down to, well, to one of her most favorite parts of him, actually. She followed it down, grasping his cock and gently stroking it.

"You're driving me crazy," Chandler groaned, pulling at the cuffs. The Velcro complained, but it held.

"Good," Eliza said, bending down to press a kiss to the swollen head of him. His cock twitched in her grip, becoming harder. As much as she'd like to suck him off, well, that just wouldn't be fair. He was supposed to be doing what she wanted now, right? She pulled off her panties and tossed them aside. Now she was as naked as he was.

Straddling his chest, Eliza looked down at her temporary slave. He was beautiful, so strong, and he was all hers.

"How long do you think you can hold out?"

The question was a little presumptuous, but Eliza didn't call him on it. She just smiled and scooted her hips higher on his chest. She was straddling his pecs now. "Longer than you can, I'll bet."

He arched a brow as she scooted a little higher. Her knees rested on the bed above his biceps now. She was almost straddling his throat. "Are you sure about that? God, Liza, you smell amazing."

She drew her legs together a bit in surprise, which only served to trap his head between them. He closed his eyes and groaned in bliss.

"Smell me? Do I stink?"

"Oh God, no. You smell like a woman. All sweet and mysterious. I bet you taste just as good."

Well, that was a convenient segue. She'd have to reward him for being so clever. She grinned. And then she raised up on her knees, moving the last inch or two so that her body was positioned directly above his mouth.

"You may have a taste."

Her pronouncement acted like a starting pistol. She gripped the headboard of the bed, trying to keep a hold on reality. But his mouth was working her body so intimately. His lips were moving on her most tender skin, his tongue tracing a path from her clit to the entrance of her body. He delicately probed her opening, and she lowered her hips to give him better penetration.

"You taste better than amazing."

His words were muffled, but she didn't care. For the moment she let herself feel everything he was doing to her. The cuffs kept him from holding her hips, grabbing her ass like she'd love for him to do, but he more than made up for it with the exploration of his mouth. Flicking, sucking, nipping, loving her, he started a rhythm that drove her wild. Tension built in her lower belly, and her hips swiveled against him. It was so good, but it wasn't enough. He was stoking her fires so hot, making her want his cock. She wanted to ride him. He was right; he'd lasted longer than she did.

"I can't wait anymore."

She fell to the side, scrambling to realign their bodies. His cock jutted straight to the ceiling, thick, hard, and proud. It was begging for her body, the tip shiny with precum. Throwing one leg over him, she began to sink down onto his hardness.

"Wait," he croaked, jerking to one side to prevent entry. "Condom."

She almost screamed in frustration, but she knew he was right. Hitting the floor at a dead run, she made it across to the desk in record time. One last condom was left from the stash she'd brought. Tearing the package open with her teeth, she fumbled the lubricated latex circle.

Slow down. Breathe. Her inner mantra helped her to slow

the crazy pace and actually put the condom on correctly. Chandler tried so hard to stay still, but she couldn't help but stroke his cock as the condom covered him.

"You like that?"

"God, yes." Chandler's hips lifted to her grasp.

"Then you'll really like this."

She turned away from him and straddled him. Bracing herself on his muscled thighs, she lowered her body onto him. He entered her slowly, stretching her, filling her body with his hard heat. For a moment she stayed still, just feeling him. They fit together like puzzle pieces, made for one another. But then she began to move.

"Your ass is so beautiful from this angle. I want to touch it, I want to grab it, spank it. Eliza, let me touch your ass, please."

Her movements became more frantic. He was asking her permission, and that made her want him even more. He twisted beneath her, his cock nudging higher inside her.

"Please, baby, this is torture. I want to touch your body."

She could come that way, but she'd rather look into his eyes as she did. So, without letting him withdraw, she slowly turned with him inside her. They moaned together, a long, low, wanting sound.

"You want to touch me?" She ripped the Velcro as she spoke. His eyes glowed while she released him, first his hands, then leaning back to reach his ankles. Once he was free, his hands ravaged her.

They were everywhere, on her breasts, down her belly, across her back, cupping her ass, gripping and squeezing and holding her tight. She let him. As fun as it had been to be in charge, now she just wanted to enjoy the fires she'd built within him. She wanted him to take her, to fuck her, to slap her ass and fill her with cum. As wild as he wanted, that was what she needed.

"Fuck me." He obeyed her command instantly.

Gripping her hips, Chandler slammed his cock into her, deep and hard. Eliza screamed as her walls stretched, the agonizing fullness within her sending a throb throughout her body.

She fell onto his chest, pressing her breasts against him, her body screaming all over for his touch. He took her, rolling her over and pulling one of her legs up to his shoulder. The penetration was so deep she bit his shoulder to keep from screaming again. He went wild for her, stroking deeply, filling her over and over and sending her body to places she'd only dreamed of.

"Are you going to come for me, baby? I want to feel your walls squeeze around me while you scream. I want to pump and pump until I fill you with cum, your beautiful breasts crushed against me. Come for me, Liza. Come now."

He reached between them and pressed against her clit, and she was gone. Light burst behind her eyes, her movements jerky and erratic as her insides pulsed with pleasure. Only a second later Chandler stiffened inside her, then groaned as his orgasm burst from him, filling her with heat.

He let her leg descend slowly, and then he left her body. But he pulled her close into his side, and they held one another for a long while.

Eliza closed her eyes and breathed in. It smelled like them. It smelled like home.

How was she really going to let this end?

He'd known it was coming, but that didn't make it any easier to bear.

The afternoon was winding down on one of the best days he could ever remember. They'd woken up late thanks to their late-night fun, then a leisurely brunch turned into a mission. Eliza had confessed that she'd been reinventing herself on this trip, and she wanted to do something daring. What could be more daring than parasailing? So he'd taken her, and she'd adored it.

Then, after they ate ice cream cones on the beach, he surprised her with a sunset dinner cruise he'd reserved a couple of days ago. As he'd predicted, she loved that, too. Standing on the bow of the boat, his arms around her, Chandler decided he'd waited long enough to make his move.

"Liza." He bent down and propped his chin on her shoulder. She leaned her head close to his and he closed his eyes for a moment. If this didn't work, he was going to hang on to this memory for a long damn time.

He hoped it worked.

"What is it?"

"I wanted to talk to you before tomorrow."

She pulled back a little to get a better look at his face. "Why do you sound serious all of a sudden?"

He forced a smile as he threaded his fingers through hers and stood by her side. She relaxed a bit and leaned on the railing in front of her.

"I don't mean to sound serious. It's just something I've been thinking about and I want to make sure I talk to you about it before we leave paradise."

Her expression got somber then. "Oh. Well, whatever it is, go ahead." She closed her eyes like she was facing a firing squad. He wanted to be offended, but he couldn't. She was too cute with her face scrunched up, waiting for the blow to fall.

Squeezing her hand, he spoke.

"These last few days have been amazing for me. Since Andrea, I haven't really had a lot of luck in the relationship department. Well, I hadn't really been trying, to tell the truth. And I wasn't really planning to try. But in the airport, when I saw you, and then had the seat next to you? I don't know that I believed in fate before, but it seems to me like things were working out that way for a reason."

Her hand was cold in his. Trying really hard not to read too much into that, he kept talking.

"I'll admit it, I wanted in your pants first. And I don't apologize for that. You're an incredibly sexy woman, and the reality of being with you was even better than I'd imagined it would be. At first, all I wanted was a fun fling over this vacation. But the more I get to know you, well, I've told you that before. And it's still true."

Eliza wasn't saying anything. She was staring forward into the ocean, the wind whipping strands of her hair across her cheek. He wished she'd look at him, give him some clue as to how she was receiving his words. But she stayed still and silent.

He surged forward. There was no turning back at this point.

"I like you, Eliza. I like you a lot. And now that this trip is almost over, I want to tell you that. I think if we gave this a shot, then maybe—"

"Chandler, I don't know." Eliza pulled her hand away from his, an uncertain look in her eyes.

"Don't be so afraid. I'm not pledging my undying love to you here."

She shot him a look and tightened her arms over her middle.

He sighed and raked a hand through his hair, but the sea breeze whipped it instantly back into tangles. "I don't know you well enough for that yet. But what I am saying is that I have feelings for you, feelings that I think could grow if we gave each other some time. And that's all I'm asking for. Hell, I don't even know what state you're from! I just want the bare minimum here. Just a promise from you that we can keep in touch, and maybe see where this thing goes. If you're even interested."

"Ohio."

His gaze flew to her. "Excuse me?"

Eliza dropped her hands to her sides, a shy smile on her face.

"Ohio. That's where I live. A little town called Appledale, in southwestern Ohio. It's a suburb of Cincinnati."

For some reason, the simple answer she gave him lifted the weight that had taken up residence in his chest. Just a bit, anyway. Now it was like trying to breathe through chocolate pudding instead of solid lead.

"Oh." He nodded. "Cincinnati is only about a nine-hour drive from the Banks, you know. Or just a two-hour flight?"

"Then one of us might have to visit the other soon."

"Maybe so."

He put an arm around her waist and together they looked out at the water. It was enough. For now, just the promise of a future in which he and Eliza were still communicating was enough.

Life did go on, after all.

"You know, my parents always travel for the holidays."

He shot her a sideways glance, trying not to betray the eagerness in his face. "Oh yeah? Holidays are kind of awkward for me. I usually eat at my aunt and uncle's house for Thanksgiving, but Christmases are on my own."

A cool breeze played up then, and Eliza shivered. Chafing her arm with his hand, Chandler held her close to keep the chill away.

She looked up at him, one of her hands holding his at her waist, the other holding her hair back from her face. "It would be a shame if both of us were alone for Christmas, wouldn't it? I mean, as acquaintances. Friends. Or, well, whatever it is we are."

Success! He kept his smile small. This was a big deal for her, for them. The chance to move forward was fragile, and at any moment he could push her too far. There was still something in her past that was hard for her to move beyond, but he knew he could help her if she'd trust him enough to share. But maybe he'd been wrong before. Maybe he could help her more by knowing what had gone on before she shared the knowledge with him.

Was it wrong for him to look into her past if it was to help her heal, to move forward? He wasn't convinced, but it was definitely worth considering. He put the idea on the back burner for the moment, though.

"It would be a shame for such a beautiful woman to be alone on Christmas. If you'd let me, I'd love to come up to Ohio and visit you. Spend a few frosty evenings in your company."

He waited, holding her close. One heartbeat. Two . . .

With a smile, she said three simple words that made him incredibly happy.

"I'd like that."

20

Eliza's suitcase wheels clacked over the tiled floor of the resort lobby. She'd just turned in her room keys and now she and Chandler were waiting for the shuttle to the airport.

"It seems like forever ago that we got here," Chandler observed, adjusting the sunglasses he'd perched atop his head. Eliza was trying really hard not to stare at him. He looked too attractive like that.

"I don't know. To me, it seems like just yesterday."

And it did. The time had flown by. She'd been so frightened, so timid when she'd gotten off this shuttle. And now? Eliza shook her head as she walked to the same van that had driven her here. Now there was something inside her other than the fear, other than the doubt that had filled her before. And she had Chandler to thank for that.

Handsome jerk. He'd ruined all her plans.

"Did you have a nice time?" The shuttle driver was all smiles again, and Eliza couldn't help returning the expression as she handed her suitcase to him to be loaded into the back of the van.

"The best time," she agreed. "This is the most beautiful place I've ever seen."

"You will have to come again. We are here all the time!" The shuttle driver laughed, and took Chandler's bag.

"We will," Chandler said, and laced his fingers through hers. Eliza's heart gave that funny little tug it had started over the past few days whenever Chandler touched her. It was a disconcerting feeling, one that she was getting dangerously attached to.

A few other passengers were using the same shuttle, so she and Chandler climbed into the back row of the van. Conversations and laughter floated around them, but they didn't really speak. Eliza just leaned into Chandler's side, and he traced patterns on her palm with his finger.

It was enough. There was so much inside her that she just couldn't voice it all.

The ride was over much too quickly. Of course, it could have lasted three weeks and still been too short for her. She didn't know how to do this. How could she say good-bye to someone who'd been there while she changed? She wasn't the same Eliza. Chandler knew this Eliza; he liked this Eliza. What if no one else did?

They got their suitcases and Eliza gave the driver a larger tip than she'd intended to. Just because he'd driven a bit slower than the rest of the surrounding traffic, she felt like she owed him.

"So where's your layover?" Chandler said as they moved toward the security checkpoint.

"I'm in LAX again. You?"

"Dallas," Chandler said, his chin falling slightly. "I guess it was too much to ask to have the same flight out of here again."

"Yeah." Eliza blinked hard. Was something in her eye? Damn dry air in airports. Making up her mind to get some eye drops inside the terminal, she began the process of prepping her bags for the security checkpoint. The line was blessedly short, but she didn't feel all that grateful. Even in the security line she was being robbed of extra time with him.

"I never asked you," Chandler said as they moved their gray tubs toward the conveyor belt. "Did your tablet make it okay?"

Eliza laughed at the memory. It was a little less embarrassing now. "I haven't even turned it on since I've been here."

"If it's broken, let me know and I'll replace it."

Eliza glared at his back as he stepped onto the yellow footprints of the scanning booth. "I dropped it, not you."

"I still feel bad." He moved on, but Eliza just stood there and looked at him.

"Step forward, please." The TSA agent looked both bored and pissed that he'd had to speak to Eliza.

"Sorry." She stood on the mark and held her arms above her head. Chandler caught her eye, looked directly at her chest, and waggled his eyebrows suggestively. Her cheeks heated, but she couldn't move, or risk the wrath of the TSA.

"Step through."

Once they'd both been cleared by Security, they stopped by the bank of monitors that held all the flight numbers and gates.

"What's your flight number?"

Eliza checked her boarding pass. "1328."

Chandler adjusted the strap of his bag on his shoulder. "Looks like you're in the D Terminal."

"And you?"

He gave her a rueful half smile. "A Terminal."

She didn't answer, just looked at him. Why was this so hard? She hadn't known him long enough to be so strongly attached. They weren't in love; they weren't even in a relationship. They'd fucked a ton, yeah, but casual sex was a thing, right? Eliza coughed, trying to clear the lump in her throat. Damn it, this wasn't happening to her.

"Are you okay?"

"Sure," she croaked, a hand at her throat as she waved him away with the other. "I'm good. Just swallowed my tongue or something."

"I thought that was my job."

She smiled, but he went curiously wavy. What was up with that? She blinked, and his outline didn't clear.

His smile faded and he stepped close to her, wrapping her in his arms.

"Come on, Liza, don't cry."

"I'm not. Don't be stupid," she sniffed, squeezing her eyes shut tight as she buried her face in his chest. "Why would I be crying? That's insane."

He ran his fingers through her hair, pressed his lips to the top of her head, and just held her there for long moments. She wasn't crying. She wasn't. That wet spot on his shirt had to be from some spilled coffee or something. It had nothing to do with the fact that she couldn't breathe without making little sobbing hiccup noises.

Ridiculous. She was completely ridiculous.

"You need to hurry," Chandler said in a soft voice. "Your flight will be boarding soon."

"I don't care." He probably couldn't understand her, because she'd said the words straight into his chest, but right now she didn't give a good damn. All she wanted was to stay right there in that spot with his arms around her.

"I can come with you."

Her heart jumped inside her chest and she jerked back to look at him. "What?"

"To your terminal. See you off? I've got a little while before I've got to board my flight."

It was unreal how disappointed those words made her. For a moment she'd dared to imagine Chandler coming home with her. Snuggling against his chest again, Eliza shook her head. "No, I can't walk on the plane with you there watching."

"Hey," he whispered against her head. "You've got my cell number, you've got my e-mail. Text me. Call me. Write me. Send me stupid pictures and corny jokes. I'm not far away. And as soon as I get home, I'll check my work calendar and book the flight out to see you for Christmas. We can hang out in your cute little small town, and you can show me that main street that you love so much. Okay?"

She just nodded. What else could she do? She was an idiot, an overemotional moron. It was like leaving summer camp when she was ten. She'd had the best time of her life there, had made new friends, and when the bus had pulled away she'd spent the whole four-hour drive home crying like a baby. And she hadn't kept in contact with anyone. They'd traded addresses, and she'd sent letters, but her so-called friends had never written back. So was it any wonder she was squeezing Chandler like this was the last time she'd ever have the chance to?

She turned her head to the side, pressing her cheek against his heart. "Will you call me?"

"Of course." His voice was extra deep with her on his chest. "As often as you want."

"And you're really coming for Christmas."

"I swear. I can probably stay for two weeks, if that's what you want."

Her heart leapt and she looked up at him. "Really? Promise?"

He nodded and tucked her hair behind her ear. "Swear. We'll decorate a tree and find some mistletoe and everything."

"I—" She stopped. What had she been about to say? She didn't know, but whatever it was, she couldn't do it. So she settled for something close. "I'll miss you."

Chandler bent down and kissed her, desperately, passionately.

She tasted her own tears, her hands digging into his shoulders like she could imprint his whole being into her memory. If only.

When he pulled away, his own eyes looked curiously misty.

"I'm going to miss you, too, Eliza Jackson. Now get your adorable ass on that plane, or I'll have to drag you to the Banks with me."

"Worse things could happen," she joked, but stepped away. Her body felt curiously cold without his touch to warm her. She backed away, step after step, widening the gap between them.

"Take care of yourself," Chandler said, his gaze never leaving hers.

"You, too."

Before she lost her nerve, she turned and walked away as quickly as she could stand it. Hopefully he didn't hear the sob that escaped her before she stuffed her fist against her mouth.

This was stupid. She was stupid. But damn, was she glad for his promise to see her at Christmas. It was the only way she was able to convince herself to leave him now.

Way over her head. That's how far she was in.

Chandler stood in front of the bank of monitors, watching until she'd disappeared down the hallway, hidden by the milling bodies.

That was unexpected. He'd known that he'd have a hard time saying good-bye to her, but he hadn't expected tears from Eliza. After all, she'd been switching from hot to cold very frequently over the past few days with him. Could her attachment to him be scaring her? Was she just nervous at what was growing between them?

It appeared so, but Chandler didn't exactly trust his own intuition where beautiful women were concerned anymore.

"Excuse me," a young guy said as he approached the board. "Can you move over? I can't see my flight number."

"Oh yeah, sorry." Chandler gave the guy an apologetic wave and walked in the direction of his gate. It might be for the best that they weren't sharing a plane out of here. He might be tempted to jump into her suitcase and follow her straight home.

Damn. He had it bad. Shaking his head, Chandler ducked into the convenient mart beside gate A-22. Grabbing a granola bar and a fruit juice, he prepared himself to wait the two hours for his flight to board.

So he was a little early. It was worth it to have gotten the extra time with her.

He settled in at his mostly empty gate and crunched his granola bar thoughtfully. It had been an eventful week. His cousin was hitched, he'd delved into some light bondage, and he thought he might finally be getting over the whole divorce thing.

Chandler smiled as he crumpled the empty granola wrapper. Yup, definitely a good week.

He pulled his MacBook from his bag and flipped open the screen. There were probably a good number of work things that needed his attention. He employed an administrative assistant, but she'd had the week off, too. So the company e-mail was probably full to bursting, despite the out-of-office message on the website and the in-box.

Oh well. Such was the joy of owning his own business.

He hovered the cursor above his e-mail application, but before he could click it and get started, he changed his mind. He couldn't think about work right now. There was only one person he wanted to think about.

"Let's see, flights to Ohio."

He frowned at the screen. She'd mentioned what town she lived in, but what airport was closest? He contemplated texting her, but when he checked his phone he realized that her flight was more than likely taking off right now. He'd have to Google to find out.

His browser took a moment to open, and before he could

198 / *Regina Cole*

think about what he was doing, he typed "Eliza Jackson Appledale, Ohio."

Four pages of results. The first was a LinkedIn profile, and he clicked it.

"Quality Testing." Her current employer was listed. His analytical brain kicked into gear without his permission.

Wandering through Google, he picked up threads of her life, her town, her surroundings. She'd won three science fairs in a row during high school. Scholarship to Ohio State University. Graduated with honors.

As he closed out a newspaper article about her promotion to supervisor at Quality Testing, he found himself wondering. She loved Appledale, loved her job, too. But there was something in Eliza's past that made her feel unwelcome in her hometown. That made her feel like a monster. So why wasn't he finding anything about that?

"You know you're desperate when you hit the fifth page of Google results," he muttered beneath his breath as he forged on. And there, buried three-quarters of the way down the page, was a hit from a blog post. "Appledale Tales and Rumors." The post title was "Chemist brings filthy bedroom habits to Appledale."

Chandler clicked the link, but before he could start reading the blog post, his cell phone buzzed in his pocket. Jumping guiltily, he slammed the lid of his laptop and pulled the phone free.

The text was from Eliza.

Hey, you. :)

His heart thumped harder, but not from excitement. It was guilt. Damn it, he was breaking his own rules. Eliza's story was her own, and he had no reason to go searching behind her back.

His personal moral code was broken, and he had no one to blame but himself. So he opened his computer, closed out the browser without reading any more of the words on the screen, and put the laptop back in his bag before replying to her.

Hi yourself. Is your flight delayed?

Three little dots on his smartphone screen indicated she was typing back to him already. Those little dots made him inexplicably happy, for some reason.

Nope. There's free wifi on this flight. So I can text you. Don't you feel lucky?

He smiled.

The luckiest. Question, what airport should I fly into for our Christmas fun?

Another passenger sank into the seat beside Chandler, but he didn't pay her much attention. He was waiting for Eliza's response. Luckily, he didn't have to wait long.

Cincinnati/Northern Kentucky International is closest. Only about an hour's drive from my house.

Then that's where I'll fly. I'll book my trip tonight.

Can't wait.

She put a little smiley face emoticon with its tongue sticking out after that. He could picture her making that face. Damn it, he was really taking this much too far.

"Will passengers here for flight 1231 with service to Dallas please come to the courtesy desk? Anyone here for flight 1231 to Dallas."

Chandler looked up. That was his flight number. So he fired off a quick message to Eliza to let her know he'd be tied up for a few, and then he lined up behind an elderly man at the desk. Then he looked over to where he'd been sitting.

The woman who'd picked the chair next to him, despite there being several empty seats spread through the area, was completely gorgeous. Tall and willowy, with a creamy complexion and deep reddish-brown hair. She gave him a smile, her eyes saying something to him that he thought he could understand.

But he only gave her a polite nod and turned away.

A week or two ago, he'd have been thrilled to talk to a gorgeous stranger in an airport. Hell, a week ago, he *had* talked to a gorgeous stranger in an airport. But now? He couldn't think of any woman but Eliza.

He had it bad, that was for sure.

Once he'd spoken with the desk attendant and secured a free upgrade, he found another seat and sent Eliza another quick text.

I'm sitting in first class all the way to DFW. Feel free to envy me.

Are you KIDDING? You suck. I'm stuck by the bathroom, and there's an angry toddler across the aisle from me. I think she's trying to pelt me with Cheerios.

Chandler snorted aloud. Eliza was almost at her most attractive when she was irritated. He wished he could see her now.

It won't be long now.

It's already too long. Too far away from you. I miss you.

His chest squeezed, and he put the phone down for a minute. There was a crowd around him now, the time having slipped away from him. Like the whole week had. Too much time was moving too quickly for him. But that was part of what made Eliza special. His whole world seemed to fly by, happier and better for the fact that she'd been in it with him.

It was a heady feeling. And the memory of her in bed with him took that over the top. He'd have to think of some ways to keep things going during the few weeks they'd be separated.

I miss you, too, he typed back. **But don't worry, I'm not going to let you forget me in the meantime. I've got some tricks up my sleeve.**

It took her no time to fire off a response.

Tricks? Like what?

He grinned evilly.

You'll just have to see. Oops, they're calling my section. Talk to you soon.

Chandler, pleeeeease tell me.

Shutting off the screen, he tucked the phone in his pocket and lined up to get on the plane. Her anticipation was going to be part of the fun. As far as the other part, well, she'd have to wait to see. But he was fairly certain that they'd both enjoy the hell out of it.

21

Three weeks later, Eliza bent low, goggles level with the countertop. Her hand was steady as she added acid to the beaker. Nothing would explode if she screwed up these measurements, but she didn't want to have to repeat this test if she didn't have to.

Her hand was steady as she piped another drop into the glass container. The clear liquid waved, then settled exactly on the line.

"Yes," she whispered as she straightened. "Perfect."

Humming to herself, she capped the hydrochloric acid and set it inside the cabinet. Just a few more preparations to make, then she could set the high performance liquid chromatograph instrument and leave it running for the weekend. Lacing her fingers together, Eliza stretched toward the ceiling, letting out a low groan as her spine crackled like breakfast cereal. She needed to invest in better shoes if the company expected her to keep testing at this rate.

Here at the office, she could pretend that things were normal. That her little escapade on a beautiful island hadn't happened. That Chandler was only a beautiful dream that she'd had to wake up from. It was easier than remembering that he was there in the world, far away from her reality.

"Hey, Jackson, the nineties called. They want their grunge look back."

Her arms dropped, hands instinctively covering the ragged hem of her Green Day tee. Fighting the rush of hot blood in her cheeks, Eliza glared at the doorway to her lab. Her boss/ex, Tyler Hagans, stood there, a self-satisfied smirk on his chiseled face.

"Tell Schweitzer to be more careful pouring acids and then maybe my clothes won't look like Swiss cheese." Eliza wasn't afraid to snap back, but she kept her eyes locked on the scarred black surface of her worktable as she did. "Maybe you guys could try hiring some chemists with experience instead of these clueless college kids."

Tyler clicked his tongue as he sauntered into the room. Hands shaking, Eliza continued with her test. Tyler made the room feel small. He always had, even when he and Eliza were dating. It used to be a good feeling, a comforting one. Now it made her want to run.

"Quality Testing took a chance on you when you were a green college kid, and look at you now. Only twenty-six and already a supervisor. Don't these other kids deserve a chance?"

She didn't bother to answer. The acid hissed and popped as Eliza poured it into the half-full testing vessel, much faster than she should have. Tyler moved back a step, frantically wiping at his unblemished jacket sleeve.

"Easy there, you're going to wreck my suit. This is Armani, you know."

"Did you need something, Tyler? I know you didn't come in here for a social visit. It's not like you want to be caught dead talking to me." She wished she could bite back the words, but instead she turned away and yanked open the instrument door. Looking busy was her only defense against the asshole. If Chandler were here—No, this was her problem, and Chandler knowing Tyler's stories would just make everything worse.

"Yeah, I did." Tyler rounded her worktable and stopped only a foot in front of her. Marshaling her courage, she tilted her chin and looked him straight in the eye. She knew that tone of voice, and it usually meant an insult was coming.

"So, spit it out." Crossing her arms, Eliza concentrated on keeping her breathing steady even as her shoulders tensed in preparation.

"Dad just went through a bunch of applications and he's down to two that he likes to fill that gap in the agriculture department."

"So?"

"They're both women." Tyler moved a step closer, the overpowering smell of his cologne clogging Eliza's nostrils. "You know the new office policy on dating, so I hope I can count on you to stay away from them."

The cold wave of hurt washed over her, but she didn't give him the satisfaction of seeing it. "I'm not gay, Tyler."

His laugh was full of cruel bitterness. "I think we both know better than that."

She tightened her fists so hard her knuckles cracked. "You're purposefully misunderstanding what I was asking for. And anyway, can we leave our past relationship out of work, please? You've already told the world what you think of me, and most of them agree with you now."

Tyler's mouth twisted in a mocking smile. "I'm not the one who turned out to be a freak, Liza. Now just promise me you'll let the new girl get settled in before you break out your whips and chains."

The urge to knee him in the groin was strong, but Eliza didn't do it. She couldn't afford to lose her job. As lovely as it would be to turn tail and run for North Carolina and the safety that Chandler offered, she refused to be run off like a stray dog. This was her home, and damn Tyler for ruining it.

"You're an ass, Tyler. I can't believe I ever thought we could work."

His face went an ugly shade of red, but she turned her back to him and slammed manuals back into their place on the shelf.

"You smug bitch. How dare you? I'm not the bi sex addict here. Seriously, Eliza, were you abused as a child? There's no way shit like that is normal."

A burst of laughter from the hallway shook her confidence for a second. She glanced at the still-open doorway.

A couple of the younger chemists were hurrying down the hall, but their hushed words carried anyway.

". . . had heard she was bi, but I didn't know she was an addict."

"Yeah, I heard when she was gone she went to some swanky sex addiction treatment center in LA. Like that guy from *Californication*."

She rounded on Tyler, her patience way past snapping. "Would you mind getting the fuck out of my lab? I have a job to do."

Straightening his jacket, he nodded. "As long as we're clear."

"I'm definitely clear on the fact that you're a selfish, grasping son of a bitch who's—" Eliza bit off the rest of her retort. It wouldn't do any good. Tyler wasn't interested in the truth. When he'd started at Quality, no one had taken him seriously. After all, he was the boss's son. But as soon as he'd started spreading rumors about Eliza, the employees had gone to him for the juicy tidbits. He'd eaten up the attention, and the stories got more and more outrageous. As Eliza's reputation suffered, his own had grown. Oddly enough, it seemed that her ruined reputation had paved the way for his acceptance here.

Tyler walked toward the door, and Eliza cranked the knob

on the instrument hard, wishing it was his damn arm she was twisting. But before he could leave the room, he turned and trained his icy stare on her.

"If I had my way, you'd have been out of here months ago. But for some reason Dad likes you." Tyler snorted. "Did you offer to let him watch you and your new girlfriend together?"

Her brain fogged with a red haze of anger, and she looked around for something handy to throw at his head. But before her hand closed around a hefty book, Tyler had disappeared down the hallway.

Carefully setting the text down, Eliza held out her hands and watched them tremble. God, was something really wrong with her? Or was Tyler just a fucking asshole?

This was why she should have walked away from Chandler when she had the chance. How could she possibly think it was okay for him to be here, surrounded by the rumors Tyler delighted in stirring up?

Shaking her head, Eliza punched the Start button on the HPLC and picked up her purse from the little shelf behind the door. Time to go home and curl up with a pint of ice cream and some stupid TV. Chandler was going to Skype her later tonight, but maybe she should just skip it. She wasn't the same girl she'd been in Hawaii, and when Chandler saw that, he wouldn't want anything else to do with her.

So she'd stay alone the rest of her life. So what? Lots of people were happy alone.

Weren't they?

"Thanks for all your help today," Chandler called as Wendi pulled her jacket on.

"No problem, boss. Oh, and Gregory Trailwick called while you were in that meeting earlier. I stuck the message to your phone." Wendi nodded at the desk where his cell usually lay.

"Great, thanks."

Wendi waved and left the small office, the door swinging shut behind her.

Chandler glanced at the shiny black clock on the wall. It was after five. If he was going to make it to the post office before they closed, he'd have to hustle. The investigation he was on, looking into a shady accountant for a locally owned hotel chain, was winding down anyway. He could finish the details tomorrow morning. Bundling his jacket under his arm, he grabbed the box he'd stowed beneath his desk so Wendi wouldn't see it, then left his office behind, locking the door behind him.

His name was posted in white letters on the door, the words *Private Investigation* beneath it. He'd been so proud when those letters had gone up, but now his work was the second most interesting thing in his life. The first just so happened to be a girl he'd met on a trip to Hawaii, one to whom he was determined to mail this package before he spoke to her tonight.

He hummed along to the radio as he drove. Eliza had seemed different the last couple of times they'd chatted, but he chalked it up to the stresses of home piling up on her. He knew how that went. His job could get hairy, and it had been nice to talk to someone about it. Of course, Eliza didn't ever really share her problems with work, or friends. It was something they'd have to work on, just because Chandler knew she'd be happier if she could vent about things. Even if it wasn't to him, he wanted her to get those things off her chest. They could both be happy; he was convinced of it. And he had a little surprise that should please her. At least he hoped so.

There was a line at the post office, of course. Chandler held the box in front of him, moving a foot forward every time someone advanced to the counter. Finally, just one person was left.

The clock ticked loudly on the wall, and he looked over at it. Damn, not enough time to pick up dinner on the way home before his Skype date. No biggie, he'd just throw a frozen pizza in the oven after he talked to Liza. Of course, that could be pretty late, but he didn't mind. Time spent with her was much more fun than eating.

"Sir, can I help you?"

He'd been standing stock-still for much too long. An embarrassed smile crossed his face.

"Sorry about that, daydreaming. I need to send this priority, please."

The woman didn't even bat an eye, just plopped the box onto the scale. "Anything fragile, liquid, perishable, or potentially hazardous?"

"Um, no." At least he didn't think so. He hadn't heard of anyone dying because of sex toys. Of course, anything was possible.

"That'll be twelve-fifty."

He swiped his credit card, thanked the woman, and pocketed the receipt. If all went according to plan, Eliza would have some interesting new toys in about three days. He couldn't wait.

Driving much too fast, he made it home just in time to sit down in front of his laptop and boot up Skype. His heart thudded like he was a teenager about to climb into the backseat with the prom queen. Much too excited to be calling a girl. His girlfriend? No, that didn't seem right. Eliza was all woman. Calling her his girlfriend somehow made her seem less important than she was, even though it was probably the best term for what they were to one another. After all, he wasn't seeing anyone else and she'd made it clear that she wasn't, either.

He clicked Eliza's picture and selected "call." The cheerful beeping tone sounded through his computer's speakers, and he waited. The little screen in the upper right corner showed his webcam's picture, and he frowned. Maybe he should have taken the time to shave.

The call picked up, and Eliza's beautiful face appeared. She looked a bit tired, or maybe even sad.

"Hey," he said, smiling warmly. Even with the corners of her lips drawn down, and dark circles under her eyes, she was the most beautiful woman on earth. When he closed his eyes at night, he could still smell her. Christmas couldn't come soon enough.

"Hi."

"Are you okay? You seem down."

She sighed and pressed her chin into her palm. "Sorry, I had a rough day at work. I won't be fun to talk to tonight. Could we maybe chat tomorrow?"

Hoping his disappointment wasn't showing on his face, Chandler nodded. "Of course. But if you want to vent, I'm here. I'm a great listener, just ask Greg. He spends more time talking drunk than he ever does sober."

Eliza gave a little laugh, raking a stray hair behind her ear. Even her ponytail looked listless. "It's no big deal, really. Just office politics."

Chandler nodded. "I get that. Used to happen a lot when I worked with a larger firm. But since I changed jobs, I get along really well with all my superiors. They agree with all my suggestions, let me take time off whenever I want, and even give me raises without having to ask for them."

Eliza hiked a brow at him. "I thought you were self-employed."

He grinned. "Guilty as charged. But hey, still applies. Could you maybe find a different company to work for?"

Crossing her arms, she leaned forward on the desk. His gaze wandered to the neck of her vee-cut tee, where her cleavage was on lovely display. God, she was gorgeous. He couldn't wait to touch her again.

"There aren't a ton of places for my line of work around here. It was lucky that I got on at Quality so early. And to be honest, I love the job I do. It's just that, well, sometimes my coworkers are tough to deal with."

Her voice got small at the end, and he had to strain to hear her.

Aw, damn. She was sad. His protective instincts came shooting to the fore. But what could he do? He knew nothing about her company or her job. It wasn't like he could give her career advice.

But maybe there was one thing he could do.

"It might spoil the surprise, but do you want to know something?"

She looked straight at the screen, almost as if she could see through him. "What?"

"I sent you a little care package today. In the mail."

A little smile curved her lips. "Really?"

He nodded. "I did. You should have it in a few days."

"It's not even my birthday. Why'd you do that?"

"Because I saw something that reminded me of you." He didn't bother to point out that he'd been shopping for said object for probably two weeks before he'd settled on the one currently making its way through the postal system to her. "It's just a little warm-up for the trip. Something to remind you that there's someone who's thinking of you nonstop."

Her eyes glowed with a warm light that he'd come to crave. "You're a really nice guy, Chandler, you know that?"

"Don't say that. I thought girls liked bad boys."

Shaking her head vehemently, Eliza caused her webcam to shake. "Not at all. Assholes are appealing for a week or two, but nice guys? Much better. Especially nice guys who can pretend to be bad when they need to be."

"Well, if you want a pretend bad boy," he growled, "I'm your man. Bend over, baby."

She did, waggling her ass at the camera while giggling. He mimed spanking her, and she collapsed in laughter.

"Thanks, Chandler. I needed that tonight."

"Me too," he said, relaxing into his desk chair, hands atop his head. "Ten more days and I can do that in person."

She nodded. "Yup. Only ten days."

He thought about asking her why she got quiet after that, but then decided he'd pried enough. Time would tell, and he could be patient. Although he was really getting tired of constantly reminding himself to bide his time.

He knew what—and who—he wanted.

22

Eliza hadn't spoken to Chandler for a few days, and it was easy to tell. She was jumpier at work, too easily startled when someone ducked their head into her lab to ask her a question. Tyler was applying more and more pressure to her, almost as if he was trying to either get her fired or make her quit. She just put her head down and did her work as quickly and quietly as possible. Arguing would just make her look worse.

Tuesday, when she was finally finished with the seemingly impossible number of tasks for the day, she packed up and left the office. Tyler waved and called to her before she got to the door, but she pretended not to notice.

As she started her car, she wondered what Chandler was doing. Who he was with, what he was thinking. Whether he thought this long-distance thing was as hellish as she did.

It'd been hard to imagine that this could be as difficult for her as it had been. After all, she'd kind of gotten used to being alone. But those few days with Chandler had shown her how amazing being with someone could be, and that made the distance even harder to swallow. Knowing that there was a man out there like Chandler, and knowing that they couldn't really be together sucked.

She missed him. And not talking to him had made it worse. He was busy, and she knew it, but his absence sharpened her longing.

Her stomach was in knots by the time she got home. Taking a few deep breaths, she exited the car and ran through the cold to her front stoop.

A box was there on the steps.

Warmth filled her chest as she remembered. That was right. Chandler had sent her a surprise. "A warm-up," he'd called it, a mischievous sparkle in his eyes. She loved that look on him. Made him look like a kid who was up to no good.

With a lightness she hadn't known was possible, she picked up the box and unlocked the door. Humming to herself, she grabbed a knife from the kitchen counter and carefully slit the packing tape.

A letter lay atop some brown packing paper. She lifted it, examining the swirls of her name written in neat handwriting.

The paper crinkled as she smoothed it out and read.

> *Eliza,*
> *This is for you. But I want to see your face when you open it. So don't go any further. Skype me when you're ready, so I can have the pleasure of seeing your beautiful face when you open the box.*
> *Yours,*
> *Chandler*

What had he done? Eliza peered into the box, poking the paper with her index finger. No clue.

As excited as she was, as happy as this gesture made her, she stopped. Honestly, was there any point to getting even more attached to Chandler? Long-term, was there any way to pursue a relationship with him? She loved her home, despite its problems. She'd never ask Chandler to leave his, either. Would they still be having Skype dates years from now?

The thought of being apart that long made her set the knife down and slowly fold the box closed.

What should she do? With every day that passed, she found herself more and more drawn to him. Would it be smarter for them to just end this now, rather than prolong the eventual pain of their parting?

"Shit."

She had no freaking clue. What she needed was a little time to figure out what was going on inside her head and her heart. She needed clarity.

She needed to get drunk. But without a buddy, she wasn't about to find her way to the bottom of a bottle of wine alone. So she picked the next best thing. She shed her clothes on the way to the bathroom and stood under the scalding-hot spray for a solid half hour.

The steam curled as it rose around her, and her skin turned pink from the high temperature. She scrubbed herself from head to toe, even washing her hair three times. But eventually the warm water ran low, and she had no choice but to leave the sanctity of the shower stall.

Wiping her palm across the steamed-up mirror, Eliza looked at herself. She looked confused and tired. Despite the emptiness of her water heater, she was no closer to an answer. But who else could she ask about any of this?

A name popped into her head. There was probably a long list of reasons why she shouldn't bother that person right now, but Eliza didn't have much other choice.

She threw on a long T-shirt and a pair of panties, then grabbed her cell. There were only four names in her favorites list, and she picked the third one without hesitation.

Bree picked up on the fourth ring.

"Hey, sunshine! Oh my gosh, I haven't talked to you in forever!"

"Hey, Bree." The lead feeling in Eliza's guts lifted just a little. She tucked her feet beneath her and leaned back on her bed. "How was the honeymoon?"

"It was . . . Well . . ." An odd note entered Bree's voice, but it was gone just as quickly as it had appeared. "It was great! Really spectacular. So, how are you? Anything happening in Smalltown, USA?"

"Well . . ." Eliza drew circles inside one of the flowers on her comforter. "I've been talking to Chandler a lot since I got back."

"Ooh, really? Do tell."

So Eliza did. She didn't go into detail, but she did let Sabrina know how close they'd become before leaving Hawaii. And then the whole Skyping thing, which was good, but then it wasn't, because she missed him even more. And when Eliza told her about Tyler's stepping up his insults, Bree lost her shit.

"Are you fucking kidding me? How is that asshole still your boss?"

"Because his dad owns the fucking company."

"Did you ever complain to HR about him?"

"How can I, Sabrina?" The anxiety was back, so Eliza jumped up and started pacing in front of her closet. "He's not going to be punished. If anything, I'll be considered the problem and let go. Harold's done that kind of thing before for Tyler. And if Tyler hasn't already told him about my weird, well, fetish, I don't want to be the one who lets him in on it."

"For the last freaking time, Liza, it's not a weird fetish. Plenty of people get off on stuff like that. Hang on a second." Bree's voice went muffled for a moment as if she'd covered the mouthpiece of the phone and was talking to someone else. Her voice got sharp, angry, but even though Eliza strained she couldn't understand her friend's words. In a minute, though, Bree was back.

"Sorry about that. Little misunderstanding with the husband. Anyway, as I was saying, you're perfectly normal. You like Chandler, don't you?"

"I do." Eliza stopped in front of the dresser, staring at herself in the mirror. Her damp hair was leaving dark splotches on her aqua shirt. "But I just don't know how we're going to get past this distance thing. And if it goes south, I don't want Chandler to see me like Tyler does now. I've already told him too much, and I can't stand the thought of him hating me."

"He won't."

"How can you know that?"

"Because Tyler is a bag of dicks, and Chandler isn't. I know it's scary. I know." Bree's tone was soothing now, and Eliza shut her eyes and breathed deeply.

"You can't go through life mistrusting every guy because one of them dicked you over. Tyler is an ass, and he hurt you. But the only person you're cheating by shutting everyone out is yourself. It's hard to put yourself out there. But when it's for the right guy? It's worth it, babe. Totally worth it."

When Eliza opened her eyes, she wasn't surprised to feel a tear slip down her cheek.

"You're an awesome friend, do you know that?"

Bree sounded a little choked up, too, when she replied, "You are, too. I love you, you dork. Now go call that boy and see what he sent you. And then send me a text, because I'm nosy and I want to know what it is."

Eliza laughed and dashed the wetness from her cheek. "Okay. You got it."

She ended the call and set the phone down on her nightstand. Then she walked directly to the kitchen, picked up the box Chandler had sent her, and sat down in front of her laptop.

Her hair was wet, she was wearing no makeup, and no bra. She didn't care. Chandler was waiting for her call, and she wanted to do this.

Bree was right. Eliza was brave enough to try.

Chandler was in his kitchen when his laptop began to trill the alert for an incoming Skype call. His heart quickened the pace of its beating as he dried his hands on the dish towel that hung on the front of the oven door.

Eliza. Had to be. Nobody else would Skype him out of the blue, right? Of course, this wasn't exactly out of the blue.

His surprise must have arrived.

He clicked the green Accept button as soon as he sat down at his computer desk. It took just a moment for the video call to connect, and then there Eliza was on his screen.

He wished she was in his office with him, but he'd settle for this for now. Just a few more days, and they'd be together again. Hopefully it would be as wonderful as Hawaii had been. Who was he kidding? Of course it would be.

"Hi," Eliza said, pushing her wet hair back from her shoulder. Her T-shirt was damp where the ends had rested. She looked completely delectable.

"Hi. You look good enough to eat."

She shook her head and cut her gaze at him. "I look like death warmed over. Don't lie."

"I'm not lying. You look great. Like, good enough to strip and fuck the brains out of."

"And there's your problem. You shouldn't look with your cock."

He laughed, adjusting the lean on his desk chair and rubbing his hands on the arms. "It's the smartest part of my body, after all."

"Smartest? Hardly. But it's not bad. I'd give it an A for effort."

"Now you're just being mean." He gave her his best lost-puppy imitation. She shook her head and adjusted the box in her lap.

Oh yeah, the box!

He raised one eyebrow at her. "So I see you got my little gift. Ready to open it now?"

Eliza looked down at the box in her hands, her brows lowering slightly. "I don't know. It's not something that'll make me want to throttle you, is it?"

Hardly, but he wasn't above teasing her a bit. "Maybe. How do you feel about live reptiles?"

She shrieked and dropped the box. Chandler just laughed.

"I'm kidding you. Come on, open it. Nothing alive. But it will move if you treat it right."

"Oh yeah?" She shot him a distrustful glance as she picked up the box and began to remove the brown packing paper. "I will kill you if something jumps out of here and scares me."

"You'd be totally justified. But I didn't do you like that. I promise." He waited, anticipation prickling the hairs on his arms as he watched her methodically remove each bit of packing paper until the plain white box inside came into view.

"More and more mysterious. Unlabeled box." Eliza pulled it free and pushed the brown cardboard aside. Picking at the tape that sealed the side, she frowned. "Is this a gift, or is it Fort Knox?"

"I couldn't risk a nosy postal worker checking out your goods. Get some scissors."

She did, and her disappearance gave him a second to breathe. He'd done the right thing, he knew it. Was it super-kinky? No, he hadn't been able to come up with something that far into left field on such short notice. But it was unique enough to give them a good time tonight, and that was all he wanted. A little reminder for Eliza of what it would be like when he got there, when they were together again.

"Back," she said, and ran the scissors over the sealing tape. "There."

Chandler held his breath as she lifted the lid off the white box and examined the objects inside.

"Well, obviously I know what this is," Eliza said wryly, pulling the sleek blue and white vibrator from the box. A small protrusion on the top side of the shaft held a secondary vibrator, the shape reminiscent of a jackrabbit. It was soft, modern, and completely charged. He had been thoughtful enough to do that before he'd dropped it into the mail.

He folded his arms and grinned. "There's a little more to it."

Eliza set the vibrator down and looked in the box. "Well, the lube is obvious."

"Got to ensure your comfort."

"Naturally." And then she pulled the small plastic square from the depths of the box. An auxiliary jack extended from the narrowest side, with an empty port on the other. Eliza turned it around and around in her hands, fumbling with the wheel atop the box, examining the jack. "Okay, you've got me. I'm stumped. What is this supposed to be?"

Chandler rubbed his hands together to deliver the sales pitch he'd been practicing for the past couple of days.

"That vibrator is controlled by sound. So you plug it into the speaker of whatever you want. Your MP3 player, or phone, or maybe your computer. And then the vibrator moves according to what it hears."

Eliza's eyebrows climbed nearly to her hairline, and her smile was one of bemused pleasure. "Oh. Okay."

"So if, for instance, your boyfriend was a few hundred miles away, and wanted to make you feel extremely good, you could connect it to your computer. And then my voice would do the delicious, dirty things to your body that my hands, mouth, and cock really wish they could."

Eliza stared directly at him. "That's brilliant."

Chandler grinned. "I know. So plug it in, baby. We've got all night, but I don't want to waste a minute."

As Eliza stood and began to plug the receiver into her laptop, Chandler pulled off his shirt and loosened the button on his pants. Even just watching her move was good to him. Her nipples were hard beneath her T-shirt, and every time they pressed against the thin fabric he longed to reach out and touch them. But he couldn't. So he told her.

"Your breasts are calling to me, Liza. Your nipples look amazing."

In response, she stopped moving and pulled her shirt tight over her chest. Chandler's hand slipped into his underwear and he palmed his cock as she teased him.

"God, yes."

"Move your camera," Eliza said, her voice growing a bit husky. "I want to see you touching your cock."

He tilted the laptop screen down a bit until he could see what was going on in the preview window. Eliza's eyes darkened as she saw his hand moving up and down on his hard erection.

"It makes me crazy to watch you touch yourself."

"Then get ready to be insane, baby. Take your shirt off."

She did, and then replaced her earbuds. She turned the receiver and the vibrator on, jumping and smiling when the blue vibe started to pulse in her hands. But then it went quiet, and she frowned.

"What's wrong?"

Chandler grinned evilly. He'd tested out some things before letting that little gem leave the house, so he had some plans for her.

"Eliza, I want you to remove your panties and put the head of that vibrator against your clit."

With each of his words, the vibrator jerked and rumbled in her hands. Eliza let out a delighted laugh.

"Oh God, you're going to enjoy this way too much."

"And so are you," he said, rubbing his cock faster as she stood and shimmied out of her panties. She'd moved the laptop to her living room, and when she placed it down on the coffee table he was right at eye level with her beautiful pussy. It was a bit shiny, as if she'd been getting wetter and wetter over the past few minutes. He closed his eyes, imagining he could smell her body, taste her skin, plunge his hard cock into her wet, hot depths. Shit, he was going to come soon.

"Okay," Eliza said, nudging her beautiful lips apart so the blunt head of the blue shaft was barely penetrating her. "Now what?"

"Now, listen to me. And this." And then he pressed Play on the bass-heavy playlist he'd crafted over the weekend. Quiet storm? This was more like a category-4 hurricane.

"Ohmygod," Eliza moaned as the vibe kicked into high gear. "Oh God."

"Now listen to my rhythm as I fuck you from here, okay? In. Out. In. Out." Chandler timed the strokes of his cock to the strokes of her vibrator. Her hips were twisting, her mouth opening as she gasped and writhed on her couch. He could see all of her, her legs spread wide, her hand moving between her legs as she thrust the toy inside her, the smaller shaft on top bumping against her swollen clit.

If only he was there, his balls smacking hard against her as his cock filled her. Chandler's breath was loud and ragged, but he had to keep talking. His voice was his direct connection to her hungry body, and he didn't want to deprive either of them.

"In. Out. Fuck yourself harder for me, Liza. Your body is so hot, so beautiful. I can't wait to fuck you again. Your mouth is so hot, I love the way your pussy walls grip my cock. I want you to come for me, Liza. Feel that vibration inside you? That's me. That's mine. You're all mine, and I'm going to fill you with my cum. So don't wait. Don't you want it? Show me. Come for me. Now."

He shouted the last word, and her hips lifted clear off the couch. The vibrator was so far inside her he could only see the white handle jutting out of her. Her scream was loud through the microphone, but he didn't care. She shuddered, moving slower and slower. And then he let himself go. Spurts of hot white cum covered his hand and dripped onto his shorts.

They stared at one another through the screen, both out of breath for several long minutes.

"Holy shit," Eliza said, wincing slightly as she withdrew the toy from her body. "How long till you get here again?"

"Not nearly soon enough."

23

Eliza hummed to herself as she put away the instrument from her last test. Gosh, it was good to be packing up. Somewhere down the hallway, Christmas music was blaring. Normally it would annoy her, but today? Screw it. Nothing could get under her skin.

Chandler was in the air and soon he'd be in her car. Once things were cleaned up here, she was heading to the airport to wait for him.

A giggle escaped her as she removed her lab coat. She felt like a twelve-year-old girl waiting for her first date. The last few days had been hard to wait through, but nightly Skype sex had eased the anticipation just a little. That setup he'd sent her was genius. She'd have to thank him again for that.

As her depraved little brain descended into multiple lusty ways for her gratitude to be shown, a knock on the door made her jump.

"I'm sorry, Miz Jackson." Tyler drew out the title as if it were an insult. "I'm going to need you to stay late tonight. There's a problem in the Tobacco Products Department, and their shift supervisor's already gone."

"Sorry, I can't." Eliza didn't look at him as she packed her stuff into her backpack. "I'm picking up a friend at the airport."

Tyler sneered. "I bet you are. Let me guess. Female? Buzz cut, leather bra, complete dyke?"

Cold rage fell through her veins like icy daggers from the sky. She gritted her teeth and took a deep breath before answering.

"No. And my private life is none of your business, Tyler. Sorry I can't help you tonight. Besides, Tobacco's not my department."

Tyler stepped close to her, and Eliza fought the urge to scramble backward. *Stand your ground. He's just trying to intimidate you. He can't hurt you.*

"I'm your boss, and you're salaried. When we need you, you've got an obligation to be here."

Eliza leveled her gaze at him, even though looking at him made the bile rise in her throat. The thought that she'd once been intimate with this guy, thought she could love him, made her want to puke. "I'm on vacation starting now, and it's been approved. You can take it up with HR if you've got a problem with me. Now, if you don't let me go, I'm going to be late to the airport."

Tyler's gaze raked her up and down. Eliza curled her hands into fists to keep from shuddering in disgust. He looked down his nose at her. "I'm sure she can wait an hour or two while you fix Tobacco's problem."

"No, *he* can't." She leaned on the pronoun, just for the satisfaction of seeing Tyler's face go white with surprise.

"He? Oh really. Trying to fake some other guy out with your bisexual tendencies?" Tyler bent down, his face only inches from hers. "How long before you beg him to do some of the sick shit you forced on me?"

She'd swallowed all this for so long. She'd bided her time,

sure that Tyler would eventually get tired of spreading rumors and tales about her. Turning the other cheek had only gotten her more and more abuse at his hands. Now his breath was blowing across her face, his hands were much too close to her body, and every cell in her was glaring red and shouting Klaxon-like warnings at her.

Defend yourself, now.

She'd ignored her inner voice for much too long.

"Back away from me," Eliza said, carefully keeping her face turned to the side. She didn't want to smell his breath, didn't want to take the chance that his lips would come any nearer to hers. His body was so close to hers, much too close. "Right now. You're invading my personal space."

"Like you invaded mine when you invited some bitch to fuck you instead? You don't understand just how screwed up you are, do you?"

He was yelling in her ear now. Fear leapt up and clogged her throat, and she wanted to turn and run. She wanted to, but she wouldn't give him the satisfaction.

"Back away now, Tyler. I'm warning you."

"What'll you do, you fucked-up little cunt? You can't lay a finger on me because I'm your boss, and you know it. So what now? Is your guy friend some kind of transgendered freak? Someone who can satisfy your greedy, fucked-up fantasies? I bet he is. Or is it she? Shim? How the fuck should I know?"

It wasn't the hateful words that did it, the terrible things he said. It wasn't even the way he was using his size to intimidate her. She hated that, but she was used to it. No, it was the laugh that caused her to snap. That caustic, evil son of a bitch was laughing at her, mocking the very real pain he himself had caused her. So she stopped being afraid, and she started getting mad.

"Back off, Tyler!" She planted her hands on his chest and shoved backward as hard as she could. Tyler wasn't expecting the attack, so he flailed backward, off balance. Knocking into a table, he grabbed at it for purchase, but his hands slipped. He hit his ass on the floor, hard. He sat there and stared up at her, his mouth hanging open like a fish's.

Eliza's heart was pounding so hard it was difficult to hear anything. Her head throbbed in time with her heartbeat, her breathing ragged like she'd spent the last half hour sprinting. A surge of adrenaline was still coursing through her, and for a moment, she didn't care. She let her feelings out, and unfortunately for Tyler, the perfect target was sitting stunned at her feet.

"I told you to back off, and you didn't. So fuck you, Tyler! Fuck you for making me trust you. Fuck you for taking what I told you in confidence, in the privacy of our relationship, and exaggerating it to everyone you've met since we broke up. Ninety percent of what you've said about me is a lie, and you don't even realize how much you've hurt me. So fuck you. You've got two choices. You can shut up about me and leave me alone, or you can understand when I cut off your balls and mail them to your mother for Christmas. So what's it going to be, dickbag? Your move."

She was standing between his legs, her fisted hands between him and her as she screamed at him. God, it felt good to finally tell him off. Retribution was so sweet. Too bad the feeling didn't last that long.

"Mr. Hagans!" Schweitzer, one of the youngest chemists on staff, was standing in the doorway. He looked petrified. "Do I need to get Security?"

What? No! She wasn't the one. . . . Well, it probably looked that way. She opened her mouth to defend herself, but Tyler spoke before she could.

"Yes. That'd be great. Tell them that Ms. Jackson has been fired, and needs an escort off the premises."

"What?" As quick as it had come, Eliza's adrenaline surge

disappeared. She felt empty, dumbfounded. "You can't do that!"

"I can, and I did." Tyler struggled to his feet as Schweitzer took off down the hall. "Collect your belongings and leave immediately. You're being terminated for physically attacking me."

"But you started it! I warned you, and I—"

"Feel free to take it up with HR, but it won't get you anywhere. They know all about your deviant habits, so who do you think they'll side with?" Tyler shot her a glare, then dusted off his pants and left the room.

Eliza stared after him. Had a bomb just gone off in this room? Had an experiment gone badly and left rubble spread around her? Because that's what she felt like. The only thing she had left, the only thing in the world she'd gotten up for since Tyler had fucked her over was this job. And now, just like that, he'd taken that from her, too?

"It's not fair," she whispered as tears tracked down her cheeks. "It's not fucking fair."

HR would bury the problem in paperwork. If she wanted this termination reversed, and fast, there was only one way. If she didn't hurry she wouldn't make it. Eliza grabbed her purse and ran down the hall in the opposite direction of the Security offices. If she made it up the back stairs to the executive level, they wouldn't be able to intercept her before she talked to the CEO.

There was only a slim chance this would work at all, but she'd never forgive herself if she didn't try. Her silence had gone on long enough. She just hoped Chandler would forgive her for being so late to pick him up.

The thought of Chandler's visit actually brought a small smile to her face as she took the back stairs two at a time. Even when her world was falling apart around her, there was something to smile about. She'd have to thank him for that.

* * *

"Can I get you something else?"

Chandler shook his head at the waitress with a rueful smile. "No, I'm good. Sorry I'm kind of camped out here on you."

She laughed and winked as she took his empty glasses. "It's fine! You'd be surprised how many people end up killing a few hours here waiting for their ride."

"Yeah, I bet." Chandler took a sip of the fresh beer she'd brought him and watched as she walked away. She was pretty cute, actually. She couldn't hold a candle to Eliza, but then again, nobody else really could, either.

He wiped the froth from his upper lip with a sigh. Where was she? She'd promised to pick him up almost two hours ago. He'd sent her a couple of texts, even called her, but the phone had dumped straight to voice mail. The negative side of him wondered if she was ditching him. It wouldn't be the first time something like this had happened, but it was certainly not something he'd expected from her.

No, he was being ridiculous. Eliza wouldn't do anything like that to him. She probably got held up by work, or traffic, or something equally as innocent.

Taking another sip of his beer, he looked around the airport. It was smaller than he'd anticipated, but this little restaurant and bar, placed just beyond the security barriers, made for a decent place to keep an eye out for her. He had a pretty good buzz going. He only hoped it wouldn't take a nosedive when he finally heard from Eliza.

He checked his phone again. No texts. Maybe he should check his e-mail, just to be sure. . . .

As soon as he tapped the app to open it, his screen lit up with an incoming call. Eliza.

He answered it with a quick swipe. "Hey, what's up?"

"Chandler, I'm so sorry. I'm on my way right now. Don't hate me."

"Don't worry about it, I'm fine. Seriously. Are you okay? You sound a little upset."

She sniffled, and the sound was so pitiful it broke his heart. "No, I'm fine. It's no big deal. Just a misunderstanding at work. I'm sure I can clear it up soon. But anyway, enough about that. How was your flight?"

"Uneventful. I was able to get some work done, so that was good."

"Great. Okay, I should be there in about twenty minutes. I'm sorry."

"Stop apologizing. I'm fine. See you in a few."

Chandler killed the call and spun his phone thoughtfully in his hand. It would take some work to draw Eliza out of her shell enough to figure out what was going on. At times like this, his vow to keep from investigating her behind her back was decidedly inconvenient. Oh well. It was for the best.

He drained the rest of his beer, left enough cash to cover his tab and a sizeable tip, and wheeled his suitcase to the exit. There was a row of benches near the doors. He'd hang out there and wait for Eliza, spending the time thinking about ways to distract her from her work problems.

That shouldn't be terribly difficult if she'd missed him as much as he'd missed her.

He sank down onto the bench, watching as a family walked out the glass doors. The chill of the air swirled past, sending a shiver through him. It felt good, though. Cleared his mind a little.

Once he'd gotten down to it back home, he'd realized just how obsessed he'd become over Eliza. His thoughts centered on her, even when they hadn't spoken in a day or two. He kept imagining what it'd be like to bring her back home with him, to show her the places that he loved. To walk along the beach with her, hold hands as they navigated the windswept and rickety old pier. Would she go fishing with him? Lay out on the sand during the warm spring days? He could picture here there so perfectly that it was kind of scary.

He wondered if he was just using Eliza to replace Andrea. After all, he'd thought his ex-wife would do all those things with him, too, hadn't he? Chandler frowned as a cab pulled to a stop at the curb. No, he was wrong. Andrea hadn't ever been interested in his home, or their life together. After her initial bout of sympathy for him, she'd stayed attached to Chandler because he was stable enough to support her so-called art career. She hadn't sold so much as a piece in the three years they'd been married. Money was a problem between them, but he could have dealt with that. What he didn't understand, and what had finally split them up, was his asking for sex what she termed "much too often."

He snorted. Twice a week was too often? And it wasn't like he didn't take no for an answer; he always did. He'd made sure to listen to her, to try to do things to get her in the mood. But rather than deal with his "overactive libido," she'd opted to walk out.

Chandler looked down at the bland, beige industrial flooring beneath his feet. He'd blamed himself for a long time. But eventually he'd come to the conclusion that he and Andrea were just wrong for one another. And if that was the case, then there was a woman out there who'd be much happier to see him.

He looked up, and his face relaxed into a smile almost instantly. Eliza was standing behind the open driver's side door of a green Honda. Her face was lit with that happy, overwhelmed expression that people got when they'd received a pleasant and unexpected surprise.

He grabbed his suitcase and ran out the doors, directly to her. Dropping the handle, he picked her up and held her so tight. She clung to him, her arms wound around his neck, her face buried against his shoulder as sobs shook her. Or was it laughter? He couldn't tell. It didn't matter.

He set her down gently and kissed her as hard and deeply as he'd been longing to for the last few weeks.

A honk from behind them forced him to let her go.

"Hey," he said, holding her hands.

"Hey to you," she said, rubbing at her cheeks. "I'm so sorry I'm late. You ready?"

He nodded and picked up his suitcase. "Let's get out of here."

Stowing his suitcase in the trunk, Chandler tried to calm his insides. It was so good to see her. These last couple of weeks had been unexpectedly difficult. But they'd been good, too. Eliza had actually talked to him. She hadn't revealed her darkest secrets, not even close, but she'd showed him glimpses of her life, her likes and dislikes, the person she really was.

It was so easy to like her, so easy to want to spend more and more time with her. So when he climbed into the passenger seat, he didn't hesitate to reach over and lace his fingers through hers.

"Sorry again," Eliza said as she turned on her signal to merge into traffic. He gave her hand a quick squeeze and released it so she could drive.

"No, totally fine. I had a couple of beers, did some work. It was cool."

"Okay. If you're lying to me, though, just know that I'll make you sleep on the couch."

Chandler snorted. "As if. As soon as you figured out what's in my suitcase you'd graduate me to the bed again."

She shot him an interested look. "Did you bring fun stuff? Like the things you had in Hawaii?"

"I did."

She grinned, but just as quickly her expression faded. "That's great."

Chandler shifted in his seat to get a better look at her face. "Okay, that's enough. What happened at work today?"

"Nothing."

"Liza. You're acting like you lost your job."

She winced visibly, and Chandler instantly felt like shit.

"Oh damn. I'm sorry, I didn't—"

"It's fine. Don't worry about it." Eliza rubbed a tear away from her cheek. "It's something that's been coming for a long time anyway. My boss and I . . . Well, it's not important."

Chandler looked at her for a long moment. It wasn't really his place to interfere, was it? Well, if she was his girlfriend, and he hoped she was, then he had a vested interest in her well-being. Aw, hell. He'd go for it. Worst she could say was no.

"If you've been wrongfully terminated, your boss can get in trouble for that. If you tell me the situation, I can help you try to get your job back."

Her mouth fell open, and she slammed on the brakes.

24

Eliza's heart leapt into her windpipe, her foot pressing hard on the brake pedal. Fortunately, the cat scampered across the road, seemingly unhurt.

"Sorry about that," she said when she could breathe again. "I didn't want to hit that stray kitty."

"It's okay." Chandler's voice was just the tiniest bit strained. "I thought maybe you were mad at me for sticking my nose into your work."

Eliza bit her lip. Selfishly, she'd love to have his feedback on the job situation. But was that really wise? What if he asked her about the rumors Tyler had spread? Chandler had been open to her sexual suggestions so far, but that secret fantasy of hers had already blown up in her face one time. This long-distance relationship was hard enough without adding another layer of worry on top of it, right?

Her grip tightened on the steering wheel. It'd be so wonderful to lay all her troubles out for him, but she wasn't there yet. She'd have to give her own solution time.

"I've taken some steps to try to get things settled out. There's a personal issue with my boss and me. Of course, my boss is the CEO's son, so that complicates things. But you don't want to spend your trip here talking about my problems."

This relationship wouldn't last forever, she was fairly certain of that. If the distance didn't kill it, the fact that she wasn't the person she'd pretended to be definitely would. So she might as well do her best to enjoy what little time she had left with him. Stupid? Maybe. But a few days of happiness would definitely make her feel less lonely in the coming days ahead.

"I know it's not really any of my business, but I'm a good listener if you want to tell me what went on."

Why wouldn't he let it go? Eliza braked slowly at a red light, biting her lip to keep from saying something stupid. Maybe just a change of subject would fix things.

"So, it's getting late, but have you had dinner? You probably ate while you were waiting for me, didn't you? If you didn't, then there's this great little pizza joint not far from my house. We can call something in, maybe go pick it up. . . ."

She trailed off as Chandler's broad hand lay atop her knee and squeezed gently.

"If you're hungry, that's what we'll do. Pizza sounds fine to me."

For some reason, the fact that he didn't press her for more information made her even more emotional. The breath that she drew in next was kind of shaky, and she pursed her lips to blow it out slowly.

Maybe she needed medication. Surely she shouldn't be getting this upset over every little thing.

Well, you did just get fired by your ex-boyfriend, then talk to the big boss about the nasty rumors flying around about you for an hour or so after that. Then someone you care a lot about was nice to you and offered to help. Yep, you're definitely stressed and in need of drugs.

Wait a minute: *care a lot about?* Eliza swallowed hard. It was true. She cared for Chandler more than she had any other guy since, well, ever.

It was a startling realization.

"This is a cute neighborhood," Chandler observed as she turned in at the front of her subdivision. "Have you lived here long?"

"Ever since I got out of college. My job helped me find this place. It's quiet, I like it."

She pulled into her driveway and killed the engine. For a moment they sat there in the silence. Eliza closed her eyes and breathed.

It was nice, him being here beside her. She felt safer somehow. Normally just coming home was stressful. She always imagined that some neighbor or other was staring out their windows at her, making reports to the neighborhood watch about her comings and goings, just in case she ever showed up on a sex offenders list.

"You okay?" Chandler's deep, soft voice came out of nowhere. His hand rested lightly on her thigh, caressing softly.

Chandler. Her blood fired then, the tension she'd felt at work flipping into something else entirely. He was here, in the flesh, and there was nothing between them except the center console of her car and a few pesky clothes.

Easy obstacles to get around, really.

She leaned toward him, and fortunately for her, he met her halfway. Their lips touched and she instantly opened her mouth to him. He delved deep with his tongue, his hand tangling in her hair. Her hand ran down his chest, memorizing the planes of his body. It felt like a year since she'd touched him like this, much too long. With her fingers playing over his flat abdomen, she moaned as he pulled her hair gently.

"We should go in the house," he said softly against her mouth. "Unless you've always wanted to do it in your car?"

Eliza shook her head as reason came crashing into her. No,

she didn't want to climb into the backseat like a naughty teenager. Well, she did, but not here. Not with all the eyes that surrounded her here. She didn't need more rumors spread about her sex life. Better get Chandler inside before someone noticed them steaming up the windows.

"Sorry. I kind of got carried away." She reached for the door handle, but he laid a hand on her thigh before she could leave the car. His gaze was direct, serious.

"Don't ever apologize for kissing me, Liza. Ever."

She looked at him for a moment while her brain whirred. Chandler was definitely unexpected. As soon as she thought she had everything figured out, he'd do or say something that took her aback, but always in the best of ways.

A smile crept across her face and she glanced down at the console between them. "Okay."

They got out of the car then, Eliza opening the trunk so Chandler could remove his suitcase. As they walked across the yard to her front door, Eliza fumbled with her keys.

She'd cleaned up a little, but she probably should have made more of an effort. What would he think when he saw her junky house? She wasn't ready for an episode of *Hoarders,* she did clean regularly, but there was just a lot of, well, stuff lying around.

As the key slid into the lock, a nervous string of words came out unbidden. "Sorry about the mess. I work a lot of overtime, and well, I've been meaning to get a storage unit for some of this stuff. When Mom and Dad sold our old house and moved away, I kind of inherited a lot of the unsold furniture and knickknacks."

The door creaked as she swung it open. She scooted inside, her back to the house as she waited for Chandler to enter. As he did, his head swiveling to take a look around, her embarrassment grew.

Putting a hand on her stomach, she laughed weakly. "Well,

it's rough, but it's home. I'm sorry. I guess it's a lot worse than you expected. I can take you to a hotel, if you'd rather sleep somewh—"

A finger appeared on her lips, silencing her.

Chandler's suitcase fell to the floor, a dull *thump* against the hardwood. His gaze locked with hers as his finger drew downward, pulling her lip slightly. Instinctively she puckered, kissing the tip of his index finger.

"There's nothing for you to apologize for. Your house looks great. There's only one problem."

"What?" Eliza's voice was breathy, Chandler's fingers tracing their way down her throat.

"This isn't the bedroom."

Eliza had appeared ready to jump out of her skin ever since they'd pulled out on the highway. The closer they got to her home, the more Chandler worried. She was almost like a different person from the one he'd met in Hawaii. There had been traces of this frightened creature there, sure, but they'd only been a tiny part of her. Here? They were the majority of Eliza's outward character.

Something was very wrong here for her to feel so threatened. But for now, all he wanted to do was distract her. When Eliza got turned on, her problems melted away. She was honest, and beautiful, and free. He wanted to give that to her almost as much he wanted to sink deep into her.

Almost.

"Bedroom," he repeated, his fingers dancing along her collarbone. A delightful shiver went through her. "Where?"

"This way."

Threading her fingers through his, she led him down a narrow hallway. The door at the end was painted blue. It reminded him of the ocean they'd spent so much time next to in Hawaii. Eliza turned the knob and let him inside.

The bedroom was different than he'd expected. Even though Eliza had told him she wasn't really the kind of woman who dressed up and liked pretty things, somehow he'd been picturing a lacy, white, feminine kind of bedroom.

A queen-sized bed dominated one wall, dark wrought-iron head- and footboards standing out starkly against soft gray walls. The curtains and bedding matched, muted colors swirling together and reminding him of plumes of smoke rising from a campfire. Dark furniture lined the other walls, simple, plain.

All in all it was a pretty plain room, but the more he looked around, the more he realized it suited her perfectly.

"I'm sorry it's not fancier." Eliza tucked a stray hair behind her ear. The simple gesture gave him a better view of her jaw, her long neck, the sweet places he loved to kiss and nibble.

Damn. He was getting hard again.

"It's perfect." He steered her toward the bed. She hesitated a moment before sinking down onto it. "Wait right there. I brought a few surprises with me that should help keep your mind off work and on me."

She arched an eyebrow. "Surprises?"

He grinned but didn't respond. He just left the room and headed back for the suitcase in the hall.

He'd wondered if there would be a problem getting this stuff on the plane. Fortunately, he'd checked this bag. Of course, when he plucked the suitcase from the carousel, it'd had one of those "Screened by TSA" tags on it. At least he hadn't been there for that part.

Now, as he wheeled the suitcase down Eliza's hall, he wondered which toy he should use. The flogger? No, too soon for that. He wanted to get her mind into a more sensual place before they played that way. The image of her bare ass, dappled with sunlight through the trees above, popped into his mind.

She'd begged him. *"God, Chandler, please. Tie me up. Spank me. Fuck me in the ass, in the mouth, however you want to."*

He'd tied her up and spanked her back in Hawaii. Well, it was a fun list. Why should he stop there?

As he entered the bedroom again, Eliza had crawled up toward the headboard and nestled against the fluffy pillows. She looked at him with wide, interested eyes.

"What have you got there?"

"It's my box of tricks. No peeking," he admonished as she leaned over to get a look inside the suitcase's now-open lid. "There are surprises in here for good girls."

That wrenched a laugh from her. "You're not going to find any good girls in this bedroom."

"Fine, then. For girls so bad they're good." He removed the small pink plug from the suitcase, along with a bottle of lube. Kicking the lid closed behind him, he grinned.

"Strip for me, baby, and I'll show you what I've got."

Her tongue darted out to wet her lips. "I've seen what you've got, and I know I want it."

Crossing her arms in front of her, Eliza lifted the hem of her T-shirt straight over her head. Chandler watched hungrily as she unbuttoned her jeans, shimmying them down her thighs. He set the plug on the table behind him and began to take his own clothes off as Eliza's hand reached behind her to unfasten her bra.

"God," he moaned aloud when her breasts came into view. They were more beautiful than he remembered—round, their points a dusky, delicious pink. The tips hardened under his gaze, causing a similar response in his cock.

"Panties, too," he said when she stopped to watch him remove his boxers. His erection sprang free, pointing directly at her. Her lips were glistening from where she'd licked them, and he longed to press his hungry cock past their softness and into the heat of her mouth.

God, he was killing himself. He had to stop, had to slow down his headlong descent into heedless lust.

Her. He had to watch her, help her past that threshold of anxiety into pleasure. She was halfway there already, her eyes dark and her hands wandering the planes of her nudity. Her panties had been tossed aside, a splash of pink against the dark floor.

"Excellent," he growled low, reaching over and picking up the plug. Without showing it to her, he placed it on the bed beside her.

He stretched out beside her, his hardness probing against her thigh, and he kissed her. Slowly at first, tentative, gentle touches. Coaxing her into a higher plane. His tongue licked along her teeth, her tongue, seeking out and finding all those warm places in her mouth that he'd missed so much.

Her arms wound around him, her leg hitching high on his hip. The slick wetness of her pussy came into contact with his thigh, leaving a hot, wet patch there. God, she was so wet and ready for him, and all they'd done was kiss! Eliza was amazing. Simply amazing.

His hands wandered down her body, one hand finding her breast, the other caressing her ass. Her hips lifted against him and she rubbed her clit hard against his thigh. Tweaking her nipple, Chandler deepened their kisses. She met him, stroke for stroke, caress for caress, her fingers wandering over his shoulders, down his chest, between them to grasp the base of his cock. She squeezed lightly, moving her hand up and down in time with the thrusts of her hips.

His balls tightened in warning, and he slid his hips back regretfully. Not yet. Soon enough he'd sink into her welcoming body, but for now he had other plans.

He rose onto his knees and looked down at her, stroking his cock with one hand. She lay splayed open to his gaze, her breasts heaving with her ragged breaths. The glistening pink folds between her legs begged for his touch, his taste, but not yet. Something else first.

"You're beautiful," he said, reaching forward to touch her. She shivered as his fingers drew down between her pussy lips, sliding with her wetness. Pressing inward at her entrance, Chandler smiled at her gasp of pleasure. "But I want to experience more this time."

His finger, coated with her moisture, dragged lower until it was pressed against her puckered hole. Eliza's eyes went wide and she scooted away from his fingers.

"Did I hurt you?" He stopped, not moving his hand away.

"No, I was just surprised." Her words sounded breathy. He liked that.

"You said you wanted this," he reminded her as he pressed against her nether entrance again. She gripped the backs of her knees, squeezing her eyes shut tight as his finger slipped past the barrier. "Do you still?"

"God." The word hissed through gritted teeth. "That feels— Oh my God, Chandler. I can't . . ."

"Relax," he said, stroking his aching cock with his free hand while one finger slid even further inside her. She was so tight, her body quivering with his invasion. Arching her back, she moaned his name, gripping her breasts and squeezing.

He'd never seen anything sexier in his life.

25

Eliza gritted her teeth to keep from yelling aloud. She'd never imagined it could feel like this. She hadn't ever had a partner willing to do all the things she'd dreamed of. She'd tried on her own, but it just wasn't the same. Her experiments hadn't adequately prepared her for Chandler putting his fingers there.

It stretched with a decadent kind of burn, one that twisted her insides and made her long for more.

Her hand wandered down her body and began a slow, easy motion between her legs. Her clit was begging for more as Chandler began to move his finger slowly, carefully, in and out.

"You like that, don't you."

It wasn't exactly a question, but she answered him anyway. "God, yes. More."

The sound of a plastic lid popping open broke the quiet of the room, and Eliza opened her eyes when Chandler's finger left her. It came back a moment later, its entrance aided by the slick feeling of lubricant.

"Oooh," she moaned, penetrating her pussy with two fingers. The pressure of Chandler's fingers and her own inside her made her blood fire. An orgasm was mounting deep in her body, and she wanted it so, so bad.

"Slow down, baby," Chandler said, easing his fingers out of her. "The main event is coming. Don't leave me behind."

She smiled at his unintentional pun. He reached down beside her and picked up an object that she really hadn't noticed him putting there. He held it up for her examination.

"Have you ever used one of these?"

It had a small, flat base. Shaped like a small, slender Lava Lamp or rocket ship, with a narrow base flaring out slightly, then tapering to the end. She knew what it was. She'd tried to convince herself to buy one and beg Tyler to use it with her, but things had ended before she could get up the courage. Chandler didn't need to know any of that, though.

"No, but I know what it is." Her breath came quicker as he lubricated the pink toy. Biting her lip, she watched as he brought it down to her ass.

"This is a little bigger than my fingers. If it hurts, tell me, and I'll stop."

"I will." She wouldn't. She wanted it, that little flare of discomfort that fanned the flames of her lust. That brief flash of pain that reminded her she was alive, and so was he, and together they could make a little island of heaven on earth.

It started as a pressure, slipping past her resisting muscles. Gripping the covers on either side of her, she waited, counting her breaths. It filled her so deeply, so much she thought she'd break. The pain built, almost breaking her from the passionate spell Chandler had woven over her, but then he reached his free hand between her legs and gave her clit some light, delicate strokes.

"Easy, Liza. Relax. Breathe. Let me go slow."

The pain faded then, and pleasure grew in its place. Then the plug slid fully inside her, and Chandler stopped his delicate torture. Kneeling between her legs, he smiled down at her.

"How does it feel now?"

"Weird. Really good, but kind of odd at the same time."

"Just wait, baby. It'll get better." He stretched out on top of her, keeping his weight on his forearms. She kissed him, her tongue playing with his, her hardened nipples brushing against the hairs on his chest. Her insides wept for him, her pussy throbbing with the want. Somehow it felt tighter, more aching than usual. The butt plug? It had to be. It was driving her crazy, his body trapping hers against the softness of her bed, his hard, hot cock rubbing against her inner thigh. She wanted it.

"Please." She tore her mouth away, but Chandler didn't relent in his ardent assault. His mouth devoured her neck, nibbling the tendons along the side, nipping across her collarbone and kissing her shoulder.

"Not yet." His voice was almost a growl as his kisses moved downward. First one nipple, then the other, each of them getting the same kisses, nips, and nibbles before Chandler's mouth moved farther downward. Eliza's fingers tangled in his hair as his tongue dipped into her navel. She couldn't stop her hips from lifting higher, her pussy from echoing her heartbeat. She pulled his hair gently, begging for more.

She wanted his kiss.

He moved lower, his soft lips brushing against her freshly waxed pubis. Thank God she'd taken a trip to the next town over for a Brazilian last weekend. It was definitely paying off now.

His hands parted her and his breath blew across her trembling flesh.

"You're so beautiful."

She didn't have time to respond before his mouth sealed over her pussy. Her gasp was loud, her moan afterward even more so. His tongue dragged down from her clit to her entrance and up again. Playing at her opening, then suckling her clit, he moved back and forth until she thought she would die.

But then, with one hand, he started a gentle, slow rotation of the plug in her ass.

Her lower belly tightened and her clit throbbed hard. She was coming, she was so close, she was almost there. . . .

"Chandler!" Her hips lifted, begging for more, begging for his penetration.

He didn't wait. His mouth was at her weeping pussy one minute, then sealed over her own the next. The taste of her own moisture was so erotic. She suckled his tongue like he'd suckled her clit, laving and licking at his mouth. Then the hot, slick head of him prodded at her entrance.

"Please, now, fuck me!"

"I don't—Condom—" His groan nearly made her lose her mind. No. No fucking way she was going to let him make her wait any longer.

"Fuck me now, Chandler!"

His groan of surrender turned into a growl of pleasure as he penetrated her so deep. God, the fullness. She was stretched so much. The pressure wound around her mind and dragged her deep into a red mist of passion. Her body wasn't hers anymore; it was possessed by a demon. A clawing, fucking, screaming demon. His cock was so hot, and then he moved it. In and out, over and over, a sheen of sweat covering them both. He came to his knees and lifted her hips to his pelvis, fucking and fucking, deeper and harder, her wetness covering them both.

Eliza gripped her breasts, teasing her nipples, both for the feeling and for the sight of Chandler's face. His eyes were dark, his tongue darting out to wet his lips as he fucked her. Deeper and harder, the pressure from the plug and the size of his cock filling her so much. Pinching her nipples hard, just for a tiny spark of pain to heighten the sensation, Eliza cried out.

"Are you going to come for me?" Chandler kept one hand on her hip, but the other splayed over her lower belly. Drawing his index finger down from her belly button to her clit, he said it again. "Liza, come for me."

One stroke on her clit. Two. Three. He was timing his deep, quick thrusts with light circles on her clit. Over and over, the rhythm was in her blood, in her brain, driving her mad.

She couldn't wait any longer.

The orgasm washed her under like an ocean wave. For long moments, her body shuddered and shook, her insides fluttering with pleasure. Her gasps were ragged, loud, rough against Chandler's low moan.

In the next second, Chandler pulled out and shot hot jets of cum over her belly. His hands rested atop her knees, and they stared at one another for a long minute.

Slowly Eliza's brain came back online. The pink plug was still in her ass. There was jizz dribbling over one hip. She was sweaty, both from her own body and Chandler's. Her legs felt like they were made of meringue, and she seriously doubted if she was going to be able to stand anytime soon.

That. Was. Incredible.

"I'm sorry." Chandler hung his head. He was still breathing hard, like a racehorse who'd just crossed the finish line.

"What?"

"I'm sorry about that. I shouldn't have . . . Damn." Without saying anything else, he moved off the bed and left the room. The bathroom door clicked shut, and Eliza shivered, wrapping her arms around herself.

What had just gone wrong?

The faucet squeaked as Chandler killed the water's flow. Drying his hands on a worn teal towel hanging by the sink, he carefully avoided looking in the mirror.

Damn. That was beyond stupid. Even though he'd avoided orgasm while inside her, bareback sex wasn't something he'd anticipated on this trip. Why hadn't he insisted on waiting the brief second it would have taken to put on the condom?

But I have to admit, it felt fucking amazing.

That didn't matter. It was irresponsible, and Eliza deserved better than that from him. A sigh escaped him as he grabbed a washcloth from the rack above the commode and began to soap it up.

A timid knock on the door interrupted him.

"Yeah?"

"Can I come in?" Eliza's voice was small and thin through the bathroom door.

"Sure." Chandler lifted the soapy cloth from the sink as the door squeaked open.

She stood there in the doorway, a light yellow robe hanging from her shoulders. It didn't quite meet in the front, and she was still naked beneath it. Her hair was wild, her lips were swollen, but her mouth was drawn down at the corners and her eyes looked suspiciously moist.

"I was coming to wash you off," Chandler said, lifting the cloth. "I didn't mean to leave you like that. Here." He moved her robe to the side and began to clean the evidence of his orgasm away from her skin.

Eliza's hair fell forward as she looked down at his hands. "I thought you might be mad at me."

"What? Why would you think that?" He wasn't stupid. He knew she'd misinterpreted his quick departure from her bed. Kind of a dick move, but he wasn't exactly thinking clearly again.

"I don't know, maybe it was bad?"

He rinsed the cloth out and wiped the suds away from the skin of her stomach and hip. "I think you know better than that."

She looked at his face then, and his mouth suddenly went dry. Damn it, he was fucking this up.

"I was mad at myself, not you. I lost my head there and should have grabbed a condom. Too little, too late, I know, but I don't have any STDs. And if you were to get pregnant—"

"Whoa, whoa, whoa, slow down there." Eliza took a step back, but her heel caught the hem of her robe and she stumbled. Chandler caught her arm and steadied her.

"I just wanted to say I'd take care of you, no matter what. I take responsibility for my actions. And I'm really sorry that I didn't this time."

"Before I almost fell on my ass, I was about to say you don't need to worry about that. I'm on the Pill, and I've been tested, too. All clear."

A sigh of relief escaped Chandler, and he laid the rinsed-out cloth on the edge of the sink. "Good. It doesn't excuse what I did, but I'm glad to know that it should be okay."

A smaller hand crept into his, feminine fingers curling between his own digits. Eliza's head leaned against his shoulder, and his arm lay between her breasts as she hugged it.

"It's okay anyway. I know we haven't really talked about what to call this, I mean, you and me, but I want you to know that for me, there's really only you. So we don't have to use anything if you don't want to."

He stared straight ahead into the bathroom mirror, trying to get a look into her eyes, but her face was hidden in his bicep and her hair covered her cheek. She squeezed his hand and took a deep breath as his heart began to pound.

"I don't know why you're interested in me, but I'm glad you are. And I'm extra glad to have you here with me."

"I'm glad, too," Chandler said, then pressed a kiss atop her head. For a moment they stood there, not saying a word, Eliza hugging his arm and Chandler breathing in the scent of her shampoo. His heart felt lighter, his body felt stronger; in fact, everything was better with Eliza close to him.

After a long, tender moment, just when Chandler was starting to really believe that this was the closest he'd felt to any other human being, Eliza sighed and let go of his hand.

"I hate to bring this up," she said, her cheeks turning a bright shade of pink. She turned and lifted the back of her robe. "But what's the best way to remove this thing?"

A snort of mirth escaped Chandler as Eliza bent over and waggled her ass at him. The pink plug was still there between her cheeks.

The bathroom echoed with their combined laughter for a long moment. Chandler gripped the edge of the counter in a vain attempt to catch his breath. His chest felt full, light, and the source of that feeling was standing beside him and wiping tears of laughter from her still-pink cheeks.

He was really afraid that he might be totally in love with this woman.

"I was kidding. I can take it out myself. But somehow I think the removal might be a little less sexy than the insertion, so maybe you could give me a minute?"

He nodded in response to her plea. "Of course. I'll grab something to drink."

"Okay. Make yourself at home." Eliza raised up on her tiptoes and pressed a kiss to his lips. For a second he let himself close his eyes and revel in the simple, sweet touch. But then he backed off, smiled, and shut the bathroom door behind him.

Before wandering through the house, he pulled on his boxers. No need to shock the neighbors if he didn't have to, right?

As he made his way to the kitchen, he took in the atmosphere of the rooms. The scent of the place was like hers, only more prominent somehow. Sweet and homey. There were books everywhere, CDs and picture frames stacked haphazardly on bookshelves and decorative tables. The kitchen was made up of dark-paneled walls with checkered light green curtains. The cabinets were painted white, and the appliances were older, but clean. As Chandler pulled open the refrigerator door, a small picture stuck on the freezer with a rainbow magnet caught his eye.

Eliza, her hair shorter than it was now, with her arms around a younger-looking Sabrina. The two were laughing at something, and the smile on Eliza's face was so bright that it almost hurt to look at her.

Chandler frowned and shook his head as he ducked to look into the refrigerator. Seeing Sabrina reminded him of Gregory, and his stringent objections to Chandler's relationship with Eliza. He hadn't uncovered everything about her, but he was fairly certain he knew his own mind. Eliza was a wonderful person, and she was nothing like Andrea. They'd be fine.

He splashed some cranberry juice in a small glass he found in the drain board by the sink. The cool, tangy juice revived him a little. That sexy session with her had definitely wrung him dry.

But now he was here, and Eliza was happy. Except for the problem with her job. That was a sticky situation, and he wondered if he'd be able to help her with it. But where was his limit? She was right, they hadn't labeled this as such, but he thought of her as his girlfriend. What could he do, other than be a comforting shoulder for her to cry on, a sounding board, a giver of advice? He wished he knew.

"Hey, are you hungry?" Eliza padded into the kitchen, belting her silky yellow robe as she did. Damn it, he'd really enjoyed the view before.

"I wouldn't mind a late-night snack," Chandler said, glancing at the clock. It was nearly eleven.

"Oh my gosh, it is late. I'm so sorry. I lost track of time, and—"

He laughed and tucked her hair behind her ear. "Don't worry about it. I was the one distracting you, after all. And I did have something at the bar while I was waiting for you. But you must be starved."

She opened a cupboard without looking his way. "I am a little hungry after all that exercise."

An evil grin spread across his face as he wrapped his arms around her from behind. "I intend to make you hungry a lot more while I'm here." He growled as he pretended to gnaw on her neck like a savage zombie. Shrieking with laughter, she batted at him with a hand.

"Ease up there, cannibal. I've got popcorn, no need to eat me."

"I thought you liked how I ate you," he said, turning his play-bites into kisses. With a sigh, Eliza melted against him.

"You're going to kill me."

"Only in the best possible way."

26

The wind was bitter cold, and it stung Eliza's cheeks as she ran from the warmth of the house to the car. Her fingers fumbled on the keys and Chandler shivered beside her.

"Come on, hurry up, I'm freezing my balls off out here."

Eliza shot him a look. "Not likely, southern boy. It's only thirty-three degrees out."

"But the wind chill is like six below. So come on, gimme the keys."

When the doors were unlocked, Eliza passed the keys over to Chandler and climbed into the passenger side. A quick glance in the backseat proved that Chandler had grabbed all the bungees and rope they'd need.

The car rumbled to life and Eliza held her hands in front of the vents to warm them. Ugh, too soon. Air was still blowing cold.

"So," Chandler said as he pulled off a glove to type on his smartphone's screen, "the name of the place we're headed is . . ."

"Rockton," Eliza said, bouncing her knees to warm up her legs. "It's called Tannenbaum Trees."

He plugged in the search, and then arched a brow at her. "You know that's two hours away, right?"

Eliza nodded. "Yup."

"You know there are, like, three lots in town, right? We passed them on the way from the airport, and then yesterday on the way home from Lincolnville, and then the day before on the way back from Spring Hope . . ."

Eliza rubbed her nose. The tip was so cold, it hurt her hand. "I know. But the lot in Rockton is really nice."

Chandler didn't question her further; he just put the car in Reverse and it rolled down the driveway. Eliza started humming a Christmas tune under her breath. She was really excited about this outing, but Chandler was getting more and more suspicious with the way she was avoiding taking him anywhere inside her town. But damn it, how else could she keep those ugly rumors away from him?

As he turned out of her neighborhood, she shot him a quick glance. He was bundled up like that kid from the leg lamp movie, with coat, toboggan, and hat pulled all the way down over his forehead. She'd laughed at his intolerance for the cold, but he'd countered with the argument that it only got that cold back home in February. She'd had a lot of fun warming him up over the last few days.

The houses thinned out and gave way to trees on either side of the divided highway, and Eliza watched them roll by. She'd been so happy with Chandler, every moment they spent together in the house. And even in the car, where they were still alone. But even with the precautions she'd taken, making sure to only go to restaurants and stores away from home, there was still the chance she'd run into someone she knew, who knew about the ugly rumors.

She stopped humming as her stomach acid bubbled inside her. Maybe she should tell Chandler what had happened. He liked the kinkier things; he'd proven that. But she'd learned her lesson. There was a limit to what most people could accept, and she didn't want to push her luck with Chandler. He was one in a million, and she wanted to keep him around as long as possible. Her breath fogged up a spot on the glass, and she wiped it away with the wool of her coat sleeve.

No, it was better to leave things alone. Her weird fantasy would stay as it was, an embarrassing memory. And it wasn't like she needed it to be happy. Chandler was enough to make her happy. In fact, she loved him.

Her mouth parted as she blinked, hard. Wow. It had come on so gradually that she hadn't even really felt it coming. She loved the guy sitting next to her. He was wonderful, handsome, strong, kind, the best guy she'd ever met. And she was in love with him.

"Are you okay? You're really quiet."

"Urg," Eliza said, slamming her eyes shut when she realized she'd sounded like a septuagenarian frog right then. "Sorry. Yeah, I'm fine. Just thinking about Christmas presents."

A gloved hand appeared on her knee and Eliza smiled as Chandler squeezed slightly.

"Don't worry. You won't be disappointed with what's under the tree." He winked at her before putting his hand back on the steering wheel.

"I'm not," Eliza said and then fell silent, just looking at him. Maybe she should tell him that she loved him. Yeah. That might be a really good idea. But what if he didn't feel the same way? Her heartbeat quickened and it was a little hard to breathe. Tugging at the collar of her jacket to give her throat more room, Eliza licked her lips. Maybe she should. This was romantic, after all. A little road trip to pick out a Christmas tree together? They'd lain in front of her fireplace last night and made love on the hearth. She should tell him.

Her mind made up, she smiled, and spoke.

"Chandler, I want to tell you something."

"Okay. Shoot."

Deep, steadying breath. This is the right decision. Everything will be fine.

"I lo—"

Her cell phone's shrill ring startled the crap out of her. Hand shaking, she reached into her pocket while apologizing. "I'm sorry. I need to grab this."

"Go ahead."

Her finger slipped on the Answer button, and she had to hit it three times to connect the call. "Hello?"

"Eliza, it's me, Harold Hagans."

"Oh, hello, sir." She hadn't talked to him in days. Why now? She'd managed to shove the ugly business of her employment to the back burner and just enjoy Chandler's visit. But if the CEO was calling her on her vacation, then something was up. "What can I do for you?"

"I've been thinking about what you said on Tuesday, and I'd like to get some more information from you. I'd been waiting to hear from the head of HR, who was out at a conference until today. But now that she's back, I'd like for the three of us to sit down together and discuss this."

"Okay," Eliza said, the acid that had calmed in her stomach now roiling full-force. "When did you have in mind?"

"We can meet with you at eleven this morning. I don't want to delay this any further."

The green numbers on the dashboard clock told her it was nearly ten. "Does it have to be this morning? I had some plans, you see, and—"

"Eliza, I appreciate your honesty in telling me everything that went on with you and Tyler. I know it wasn't easy, since we are related, and I respect that. This needs to be handled immediately. If word of this got out, it could make things difficult for Quality. I'd like to move on this ASAP. I'm sorry about the late notice, but in order to mitigate the damage, I'll need to get the ball rolling as soon as possible." His voice was friendly, but very firm. Eliza tensed her shoulders and nodded.

"Okay, sir. I'm sorry. I'll be there by eleven. Thank you."

She killed the call and stared down at her lap. *Breathe, just for a minute. Get yourself back together.*

"Is everything okay?" Chandler's voice held concern. Damn it, why today of all days?

Eliza swallowed her disappointment and looked over at Chandler. His nose was wrinkled in concern.

"Yeah, but we're going to have to postpone our tree mission. I have to go to meet with the CEO at Quality. He wants to talk to me about Ty—I mean, my ex-boss." She didn't want to say his name. She'd done it once before accidentally, a long time ago on a wilderness trail in Hawaii. The less said about him, the better.

"Okay. Here." He passed her his phone. "Pop the address in there and I'll drive you."

"No," Eliza said, taking the phone from him and plopping it right back into the cup holder it had been riding in. "Let's go back to the house. There's no need for you to sit around there. I'll be fine."

"I know that, but if I'm with you, then we can go on our mission after your meeting. You were looking forward to it, so I want to make sure we get your perfect tree."

Her eyes were stinging, and she fought the urge to sniff. He'd been teasing her for the last two days about how excited she was about tree shopping. She hadn't had a real Christmas tree, well, ever. Her parents always traveled over the holidays, and the most they'd ever done was a three-foot plastic tree that the needles fell off of regularly. And the thought of her first real tree, and her first real Christmas in fact, being with the man she loved? It was like a dream come true.

Now it was hard to feel like real life hadn't just come crashing down through her delicate, blown-glass dream.

"I'll be fine. You don't have to protect me. I'm a big girl, and I can fight my own battles. Besides, it's not likely that Tyler will get in my face and scream at me again in front of his dad."

As soon as the words left her mouth, she knew she'd screwed up big-time.

Chandler drew a deep breath through his nose, holding it there for a moment before replying. His first instinct was to grill her for details, but he had to remain calm.

Flipping the turn signal, he guided the car into a gas station's lot. The car's brakes squeaked slightly as he stopped the vehicle. He didn't cut the engine, though—they'd freeze.

"What do you mean, he got in your face and screamed at you?" Chandler turned in his seat, pegging her with his gaze. He wasn't going to let her lie to him, and she wasn't going to get out of explaining this one.

Fidgeting with the hem of her coat, she didn't meet his eyes. "That sounded worse than it was. He wanted me to stay late for a project that's not in my department, and when I said I had other plans, he got mad. And I overreacted when he started yelling in my face. Honestly, I doubt he'd have hit me or anything, I shouldn't have pushed him, I just got scared."

Chandler's anger was swelling into his throat, and for a minute he couldn't say anything. Eliza must have misinterpreted his silence, because she started talking faster.

"It wasn't a big deal, honest. He probably wouldn't have fired me for it if someone hadn't seen it happen. It was just he was saying these awful things and his breath was blowing over my face and it reminded me of, well, that doesn't matter."

"Eliza," Chandler said, reaching for her hand. Damn, he wished he'd taken off the gloves. He wanted her to feel his skin, to know he was there and that he wouldn't leave her. "This is serious. I know you don't want me to worry, but I do. You were justified in defending yourself, but that might not stop that jackass from retaliating. So let me go with you. I won't go into your meeting, just let me escort you into the building."

Her head shake was vehement. "No, you can't. I don't want anyone to see me with you."

The blood in his veins that had just started to thaw thanks to the car heater began to freeze again. "You don't want to be seen with me?"

"No, that's not it at all! God, I'm sorry. I'm fucking everything up again." Her words were thin and high, and she rubbed at her cheeks. The sight of her eyes, bloodshot and teary, socked him in the guts. "I just don't want anyone to think badly of you because you're with me."

"That's crazy," Chandler scoffed. Instantly he regretted it when Eliza sniffled and rubbed away more tears.

It wasn't very easy to hold her with the center console between them, but he thought he did an okay job of wrapping his arms around her and letting her bury her face in his shoulder.

"Listen." He rubbed her back. "I know it sucks to lose your job, and I know that this meeting is probably really awkward for you. I just want to help ease your burden. And that's the truth."

He wanted to say more, but what else was there? Nothing that he knew of, anyway. So for a while he just sat there, engine idling beneath them, his arms wrapped around her, the damp patch on his jacket shoulder growing as she cried.

"Sorry," she sniffed, pulling back and wiping at her nose. "I'm just an idiot."

"No, you're not. Now, come on. If you need to be there by eleven, we should probably start heading that way."

A strand of hair was stuck to her cheek and he moved it away tenderly. God, why did her eyes look so frightened, so wary?

"You can drive me if you want to. But don't come in, okay? Just stay in the car, and I'll call you if anything happens."

That sucked, but what else could he do? It was her job, her problem, and as much as he wanted to march in there and hand her ex-boss his own ass, it wasn't something he could do. He was just the boyfriend. If that.

"Fine. But you've got to keep me updated. If it goes too long and I haven't heard back from you, I'm going in there to find you."

"Okay, but everything will be fine. Harold's a good guy, generally." Eliza picked up his cell phone. As her long fingers typed in her office address, he turned the problem over in his mind.

Her ex-boyfriend, ex-boss, had taken away a lot from her. A lot more than just her job, it seemed. What would it take to get her to open up to him about what had gone wrong? He wanted nothing more than to help her be happy, but it would take more trust than she currently had in him.

He had another week or so here to make that happen. Hey, anything was possible, right?

"Here." Eliza put the phone back into the cup holder, and the cheerful female voice announced that it was starting navigation. Chandler put the car in Reverse and soon they were back on the highway, going back the way they'd come.

"I know it's probably hard for you to talk about, but what did your boss say?"

Her sigh was loud in the car. "It's nothing, really."

The look he shot her plainly stated *bullshit*. "You wouldn't have pushed him away from you if it had been nothing. I know you, Liza. You're not the kind of person to pick a fight where one isn't necessary. Of course, if you want, I can call Stacey up. She's good at defending you from asshats."

Eliza cracked a small smile at that, and Chandler's shoulders lost a bit of the tension they'd been carrying. At least he could do that much for her. Maybe he shouldn't pry right now. The CEO was sure to do a good amount of grilling when she got up to his office, so for now, he'd talk about more pleasant things.

"Greg told me that Stacey was doing well."

"Oh yeah?" Eliza turned to him.

"Yup. She and Sabrina have been talking on the phone a lot lately. Seems like she's healed up well from her ordeal. She's always been a workaholic, but now she's actually making use of her free time."

"That's good." Eliza glanced out the window, frowning at the "Welcome to Appledale" sign on their right. "She was really nice. I wish I'd gotten her e-mail address before she left."

Chandler shrugged. "She scooted out so quickly that nobody really got the chance to say good-bye."

"Yeah." There was a furrowed spot between Eliza's brows now, and Chandler's thumb itched to smooth it out. Damn it, he couldn't fix everything.

The electronic female voice announced that his destination was on the left in one mile. He let his foot off the gas slightly, because the closer they got, the paler Eliza became. When he turned in to the lot beside the Quality Testing sign, she looked almost ready to pass out.

"You don't have to do this," Chandler said as he picked a parking spot marked Visitor close to the door. "You aren't employed there anymore, so if you don't want to, we can leave right now."

"It's not that. It's just . . ." She turned to him, and her eyes were so wide, so frightened. He wanted to drag her into his arms and protect her from whatever it was that made her so scared. "Just promise me you won't talk to anyone. Stay in the car, okay?"

It was hard not to feel like she was ashamed of him, but he shoved that notion to the back of his mind. "I won't go anywhere unless you need me. Got your phone?"

She patted her pocket. "Right here."

Reaching for the door handle, she swallowed audibly. Her

body was so tense it was almost vibrating. He couldn't let her walk off like this.

"Liza." He reached for her, turning her face to him. His soft kiss brushed her lips. Not passionate, not this time. Caring. Loving. He poured everything he wanted to do for her into that kiss, hoping that the brief touch would be enough to remind her that she was strong enough to handle whatever the meeting would throw at her.

Too soon, he pulled away. He couldn't make her late.

"Thank you," she whispered, then she opened the door. A cool gust of wind blasted into the car, and then she was walking quickly up the sidewalk and through the double glass doors of Quality Testing.

Chandler folded his arms across his chest, his frown tight. He hoped she'd be okay. If not, someone would answer to him.

27

It was weird walking back in her building like nothing had ever happened. The cheesy pictures from the employee picnic were still posted on the bulletin board. She'd wondered how quick they'd erase all evidence of her employment, but there she was, holding a marshmallow on the end of a long skewer. Eliza quickened her step. She needed to get in and get out, fast.

At the end of the entryway, she hesitated. She always used the stairs at work, mostly because her department was only on the second floor and using the elevator for such a short distance seemed lazy. And even when she had to go the fourth, and top, floor of their building, she'd always used the stairs out of habit.

But to get to the stairwell, she'd have to pass Tyler's office. No way. The last thing she wanted was to give him more ammunition. So instead of her usual right, she hung a left and punched the Up button beside the elevator door.

She gave a wave and a tight smile to a couple of people from Cosmetics Testing. The guy called a friendly hello, but his female companion shot her a look and hustled away. The same old story. Eliza smothered her shame and anger as the elevator beeped its arrival. This wasn't her fault. None of it was her fault. Chandler was right. She had to stick up for herself.

The resolution lasted her approximately half a second after the elevator doors opened. All the blood drained from her head and she swayed for a moment.

"Well, this is a surprise." Tyler stepped out of the elevator, buttoning his suit jacket. The familiar sneer was on his face, draining every bit of attractiveness from his features. "I thought you'd already cleaned out your office."

Don't say a word. He just wants to bait you. Get in the elevator and punch the Door Close button. She didn't even turn his way, just stepped into the empty elevator. Punching the button for her floor, she then hit the Close button and prayed.

Of course, Tyler wasn't letting his favorite punching bag go that easy. He splayed his palm over the left side of the door, and the machine gave a defeated alarm.

"Why are you here?"

Keeping her gaze trained on the number pad, Eliza said only what was strictly necessary. "I was asked to come in. Now, please let me go."

"I thought you were off somewhere with your 'friend'." He made an air quote with his one free hand. "Did you run her off already?"

"That's none of your business."

The anger, the disgust, the guilt she felt at ever allowing herself to be used by this guy swirled over her. She closed her eyes, wishing he'd just leave her alone already.

"Hey, Eliza, come on, I just asked a question."

Her eyes flew open in alarm. Tyler leaned his head against the palm still holding the door open. His mouth curled up in the half smile he used to give her, the one that made her chest feel all warm and bubbly. His eyes had softened, no longer the eyes of a predator, now more the eyes of a lover. "There's no need to be upset. You're going up to see Dad, aren't you? I was just up there, and he made me leave. If he's doing the exit interview, just remember something for me."

Tyler leaned close, and Eliza fought the urge to scramble back against the wall. He made a motion to touch her cheek, and she flinched away. With a disappointed *click* of his tongue, Tyler dropped his hand.

"Just remember that you were the one who touched me. And there was a witness."

And just like that, the soft eyes and half smile were gone, and the bitter mask was back. Tyler stopped blocking the elevator door and put both of his hands in his pockets, keeping her pinned with his gaze like a butterfly to a science project case.

When she finally began to ascend, alone in the elevator, Eliza's knees gave out. She collapsed against the wall behind her, sliding down until she crouched in the corner. Covering her face in her hands, she shook.

It was too much. She couldn't face the CEO right now. Not after that.

When the elevator beeped and the doors whooshed open on the fourth floor, Eliza bolted to the nearest bathroom. Locking the door behind her, she leaned against it.

Her breath was loud in the small room, the only other noise the quiet, occasional drip of the faucet.

Breathe. Come on. You're fine.

But her chest was tight. Her ribs felt bruised from the heavy beat of her heart against them. Her legs were shaking.

Come on. Pull it together.

Several minutes later, after splashing four handfuls of cold water over her face, and drying it as best she could with the wrinkled brown paper towels, she stared into the mirror.

Her cheeks were angry red. Her hat was still perched atop her hair, the fluffy red ball of her toboggan at a jaunty angle still. She pulled it off and smoothed her hair. Well, she wouldn't win any awards, but at least she looked less like a vagrant now.

One hand on the doorknob, she started to turn it. Then stopped.

What if Tyler came upstairs again? What if she ran into him?

Her hand fell into her pocket, the corner of her cell phone jutting into her palm.

Chandler. She could call him, and he'd come inside and walk with her into the CEO's office. He wouldn't let her be afraid. She loved him, and she trusted him. He'd protect her.

Her toes curled in her boots. Self-disgust swam up her spine, and she shivered. This had nothing to do with Chandler. As much as she loved him, this was a battle she had to fight on her own. There was nothing he could do for her that she couldn't do for herself.

With a decisive nod, Eliza gripped the handle and spoke aloud. "I can do this, Chandler. See you in a few minutes."

Her footsteps echoed in the hallway as she walked to the CEO's office. The fourth floor was much emptier than normal—most of the top-level employees took off the last half of December. So there wouldn't be any more awkward greetings to contend with before she made her way to the CEO's administrative assistant.

"Hi, Whitney," Eliza said, tucking her hair behind her ear. "I've got an eleven o'clock meeting with Mr. Hagans?"

Whitney smiled. She'd always been really nice to Eliza. "Sure. It's good to see you. Come on, I'll show you in."

Eliza watched the floor as Whitney walked toward the large oak door with the brass nameplate on it. Her knee-high boots had four-inch heels on them. Even at her most daring bombshell mode, Eliza hadn't worn anything that tall. A wry smile twisted her lips as she remembered. Shopping for all those fancy clothes, putting on makeup every day, flirting with perfect strangers—Hawaii had changed her. And as she remembered the guy waiting in the car for her, her smile turned into a full-on grin.

It had changed her for the better. So no matter what happened in this meeting, she'd be fine.

"Go on ahead," Whitney said, holding the door open for Eliza. She gave a wink as Eliza passed by and whispered, "Good luck!"

"Thanks," Eliza whispered back, giving Whitney a genuine smile. "I'm going to need it."

As the door shut behind her, the *click* was as soft as a prayer. She'd need those, too.

Chandler checked the time again. Seven minutes. It had only been seven minutes since she went inside, and he was already wondering if it was too soon to storm the castle.

He looked out the driver's side window at the building beside him. The exterior was a grim gray, making it look like a correctional facility, despite the large number of windows and tasteful landscaping. The cars in the lot behind him were modest, for the most part, SUVs and sedans in white, silver, and black. Other than a couple of high-end sports cars parked close to the entrance, it looked like the parking lot of an elementary school.

Chandler took a deep breath and checked the time again. Eight minutes. Damn, he thought he'd killed more time than that.

Punching the radio's Power button, he thumped his skull back against the headrest. Christmas music poured from the speakers, much too loud and much too cheerful. Nope, reminding him of the day they were supposed to be having right now wasn't helping at all. A quick scan through the channels revealed tons of commercials, the latest and greatest overplayed shit, and a whole bunch of blah. He killed the power. Better to sit and stew in silence than to break Eliza's radio in frustration.

One more time check. Ten minutes. He looked at the building again, wondering if any of the windows facing the lot were to the room she was in. He hoped so, just for the simple fact that maybe she could look out and see her car, and remember that she wasn't in this alone.

God, he was a sappy ass.

He plucked his phone from the cup holder and swiped to unlock the screen. There were plenty of ways to kill time on a smartphone, right?

Of course, as soon as he opened the web browser, the sight of the gift he'd purchased for Eliza's Christmas present slammed into him like a two-by-four. The beautiful designer purse that Sabrina had so graciously helped him to pick out wouldn't be empty. No, the half-carat diamond earrings would be tucked safely inside for her to find.

As he scrolled down the page, his previously viewed items were listed like a police lineup. Diamond solitaires weren't something you could give a girl you'd only known for a couple of months, despite how strongly you felt about her. At least, that's what his friends had said when he'd mentioned the idea over a couple of beers. And as much as Chandler hated to admit it, they were right. He loved Eliza, but she was gun-shy, and so was he. And with good reason, too.

Thirteen minutes. He wasn't really superstitious, but the number felt ominous, for some weird reason.

Movement at the building caught Chandler's eye. Three men were exiting, two of them zipping their jackets and talking animatedly. The third was wearing a suit and an ugly frown, heading straight down the walk toward the car while the other two hung a right and climbed into a beige SUV.

Chandler returned his attention to the third man. Only two parking spots over, he was fumbling with the keys to a flashy Jag. But he kept looking at something in Chandler's direction, his brow wrinkling further and his eyes narrowing.

Chandler's pulse increased and his muscles tensed. What a weird vibe from this guy. If he'd been on a job, he'd have snapped several pictures of the man. His demeanor and actions were incriminating as fuck.

Then Suit Guy moved away from the Jag and stepped into the walk again. He walked closer to Eliza's car, Chandler still sitting calmly inside. It was easy to spot the very second he noticed Chandler. His jaw dropped, mouth and eyes wide like a fish on a line.

Chandler would have to take Eliza fishing someday. She'd probably really enjoy it.

The mental side trip didn't take nearly long enough or ease his worries at all. Suit Guy was coming toward the car, that ugly frown reinstalled on his face.

Chandler reached for the door handle, ready for a confrontation, when Eliza's plea popped into the forefront of his brain.

"Don't talk to anyone. Please."

Damn it. He dropped his hand and simply waited for Suit Guy to approach. He wasn't going to talk. All he could do at that point was listen.

"Who are you?" Suit Guy accompanied the question with a quick rap of his knuckles across the window. "This is Eliza's car."

Oh well. It looked like his intuition had failed him this time. The guy was apparently being nice and looking out for Eliza's car.

Well, that would have been Chandler's thought if he wasn't on high alert already. As it stood, Chandler's hackles were raised and he had to bite his tongue to keep from defending his—and his woman's—turf.

"Listen, if you're with her, you should know about some stuff. I used to date her, and man, she is hard-core fucked in the head."

And with that, Chandler knew exactly who was standing outside the driver's side door. The infamous Tyler, the one he'd been dying to airmail a right hook to ever since he'd learned the fucker's name.

Chandler's pulse was flying now, his muscles twitching wildly with the effort to keep still.

Seventeen minutes. Still not enough time.

"Get out of the car and we can talk about it. I'm just looking out for a fellow bro."

Chandler's eye roll was impossible to stop. But he stayed quiet, keeping a cool eye on Tyler. The guy was getting more and more pissed the longer Chandler stayed silent. It would have been funny if Chandler didn't want to jump out of the car and break the asshole's nose. At least he had to be freezing out there in the cold, wintry day. Hey, was that a snow flurry? Tiny white flakes began to appear on the shoulders of Tyler's jacket as he knocked on the window again.

"Seriously, you should run. I could tell you stories, man. Has she asked you to do anything weird yet? She will."

He wondered how much trouble he'd be in with Eliza if he jumped out of the car and introduced Tyler to the blacktop. Face-first.

The door to the building opened, but Chandler couldn't see who was coming out. Tyler was blocking his view.

"Has anyone told you she's a dyke? For real, she is. Tried to tie me down and have some leather-covered lesbian rape me. You'd better run if you don't want her to do that shit to you. Eliza is a hard-core kinked-up lesbo freak, and she'll ruin your life! She's disgusting, she's perverted, she—"

"Shut up!"

Chandler's hand was on the door latch, and he'd already pulled it halfway open when he heard the female yell. Tyler stepped backward, and Eliza came into view. Her cheeks looked tear-stained, and her hat was missing.

"Back off, bitch." Chandler got out of the car while Tyler turned his guns toward Eliza. "I was just warning your friend here about what you're really like. You pretend to be this geeky innocent, but you're really just a horny devil bitch."

And with that, Tyler sealed his fate. He put a hand against Eliza's sternum and shoved. She stumbled against the curb and fell backward onto the sidewalk.

Chandler's vision went red and he launched himself at Tyler. The crack of his knuckles against Tyler's chin was so satisfying. The man squawked, windmilling his arms to maintain his footing. He couldn't, and fell back against the hood of the Mustang next to him.

"Get away from her," Chandler growled, glaring at Tyler as if he could maim him from sight alone. "Leave. And if you ever lay a finger on her again, you'll have to answer to me."

Tyler glowered, started to argue, then took a better look at Chandler. Chandler squared his shoulders. It was obvious that he was the taller and stronger of the two. Even if Tyler was stupid, he'd have no chance of winning.

Chandler kind of hoped the guy was stupid. One punch hadn't been nearly enough to quell his anger.

28

It took a long moment for Eliza to realize what was happening. She stared up at Tyler, who was leaning against the car behind him and holding his jaw in shock. Chandler's fists were raised, and his face was dark with anger. Pain was spreading in her rib cage, and she pressed a hand there with a wince.

Tyler had pushed her. She'd fallen down. Because he'd been in the midst of ruining everything.

"No," she whispered, the rough sidewalk scraping her palm. "No! Tyler, stop!"

"You fucking prick," Tyler said, shoving himself upright. "Who do you think you are? I don't give a shit what you do with this whore, I was just giving you a friendly warning. She's not into guys, she only wants to see you fucked—"

Chandler bent his head down and barreled straight into Tyler. Eliza slapped a palm over her mouth to cover her scream. She wanted to get between them, to break it up, but fists were flying, then the pair of them fell to the pavement. Blood streamed from Tyler's nose, and a bright-red smear marred Chandler's upper lip.

Scooting backward as fast as she could, Eliza finally reached the bumper of the car. Bracing herself on it, she managed to get upright. But it hurt to breathe. She wasn't sure if the pain was physical or emotional. Truth be told, it didn't matter. The end result was that she hurt, and Tyler was responsible. He'd ruined everything for her.

Again.

"What the fucking hell is going on out here?" The angry male voice jerked Eliza's gaze from the fighting men in front of her to the doorway of Quality, where one very angry CEO was striding toward them. Two security officers were behind him.

Shit. Someone from inside had seen what was going on.

"Chandler!" Her warning distracted him long enough to let Tyler land a punch in his midsection. Chandler grunted in pain as Eliza winced, and the security guards pulled them apart.

"Tyler, what the fuck are you thinking?"

"This asshole just attacked me! It's that bitch's fault." As Tyler's finger pointing raged on, Eliza hurried to Chandler's side.

"Oh God, are you hurt?" Eliza's own chest was on fire, but she ignored it as she checked Chandler over. His cheek was swollen, and his eye looked suspiciously dark.

"Ma'am, please step away. The police are on their way." The security guard edged her away from Chandler as Harold started to stroke out.

"No! Why the hell would you call the cops?" Harold's face was purpling with rage. "You idiot, this'll be all over the papers. It's going to cost me a fortune to keep this quiet now."

Chandler's gaze was still glued to Tyler, as if none of the others were even there. "I think I've made myself clear. Leave Eliza alone. She's not your girlfriend now, so you'll keep your damn mouth shut about her, no matter what happened while you were dating."

Eliza stepped back. *No, it's not like that. I didn't really do those things, Tyler's exaggerating!*

Her mind screamed the words, but her mouth just couldn't echo them.

Chandler continued, "Eliza might be adventurous in bed, but she's not a freak. And you don't know what you missed out on. She's incredible, and if she wants to leave me for a woman, well, that's her problem and mine. So fuck off."

No! I'd never leave you for a—That's not what I'd asked— You don't understand—

She was frozen like a statue, one of those angels in the garden with their hands over their faces. She couldn't move, pinned to the spot like she was frozen there. Frozen. She couldn't really feel the cold anymore.

"You're an idiot." Tyler spat onto the pavement, barely missing the security guard's boot. The liquid was pinkish with blood. "You're a fucking tool, and you deserve whatever she puts you through."

"Nice to meet you, too. Now leave her the fuck alone."

"Shut up, you two. Good God, what am I going to do now?" Harold put a hand over his forehead as if his thoughts pained him. "Come on, bring them inside. No reason we all should freeze our nuts off while the cops take their time getting here. I don't suppose there's any way to tell them not to come now, is there?"

The security guard holding Tyler responded while Eliza fell into step behind Chandler.

Her meeting with Harold had gone so well, and now everything was up in the air once more. It was happening all over again. The little slice of happiness she'd scraped up had been burned into an unrecognizable form, and Tyler was holding the blackened match.

Once they were inside the foyer, and the security guard was

satisfied that Chandler wasn't about to either leap on Tyler again or make a break for it, he stepped back and allowed Eliza to move next to Chandler.

"Liza," Chandler said. He reached for her hand, and only then did she realize that she was still gripping the painful spot in the center of her chest. He cradled her hand in his, and she winced at the sight of blood on his knuckles. "Are you okay? You fell pretty hard."

Her cheeks were stinging. Why? A trembling finger wiped her face. Oh. Tears. She'd been crying and hadn't even realized it.

"Come on. You're shivering. Lean close to me."

His arm went around her shoulder, and her teeth chattered as she snuggled close to him. She'd tried so hard to keep this away from Chandler, to prevent him from knowing the depth and breadth of her problems, but they'd literally punched him right in the face.

What would she do if Tyler pressed charges? Harold was so concerned about the public face of Quality. He'd made it clear that if she kept things quiet there was every chance she'd be re-hired at the first of the year. But now—would that even happen? And Chandler's business, oh God, what if it got back to his clients that he'd been arrested?

She'd cost him so much, so very much, and she couldn't be selfish anymore. She loved him too much.

That morning, talking and laughing while preparing to pick out a Christmas tree, felt like a lifetime away.

"I'm sorry," Chandler broke the silence. "I didn't leave the car until he came up to me and started talking through the window. I promise I didn't try to talk to him first."

"I know," she choked out. "I'm so sorry about this. So, so sorry."

"It's not your fault," Chandler said, but before he could continue, sirens and flashing blue lights moved into Quality's lot. The cops were there already, and she still didn't have a clue how to make any of this better.

"It's going to be okay," Chandler said as the security guard motioned Eliza away. "I promise."

But he was wrong. Nothing would ever be okay again, because for Chandler's own good, she'd have to end this. She refused to be responsible for Chandler's future being ruined the way hers had been.

The police station at Appledale was nice. Dated, but clean and fairly efficient for such a small town. The questioning process took a little over two hours. Neither of them pressed charges, mostly due to the fact that Harold Hagans looked just this side of a heart attack over the whole thing.

But even getting processed through Appledale's correctional system didn't worry Chandler as much as Eliza herself did. Something wasn't right. She was taking this much harder than he'd expected. And though she refused to press charges against Tyler, Chandler wished she'd at least agree to go to the hospital and get checked out. She'd fallen pretty hard. But she'd insisted she was fine, then they'd driven back to her house—silently. When they arrived, Chandler watched as Eliza bolted into the house.

He pulled the keys from the ignition and shut the car door behind him. As he walked toward the door, he looked at the sky. Thick, gray clouds hung low over him, the light dusting of snow already past. Hmm. Figured. He couldn't even get a white Christmas when he flew north for it.

As soon as he went into the house, he heard her crying. His ribs felt tight, his emotions snarling and knotting inside him.

She wants to be alone. Give her a few.

He stopped in the bathroom and took stock of the damage. Not too bad. He'd skinned his knuckles, had a blackened eye, and his upper lip was nicked and swollen from a lucky shot Tyler had landed, but on the whole he wasn't bad off. He cleaned the small wounds and raided her medicine cabinet for Neosporin and a Band-Aid for his hand.

Her cries had gotten quieter, and now as he left the bathroom, they were gone altogether. The house was eerily quiet, only the soft hum of the heating system giving any sound at all.

He used his left hand to knock on her bedroom door. The right one was bandaged. "Liza?"

The bedsprings creaked a little, as if she'd shifted. Standing? Coming to the door? He waited, but no other sound came.

He knocked again. "Liza, please talk to me."

Small footsteps then, and finally the *click* of the bedroom door's lock. She pulled it open, but only enough to let him see her face.

"I think you should go."

His lungs gave a painful squeeze, and he shook his head to clear it. "What?" No way could he have heard that right.

"I said, I think you should go. I shouldn't have said yes in the first place. I'm sorry. I'll pay for your return flight, or a hotel room for you until your original one. Just let me know how much it is. And I'll pay your cab fare to the airport."

She tried to close the door, but he blocked it with his foot.

"What the hell are you saying? I don't understand. Why do you need me to go?"

She broke then, shattered into a million pieces right before his eyes. "Because I'm fucked up, and I can't let you be fucked up, too. Didn't you hear Tyler? I'm dirty, and broken, and useless. I can't let your life be ruined by this, can't you see? This"—she waved between them wildly—"whatever it is, it's done. I can't let you, not now, I can't—"

"You're wrong. It's not over, Eliza. Why the hell would you be worried about me? No matter what you like, it's—"

"Don't you see, that's the fucking problem!" She dropped

the door and it swung a little farther open. He wasn't surprised to notice that the bed was rumpled. She'd probably been crying there since they'd gotten back.

"What's the problem?" He didn't want to yell, but he found himself matching her impassioned tone. "How can I know what it is if you won't tell me? How can I promise you that it doesn't matter if you keep me in the dark about everything?"

Her hands covered her face, and her reply was muffled. "You can't be with someone like me. The distance, the problems, they're too much."

"Too much for you, or too much for me?" He stepped backward. His head was pounding, a knife-like pain building in his temples.

"For me," she said softly. "I can't do this anymore."

He set his mouth into a grim line. He wanted to fight back, wanted to assure her that they could overcome anything. But she'd just been dragged through the police station because of him. She'd just had her whole world turned upside down over the past week. That could make anyone feel overwhelmed. And if he wasn't part of the solution, he was part of the problem.

Only one thing he could do.

"Okay. Give me half an hour to pack and I'll be out of your hair in no time."

He turned on his heel and stalked toward the living room. Sinking onto the couch, he rested his pounding head in his hands.

Everything had gone to shit in such a short amount of time. Why hadn't he seen this coming? Eliza hadn't ever breathed a word of what her hang-up was, and if she was confused about her sexuality, he could understand that. But why had she chosen to keep everything from him? Hadn't he shown her that he loved her, that he accepted her, that he was willing to try every kinky little thing she'd suggested?

Before he realized what he was doing, his smartphone was in his hand and he was calling a cab. He'd already put too much of his heart on the line, and if he was going to be able to salvage any of it, he'd have to move quickly.

Glancing at the hallway, he frowned. His stuff was in her bedroom. He'd have to go get it.

The bedroom door's knob turned easily under his hand this time. She'd left it unlocked.

"Just need to grab my stuff," he said gruffly, then turned his back to her and knelt by his suitcase.

As he folded his clothes and placed them inside the black rolling bag, it was easy to feel her gaze on his back. He moved slowly, deliberately. The tension in the room crackled, and even though all he wanted was to give her the space she needed, if not take her in his arms and kiss this awfulness away, he did not rush his packing.

"I'm sorry." Her voice was small, wavering with tears.

He paused in mid-zip and looked back at her. She was on her knees in the center of the bed. She still hadn't removed her coat and boots. It was almost funny how overdressed she was.

"What?"

"I'm sorry about this. About Tyler. About taking things out on you." She looked down at the comforter, her beautiful lips downturned. "I feel like I owe you an explanation."

He couldn't pretend he didn't want to know her side of the story, but he didn't want to push her. So he stayed quiet, nodding for her to continue.

She took a deep breath, and then said, "We dated for about a year. Tyler was nice enough, but—and I'm sorry to give you TMI—the sex wasn't all that great. I started to research things to spice it up. I'd had this fantasy for a really long time, and I finally found someone to help me do it. She was a dominatrix, I guess you'd call her. I hired her because I wanted her to dominate both Tyler and me. Together, though, like spank us both and force him to fuck me, that kind of thing. I never wanted her to have sex with me, or to peg him or anything. But he freaked out, and then broke up with me, and that's why he says those awful things about me. Half the things he accuses me of aren't even true, but everyone in town believes him. They treat me like shit. But I don't know what to do now. I'm all mixed up. I thought maybe—I thought you and I—But then . . ."

He rose to his feet and lifted the suitcase onto its end. Leaving it standing by the wall, he crossed to the bed and sank down on the edge. With his bandaged hand, he reached for hers, and gave it a gentle squeeze.

"Thanks for telling me. You need time. We both do, honestly."

She nodded, the tears still streaming slowly down her cheeks.

A horn honked outside then, and she flinched.

"That's the cab."

Her eyes went wide as she met his gaze. Her lip was trembling, and he wanted so badly to run his finger across it, to press a kiss to her lips. But he couldn't. Not now.

"I'll give you a call, okay?"

She nodded, her hair falling forward.

He waited for a second, hoping she'd say something else. Like maybe, *Don't go, I love you, I want you to stay with me, we can work this out.* But she didn't, so he stood and gripped the handle of his suitcase.

"Talk to you soon."

"Okay."

Even though she'd agreed, he found himself doubting that it would actually happen. As he exited the little house that had started to feel so familiar over the past couple of days, he began to put his brain to work.

"Take me to the Holiday Inn on the corner of Oak and Elm, please."

"You got it," the cabbie said with a nod, and the cab pulled away. Chandler watched as the little blue house disappeared behind them.

Time, he could give her. Space, he could give her. But he wasn't willing to give up on them.

He loved her too damn much.

29

When Eliza woke the next morning, it was to an empty space in the bed beside her. For just a second before she'd opened her eyes, she'd thought she'd heard Chandler's soft snore beside her. That made the reality of the lonely bed even tougher to take somehow.

She shut her emotions down and went through the habit of eating breakfast and dressing as quickly as she could.

Chandler had shown her, for a couple of days at least, that she could be happier. So she was determined to make that happen. She'd spent a long while last night researching, and today she'd go out and find work. Someone was bound to need an employee of her skills and experience. At least, she hoped so. Her savings would last for a good while, but staying cooped up in her house alone for the next six months seemed like a fate worse than death. Especially because she saw Chandler in every corner of the place now.

The sky was as overcast and snowy-looking as it had been yesterday. The forecast had warned of an impending snowfall, but it wasn't supposed to happen until later that evening. Her errands wouldn't take that long unless things went really, really well, and she wasn't expecting that.

The first place she tried, a pharmaceutical manufacturer, didn't have any openings at the moment. The second place, a sewage-treatment plant, did, but when she'd given her name the supervisor had hiked his eyebrows and smothered a laugh. Then she noted his name tag. Anyone with the last name of Hagans had no business being her boss, ever again. So she declined the interview, thanked him politely, and left.

Only three hours later, she was back home. Nowhere in her immediate area would work for a new job, unless she decided to switch careers. And frankly, she didn't want to. Her job was interesting, and fun, and she liked what she did.

As she drove down the familiar streets of Appledale, she watched the sights go by. She'd ridden her bike down these roads as a kid. Scraped her knee on the basketball court in that park. Fallen off the trampoline behind that house when her friend Melanie lived there.

Her stomach had been leaden since Chandler had left, and it only felt heavier now. She frowned tightly as she braked at a stoplight.

Why did she stay here, other than the obvious? Sure, she'd grown up here, and she had been happy here before, but why couldn't she just pick up and leave? It would be so much easier. But was that giving up? Was that letting Tyler get the best of her?

The light turned green and she made her way through the intersection. At this point it didn't matter who lost or won. Her life was a prison of rumors, lies, and half truths, and it had just cost her the best guy she'd ever known. Enough was enough. She'd sacrifice her childhood home for a chance at a brighter future.

Her mind made up, she made the turn into her subdivision. There should be a good amount of opportunity for a chemist down in North Carolina, right? Or maybe that was too sudden. She'd hurt him by kicking him out, she knew that. But what harm could checking out the possibilities do?

She turned into her driveway and frowned. There was an unfamiliar SUV parked by the curb. Shiny black with chrome rims, it was a flashy car for this neighborhood. Oh well, maybe the guys across the street were entertaining. It didn't have anything to do with her.

She mounted her front steps just as the first flakes started to fall. She turned and looked out at the fast-flying snow. Chandler had mentioned several times how he'd never had a white Christmas. She'd wanted his first to be here with her. But she'd fucked that up.

Her shiver had less to do with the cold and more to do with the fear that she'd never be able to fix things between them.

Come on, Liza. Get yourself together and move forward.

With her subconscious cheering her on, she unlocked the door. The instant her foot hit the floor of her foyer, a prickle ran up her spine and settled on the back of her neck. Soft voices came from down the hall. Someone was in her house.

"Hello?" she called out as she pushed the door open. Damn it, her Mace was in the kitchen. She'd taken it off her key chain when she went to Bree's wedding and had never bothered to put it back on. "Is someone there?"

"Come in, Eliza. Remove your shoes."

A strange woman stood in the living room doorway, her leather pants and red lace bustier clearly showing off her assets. Her hair was shoulder-length, auburn, with blunt-cut bangs. She had bright tattoos, beautiful eyes, and a wicked smile. Eliza's eyes widened as she saw the riding crop flick against the woman's leg.

"Um, who the hell are you? Why are you in my house?"

"I asked her to come. I wanted it to be a surprise." His voice was unmistakable.

Her hand flew to her mouth, and she stood there in shock. The woman had moved aside, and there, in what once had been

Eliza's living room, was a sort of makeshift BDSM dungeon. A swath of black fabric covered her couch, with assorted toys laid out like a buffet of sin. And there, in the center of the room, Chandler was strapped to a wide, low, padded table. He wore his pants, but he was shirtless.

"We got here about half an hour ago. I didn't know where you'd gone, but I wanted this to be a surprise. I hope it's okay. Please tell me it's okay."

The woman laid a gentle hand on Eliza's shaking shoulder. In a soft, motherly voice, she spoke. "Your boyfriend told me about your fantasy. I think it's beautiful. If you want to, I can help make that fantasy come true for the both of you."

Eliza looked at Chandler, wondering how her body could possibly hold all the happiness and love that was flooding her limbs. It felt as if the feelings were pouring through her, leaking from her pores and glowing through the room.

Chandler pulled at his restraints and frowned. "I guess I didn't think this through. I really want to kiss you right now. Sidney, do you think—"

" 'Madam' or 'Mistress,' please." The woman's tone was sharp.

"Sorry. Mistress, think you could turn me loose for a minute?"

Eliza didn't wait to see what Mistress Sidney's response was. She ran across the room and threw herself atop Chandler, laughing, crying, and kissing him all at once.

"You do understand," she said between kisses. Her tears were salty, and were dripping on his face, but she didn't care. "You are the best man I've ever known."

He met her kiss with every bit of fervor she put into it. Their tongues met and touched, dancing together in the wet heat. She pulled back to look down on him, her smile so wide it almost hurt her cheeks.

"I love you, Eliza. I'm sorry that I ever gave you cause to doubt that."

"Chandler." Her voice broke and she rested her head against his bare chest. "I love you, too. So very much."

"I'm glad. That makes this a lot more convenient."

He winked at her, and she laughed aloud. Her heart was so full, and her mind was so filled with the wonderful man beneath her that she'd almost forgotten they weren't alone.

A pointed throat clearing from behind them startled Eliza back into the moment.

"Well, what's it going to be? Submission for two is on special today."

Chandler wasn't sure what he'd done in a previous life to deserve what was happening to him now, but he thanked his long-lost former self for whatever it was.

After Eliza had crawled on top of him and kissed him, Mistress Sidney had ordered her down. What followed was the most erotic two hours of his life. Under the dominatrix's firm hand, Eliza tortured Chandler in the most decadent ways possible. The two women had stripped his pants from him, and he lay on the table, wrists and ankles trapped as they applied various punishments to him.

Eliza had teased him with a small, prickly wheel, the tiny metal teeth biting softly into his skin. He'd shivered as his blood pumped harder. His cock took notice, especially when she wheeled the thing over his inner thighs.

Then he'd been blindfolded, teased with a feather, and as he waited now in the darkness for whatever was next, he counted his lucky stars that he'd ignored Gregory's warnings about Eliza.

His hardness was unmistakable, and his libido was on high alert.

"What should we do now?" Eliza's voice was excited, breathy.
"I think maybe—this."

A whispered conversation took place then, and though Chandler strained, he couldn't make out the words they were saying.

"Oooh. I see."

Suddenly there were hands on his wrist and his ankle. The bonds were being removed.

He couldn't help but be a little disappointed there. But then the thought that he might get to tantalize Eliza in much the same way sprang into his brain, and he couldn't possibly feel sad about that.

The velvety restraints fell away, and he started to sit up.

"Stay right there. You haven't been given permission to move."

Chandler stopped. He wasn't really the submissive type, in general, but being with Eliza had shown him the many different ways he could enjoy sex. So he stayed put.

"Move to your right, Chandler, until you're lying on the edge of the table." Hands, presumably Mistress Sidney's, appeared beside him to show him where the edge of the table was. He moved into position, anticipation pinging in his brain.

Fabric rustled, the *thump* of something hitting the floor. Shoes? The table moved slightly, then a warm body was stretched out beside him.

"Roll onto your sides and face one another." Mistress Sidney removed the blindfold, and he blinked at the sudden light. Eliza lay next to him, a nervous smile on her face. She wore only her bra and panties, and the sight of her near-nudity sent another jolt of lust to his already stiff cock.

"Get close together, that's right. Chandler, wrap your arms around her. Now, are you comfortable?"

"Yes, Mistress." They said it at the same time, and a soft laugh escaped Eliza. Chandler smiled, too. There was no denying that this was strange, but erotic nonetheless. Her warm body was pressed against him, skin on skin, the beautiful scent of her driving him wild. He drew in another breath of her. He'd never get enough.

"Now remember, this is what Eliza asked for. If it's too much, speak the words. You're in control of this."

"Yes," Eliza said, and Chandler held her tighter.

The dominatrix held a long-tasseled flogger in her right hand, and she stood by the low table on Eliza's side, looking down on them. With an expert twirl, she gave an evil grin.

"For every strike, I expect thanks."

The flogger flicked across Eliza's backside, and she gasped. Her cheeks colored, and her fingers dug into Chandler's back. "Thank you, mistress."

The flogger twirled in the air before laying its tendrils across Chandler's hip. The tiny sting heightened his arousal, and he groaned, pressing it harder against Eliza. "Thank you, mistress."

The next soft strike was Eliza's. She bit his neck. "Thank you, mistress."

Chandler's. He moved his hand to her breast and squeezed lightly. "Thank you, mistress."

It continued in this way for long, incredible moments. The pace was never predictable, and with every touch of the flogger their passion grew. They kissed deeply, tongues moving as their bodies flinched from each tiny sting. The pain turned to pleasure as quickly as it sparked, and every time Eliza's hips thrust against Chandler he fought the orgasm mounting in his body.

He had to wait. This was the warm-up; the main event was coming soon. And so would they.

Then Mistress Sidney's rhythm quickened. Right, left, she struck them lightly, over and over, the flogger's suede strips crossing from Eliza to Chandler and back again. Chandler could feel each hit, each decadent strike on their bodies.

Eliza panted, she moaned, she rubbed against him as if she

were on fire and he was her only hope of survival. His hands roamed everywhere, her breasts with their taut nipples, down to her leg where he squeezed, then between her thighs where he rubbed her panties gently.

Their breath mingled and they clung to one another until the flogging was over.

"Now," Mistress Sidney said, stepping back and removing her leather gloves, "I will leave you. I'll return in two hours for my equipment."

"Thank you, Mistress Sidney." The words were muffled because Chandler's mouth was on Eliza's neck. He was so preoccupied with the sweetness of her flesh that he barely even heard the front door shut behind her.

"God, Chandler," Eliza cried as he ripped the panties down her legs. God, she was so wet. He could smell her arousal, and it made him crazy.

Kneeling by the edge of the table, he gripped her hips and moved her to the edge. Then he buried his face between her legs, his tongue seeking and finding her throbbing clit. From the top of her slit to the bottom, over and over, he kissed, nibbled, and licked her. Her hands tangled in his hair and she pulled, the discomfort edging his cock higher into the danger zone. Thrusting his tongue inside her, he drank her in.

Eliza. She was his.

"Fuck me, please." She was sobbing with want now, thrashing her head back and forth on the padded table. "I—I've never, God, please, I want your cock now!"

He jerked upright and sank into her in the very next second. Her body was so wet that it easily accommodated him, and he sank into her all the way to his hilt. His sac nestled against her ass, as he stood on the floor and widened his stance.

"You want this?" He pinched her nipple lightly as he withdrew his cock.

"Yessss." Her hands reached for his hips, her nails dragging down his skin.

He slammed into her again, and she cried out. Over and over he plunged his cock into her sweet depths, her body welcoming him, beckoning him further in, deeper, more. Faster. Her voice and her skin and her soul seemed to invite him in, and he was more than happy to accommodate them.

He pounded against her, his sac slamming against her ass, his hands gripping her thighs hard. He almost came, but he pulled out before he could spill himself. Too soon. He wanted to see her come first.

"Get on top of me," he directed as he lay back on the table beside her. "I want you to ride me."

She didn't hesitate. Her thigh slid over his belly and she rose on her knees to guide him to her entrance. His blood roared in his ears as she slid down his length until he was completely inside her. For a moment she didn't move anything except her inner muscles, those wonderful little creatures that begged him for his cum.

"Ride me," he growled, reaching for her breasts. She lifted her hair off her neck and began to lift and swivel her hips. Over and over she lifted and lowered, in and out, her body hot and wanting.

Her rhythm grew faster, more insistent, and she braced herself on his chest. Her eyes went wide, and her pants were gasps, hungry cries. He knew what she needed, and he'd be happy to do it for her.

He reached between them and fondled her clit. The soft touch was enough to send her over the edge. Her rhythm broke, and she slammed down on him, hard. Her inner muscles worked him, and that hot, sweet fist of her body broke his resistance. With a hoarse yell he released his orgasm, hot pulses deep within her body.

His heart pounding and his body spent, Chandler looked up at Eliza. Her mouth was open, her eyes soft, and her hair was wild.

"I love you," she breathed.

"I love you, Liza."

He grabbed her hand and brought it to his lips for a kiss. This hand was the one he wanted to hold, for now and forever. He'd wondered what it would take to heal his heart, and it was this woman. She was more beautiful than anyone he'd ever seen, especially with a halo of afterglow.

And she was his.

EPILOGUE

The sea wind whipped Eliza's hair across her face, and she tried her best to corral it behind her head. It was tough with as fast as the boat was traveling.

"You okay?" Chandler's voice was far away, even though he stood just two feet away behind the small skiff's wheel.

"I'm good!" She wrestled her hair into a messy ponytail and adjusted her sunglasses.

It was a beautiful day on the Outer Banks, and she'd been happier here than she ever had been in Appledale. For the last six months this had been her home. She and Chandler spent their free time on the beach, or riding in the boat, even kite-boarding, which Eliza had just discovered a passion for. Not to mention the BDSM classes they took once a month.

In a small shoal, Chandler cut the engine and moved to sit beside her on the small bench. Eliza snuggled against his side.

"You feeling okay?" His broad hand rubbed her hip gently, and she winced.

"Yeah. It's sore, but a good kind of sore."

Chandler's face—more tanned now that they'd spent the

past few months outside more often than not—wrinkled in a smile. "You wouldn't be so sore if you didn't keep begging me to spank you harder."

"Well, you like it as much as I do." She pinched his ass, and he gave an obligatory yelp.

"True enough. I never thought I'd be into it, but I'm glad you introduced me. What's the next class supposed to cover?"

Eliza watched as a seagull swooped down beside them, ducking its head under the water. "I think it's *shibari*—you know, the knots and rope stuff?"

"That should be fun. I'm good with knots."

Eliza's heart leapt. "I remember."

They fell silent for a moment or two, watching the gentle lap of the waves in the sound. Rushes of a nearby sandbar riffled in the wind, dappling the sunlight on the water's surface. Eliza closed her eyes and breathed in the scent of sea and Chandler. Her favorite scents now. She'd never imagined being this happy. Ever since she'd been fired from Quality, her life had improved dramatically. Harold had finally gotten tired of Tyler's shit, and he'd been let go about a month after the fight. Last she heard, he was a pharmaceutical rep schmoozing with urologists. It suited him.

She'd found a perfect job only twenty minutes from Chandler's home, and they'd been living together. Head over heels in love wasn't even enough to describe how she felt for him. In his arms, she was home. In his bed, she was beautiful. And she liked herself. More than that, she finally understood that her fantasies had never been weird or wrong. Chandler loved and accepted everything about her, including her not-so-vanilla desires.

"I thought you were going to go fishing," Eliza murmured.

"Well, we can, but I thought maybe we'd get some business taken care of first."

His voice was unusually serious, and Eliza popped her eyes open. "What?"

Chandler stood, and carefully turned to face her. As he dropped to one knee, Eliza's hand went over her mouth. He pulled a small gray velvet cube from the pocket of his swim trunks and opened it.

The diamond inside glittered brilliantly in the sunlight, throwing sparkles onto the water surrounding them.

"Eliza Jackson, will you do me the honor of becoming my wife?"

Her heart was beating so hard she was afraid she'd misunderstood him. Her fingers trembled against her lips. "Oh my God, really? Are you sure?"

Chandler nodded, and the smile on his face was full of intense emotion. "I know this is right. I love you more than I've loved anyone in my life. I want to spend forever with you, Eliza."

There was only one answer. "Yes. Oh please, yes."

She threw her arms around him and laughed aloud, startling a flock of gulls who'd landed nearby. As they took to the air, feathers flying, Eliza watched them. She was free of her past, free of her own doubts. And all it had taken was this man believing in her to change her world.

Chandler kissed her, and she kissed him back. For the rest of her life, this was where she wanted to be. In his kiss, in his arms, in his bed. She was happy in her skin, and he loved her just the way she was.

Had any woman ever been as lucky as she was?